Praise for

KATHLEEN KORBEL

"Intriguing characters that unfold
through tremendously multilayered
storytelling—a rich, remarkable read."
—*Romantic Times BOOKclub* on
Some Men's Dreams

"Yet another emotionally satisfying, beautifully
poignant romance...a superbly fashioned,
wickedly clever and witty love story. With its
exquisitely crafted characters and delectably
sharp prose, this is a romance to treasure."
—*Booklist* (starred review, a top-ten romance
of the year) on *Some Men's Dreams*

"Magic flows through Ms. Korbel's pen
as she dazzles us with compelling
characterization, outstanding dialogue
and exquisitely touching emotion."
—*Romantic Times BOOKclub* on *Sail Away*

"Any romance reader worth her salt knows
and treasures *A Rose for Maggie*."
—*The Romance Reader*

KATHLEEN KORBEL

and her evil twin, Eileen Dreyer, have published not only bestselling romance novels for Silhouette, but medico-forensic suspense, as well. She is only the fourth member of the RWA Hall of Fame, and is darned proud of it. Retired from trauma nursing (where she got a lot of her motivation for any revenge elements in her books), she can be found in St. Louis with her husband and children—when she's not feeding her travel addiction, that is. She's sung in some of the best Irish pubs in the world... and is darned proud of that, too.

KATHLEEN
KORBEL

DANGEROUS TEMPTATION

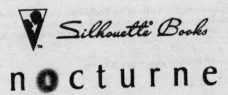

Silhouette Books

nocturne

If you purchased this book without a cover you should be aware
that this book is stolen property. It was reported as "unsold and
destroyed" to the publisher, and neither the author nor the
publisher has received any payment for this "stripped book."

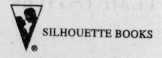 SILHOUETTE BOOKS

ISBN-13: 978-0-373-61749-4
ISBN-10:   0-373-61749-6

DANGEROUS TEMPTATION

Copyright © 2006 by Eileen Dreyer

All rights reserved. Except for use in any review, the reproduction
or utilization of this work in whole or in part in any form by any
electronic, mechanical or other means, now known or hereafter
invented, including xerography, photocopying and recording, or in
any information storage or retrieval system, is forbidden without
the written permission of the editorial office, Silhouette Books,
233 Broadway, New York, NY 10279 U.S.A.

All characters in this book have no existence outside the imagination of
the author and have no relation whatsoever to anyone bearing the same
name or names. They are not even distantly inspired by any individual
known or unknown to the author, and all incidents are pure invention.

This edition published by arrangement with Harlequin Books S.A.

® and TM are trademarks of Harlequin Books S.A., used under license.
Trademarks indicated with ® are registered in the United States Patent
and Trademark Office, the Canadian Trade Marks Office and in other
countries.

Visit Silhouette Books at www.eHarlequin.com

Printed in U.S.A.

Author Note

Fairies, like any other creature, have conflicts and challenges and a touch of darkness in their souls. (Well, often more than a touch. Wait until you meet the *leannan sidhe*.)

More surprising to me, Zeke's heroine, Nuala, had a family, too. Only hers weren't simple ranchers. Her mother is Mab, Queen of Fairies, and her two sisters are heirs to the same throne. Ah, conflict. So from the end of one series, I found another was born. And I discovered along the way that I really think this world-building thing could catch on. I love my fairies for the very reason that I wrote them. They aren't cartoon characters. They aren't wee folk or dragonfly copies. They're varied and complex and sometimes awful.

For Kieran O'Driscoll
1984–2003
The fairy child
Slan abhale

Prologue

He was the seer. The prophet of the great faerie clan, the *Tua de Dannan*. It was he who saw the way to their future and the link to their past, he who unraveled the fiber of woven time and experience to identify the pattern. He was the thread that held the world of faerie together and the eyes that bore witness to the future.

Sometimes he could forget that. Sometimes he could lay his burden down and simply enjoy his place in the mortal world, where his responsibilities were simple and his name unknown. Sometimes he could pretend that he was nothing more than a mortal with an imagination. But this was not one of those times.

He stood out in the early morning light, the grass dew-wet against his feet, the mist curling like smoke around him, the earthsounds muted and dim. The sun had not risen, but already it painted the sky in lurid crimson, so that the very air carried portent.

What was the saying? "Red sky at morning, sailor take warning"? So, too, he realized, the world of faerie. The vermillion sky held images only he could see, and they were stained with crimson. With fire and fairy blood and failure.

The time had come, then. Penance was about to be paid for the sins of the past. The precarious balance that had begun to erode would fail. For want of a stone, the world might well collapse in upon itself.

The stone was one of the Filial Set, those great gems that bestowed all power on the clans of faerie. Three stones mined by the first ones and set in royal crowns. Three stones that controlled the fragile balance between the worlds of mortal and faerie.

Donelle, the ruler, who glittered blue as sapphire, remained in the Land of the West, where capricious hands could not disturb it. Where covetous hearts could not subvert or sully it. Dearann, the fruitful female stone of diamond clarity, lay in the crown of the *Dubh-lainn Sidhe*, the patriarchal Fairies of the Dark Sword, whose realm was the air and sea. And Coilin, the virile male stone of ruby red, graced the diadem of Mab herself, queen of the matriarchal earth fairies.

It had remained so for untold centuries, the male and female powers balanced and in harmony as they cared for the earth they so loved. And then, only a hundred years ago, Dearann had been lifted from her resting place and taken away, out of the world of faerie. Mab, still in control of her virile Coilin, ascended in power, while Cathal, king of the *Dubhlainn Sidhe*, languished, his spirit growing dark and resentful for want of the power of the queen. The two great powers of faerie, once neighboring courts of pleasure and favor, broke contact, and the earth suffered.

But the time of change had come. Even as he watched the sun crest the gentle rise beyond his castle, the seer saw a dark stranger set his foot onto Irish soil. This was the mortal, he knew, who would set into motion the events that would either reestablish order or destroy it forever. This was the catalyst for upheaval.

The seer recognized the threat of the stranger, the redemption of him. He saw all the possible consequences of his arrival even before the stranger put his second foot down. And he knew that without intervention, all would be lost. Might be lost already.

The seer had to return to the land of faerie. He was needed there now, more than any of the seers he'd succeeded. For a moment, though, he remained where he was, soaking in the sound of early birdsong, the rustle of small animals in the brush, the whisper of a writhing mist. He inhaled the scent of peat smoke and freshly turned soil to take with him into that land of endless bliss. He bolstered himself with the comfort of his family, who even now slept in the castle that stood behind him, aged and stone-sculpted in the shadows. He gathered to him the power of the raw earth to shield him against the cataclysm to come. And then, the grass unbent from his touch, he turned to face his destiny.

Chapter 1

Zeke Kendall did not believe in fairies. Not merely a serious scientist but a man of the millennium, he held no truck with ghosties or ghoulies or things that went bump in the night. It didn't matter that he was standing hip-deep in what was purported to be a fairy glen in the middle—well, no, to be fair, the western edge—of Ireland, where generations had seen, spoken to, consorted with and recovered from fairies. Even standing in the middle of fairy central, Zeke could say with perfect conviction that he did not believe in the species.

Which was why the sudden sight of the delicate, sloe-eyed woman sent him reeling.

He'd been on the site most of the morning, tucked along a steep, wet hillside in between road and riverbed, in preparation for his work farther up the mountain. Seasoning, one of his Irish colleagues had called it, for the meal to come. Background and basis for an area of study he wasn't acquainted with.

"Get a feel for the magic here," the friend had said with a huge grin over a double shot of Tullamore Dew the night before. "The kind you can't get in a place with barstools and cigarette smoke."

Zeke, a trained and experienced field anthropologist whose specialty was North American Indian tribes, was here by invitation of that same friend, who wanted to compare and contrast burial and ritual seasonal customs between the migratory cultures of the western hemisphere and the migratory neolithics of the eastern.

Zeke's ancestors had come en masse from the Celtic countries: Ireland, Scotland and Wales. Back in North Carolina, his great-great-grandmother had been called an Irish witch when she wasn't needed for her healing abilities and a powwow woman when she was. So, in a rare moment of whimsy, Zeke, nursing a long whiskey at his sister's wedding, had been overcome with that common and obviously communicable malady, genealogyitis.

So here he was, up to the tops of his work boots in Irish mud, the rain dripping off the battered old cowboy hat he used for digs, and his field of vision jam-packed with green. Green rhododendron, green ferns, green moss, green holly, green yew and whitethorn and oak and birch. An explosion of green, a bouquet, an overdose to a man more used to stalking the stark, red-hued desert of the Four Corners Reservation.

Oddly enough, though, he felt almost at home here. Certainly more than on his digs, more even than in the high, wind-swept mountain valley in Wyoming where he'd grown up. It was almost cozy here, even with the steady patter of the rain. Friendly and soft and gentle in a way he wasn't used to. Well, he supposed, if you were fairies, you wouldn't want to fight a howling desert wind to set up shop.

On the other hand, if he stood still enough, he could feel something else here. Something alive, something prescient. Something darker than the shadows that collected in this little glen. Even wearing his best long johns and leather jacket, he felt an odd chill skitter up his back.

He was just about to turn back up the hill, to where an iron grill gate set among overgrown fuchsia hedges separated the third millennium from the first, when he saw her. A flash of her. A sudden, heartstopping glimpse of her farther down the walk.

He caught her out of the corner of his eye, the way you would in a dream. Creamy skin that all but glowed in the soft, watery light. Thick, curling auburn hair that seemed oddly dry in the rain. Big eyes. Wide eyes. Clear, laughing green eyes that sparkled at him and then turned away. Eyes he would swear on his grave he recognized from somewhere.

Before he realized what he was doing, Zeke was following her. Splashing in puddles up to his ankles, he shoved aside ferns and fuchsia and oak branches in his haste to catch up with her.

She was in a dress. Could she possibly be in a dress? A floaty kind of silky thing in the most iridescent shade of peacock he'd ever seen. Tantalizing over breast and hip and thigh. Compelling a man who had never had the need to be compelled.

Zeke was no monk. That had been his brother Jake's job for most of their lives. Zeke preferred to sample a bit of everything life had to offer. He'd had his share of relationships. He'd been told by people other than his family that he was handsome. Rugged, according to his latest friend, Tina. He was in shape, that was for damn sure. Hard not to be, when you did more vertical cliff-feet than a mountain goat. Wide-shouldered and tall and healthy. He hadn't needed to beg women to stop for him, nor had he ever particularly felt the gut-wrenching desire to do so.

But suddenly, after the swift, stunning sight of a woman who had not smiled at him but laughed at him, luscious strawberry lips parted over perfect white teeth—just a glimpse, as if they were illicit—and a toss of perfect copper hair, he was running as if his life depended on it.

And somehow, on a single path to a single stream in the middle of nowhere, he lost her.

Zeke got to the very bottom of the path, all but breathless from hopping boulders, sliding through mud and ducking under foliage, and stopped. Looked around. Stared hard at nothing.

He was sure he'd seen her. He couldn't mistake something that vibrant. He could almost still hear her windchime-light laugh as she spun away. Hell, he could almost feel that silk dress against his fingers. He swore he smelled cloves.

Where the hell was she?

Who the hell was she?

Zeke had only meant to spend a few minutes in the fairy glen, the one to which W. B. Yeats had lovingly ascribed magical powers. He'd just wanted to see what kind of place could invest itself a sense of magic that would survive so long.

And okay, he had found it to be something special. Something completely otherworldly, as if all that green had turned the light aqueous and the water fingered tunes among the trees. Zeke had always appreciated water, having spent so much of his professional life having to do without it. But here…here it was more elemental, more compelling. Here he could invest it with all the magic the Irish seemed to give it.

Here he could see that ferns and yew and even tropical-sized elephant-ear could transform shadows into living beings. He could almost believe that the world on this side of that iron gate was something not quite real. Not really a part of the sunlight, the banal ritual of everyday life. He could understand why Yeats and all his countrymen would want to find fairies here.

But that didn't mean there were any.

He turned away finally, deliberately, and slogged back up the hill. He hadn't really seen her. It had been jet lag. It had been all those suggestive stories whispered in his ear when Colm O'Roarke had shared a fire with him in the canyons of Utah. It had been swamp gas, for God's sake. It had not been fairies. Zeke Kendall did not believe in fairies.

Then what the hell had she been?

* * *

"Fairies, boyo!" Colm bellowed the next morning when he picked Zeke up at the B&B Colm had found for him.

An old country house, it was a little faded and ragged around the edges, and tended by a hesitant, overanxious woman named Mrs. O'Brien, who gave Zeke the sneaking suspicion he was going to Irish breakfast her out of house and home.

Colm had waved off the worry when Zeke had brought it up. "Ah, sure, don't be worrying over old Mary. She gets more people to forego their rightful breakfast by that hangdog look on her pious old face. What do you mean, you saw a beautiful woman in the fairy glen?"

Zeke realized now he shouldn't have said anything. Not so much as a word. But somehow it had just slipped out. Kind of in the "You're from around here, Colm. Do you know any beautiful redheads who hang around the fairy glen?" way of things.

And then, of course, he hadn't been able to explain it. Not her appearance, not who she was, nor where she'd gone. And certainly not the dark, disturbing dream of her that had followed him through the night.

Colm howled with delight, his ugly little face alight, his thin, stooped shoulders shaking with glee. For a short, skinny man, Colm had an amazing capacity for volume and mirth.

Colm could hardly get the car started, he was laughing so hard. "You, Zeke Kendall, man of science, dancin' with the fairies. By God, I wish I'd seen it, so!"

"I didn't dance with any damn fairies," Zeke growled, mashing his hat brim between his hands where it sat across his knees, since it didn't fit on his head in the tiny almost-car Colm piloted down the almost-roads like a Disneyland ride. "I saw a woman who didn't introduce herself and knew a different way out of the woods."

"Of course she did, lad! She lives there!" Another round of guffaws accompanied much handslapping against the steering wheel. "Tell me, you didn't by chance think to go wanderin' around that little patch of grass at dusk, like, did ya?"

Zeke was now actively gritting his teeth. This was worse than the time he'd told his sister Gen he'd accidentally walked into the girls' locker room and seen Betty Williams without a bra on. All that effort, his sister had howled in glee, and wasted on poor Betty. But even Betty hadn't bothered him like the sight of one laughing Irish girl in the dusk.

"Never mind," he snapped, staring out into the rain.

No wonder the water was so plentiful here, he thought for no reason. It never stopped coming down.

"Ah, no, I don't think we can," Colm disagreed, wiping his merry blue eyes with the back of a gnarled little hand. If Zeke had really seen fairies, he would have preferred them looking more like Colm—small, knobby, bushy-haired and merry. Leprachaunish. Not...

Not...

"See," Colm was saying, pulling out a pipe to clamp

between his teeth. Barry Fitzgerald, for God's sake. "We're going to be after diggin' around the old girl's house."

"What old girl's house?"

"Your girlfriend, boyo. If she was *sidhe,* like I'm thinking."

"Don't think."

He got another rolling laugh. "I told you we'd be siting the next stage of work on the excavation of the multiple raths and cairns in the area surrounding Knocknarea and Carrowmore." Finally, the pipe bobbing with his words, Colm sounded completely businesslike. "The one we've sited to do next is a cairn of maybe thirty meters surrounded by a rath...an old ring fort or, in local parlance, fairy fort. Fairy rath. On moonless nights, especially Mayday Eve and Halloween—which is coming up, boyo, so watch out the fairy queen doesn't steal you to go live with her in that magic hill of hers—the fairies were forever riding from the Fairy Glen around Knocknarea Mountain to Carrowmore to celebrate. Or to steal mortals to play with for all eternity. Then they'd go back home beneath our very cairn."

"So, thoughtful scientists that we are, we're going to tear it down to see if they're still there."

Colm shot him a quick, sharp look. "Scientists don't believe in fairies, boyo."

Zeke gave him a wry grin. "That's what I've heard, Colm."

"What I thought we'd do, like, is see the new site

first. Get acquainted before we start pickin' at it and all.
Then I'll zip you on over to Carrowmore and meet the
staff there. Talk about what they've found, all right."

Not "all right?" as if asking reaction. All right, as in
punctuation. Zeke just nodded. He'd already done time
researching the Carrowmore finds before ever hitting
the shores here. A vast site of megalithic remains out
on the peninsula between Sligo town and Knocknarea
Mountain with its amazing fifty-foot cairn as a cap,
Carrowmore had been a site of study for over a hundred
years. More than sixty chamber tombs, stone circles
and dolmens lay spread over the peninsula, and more
were being discovered every day with the new technology available to archeology.

The archeologists dug; the anthropologists theor-
ized. How versus why. Zeke was much more interested
in the why of a puzzle. Why would a people spend over
four generations building an elaborate sun-sited tomb
that only held a few cremated remains and then deliberately close it up no more than two generations later?
Why would they cut a triangular-shaped hole in the
back of some living skulls, and why would those be the
ones enshrined in the precious, exquisitely built
chambers?

Used to the simpler, cell-type burial chambers of
the Hopi and Anasazi, Zeke was intrigued by the elaborate Celtic structures. They called to him like poetry
or music, complex and mysterious and elegant.

He couldn't wait to actually walk around on the site.
To get the feel of the ground, the position of the sun and

sky and stars. To imagine just why the old ones had chosen this particular site, why they had ringed all their tombs to open toward one central one, even the high cairns that dotted mountain tops for miles around. He couldn't wait to help shift that first layer. Pristine sites were so rare.

At the same time, he couldn't help but regret the fact that to understand the people who had come before them, they had to dismantle what had taken such care, such reverence, such immense, focused effort that it had formed the core of a culture.

"All right, boyo," Colm said, dislodging his pipe and picking up a fisherman's hat just as battered as Zeke's. "Get on your hikin' shoes, so. It's time to meet your hosts for this trip."

They were parked on an impossibly narrow gravel lane lined in high, overgrown fuchsia hedges. The middle of September, Zeke thought, and the damn things were bursting with blossom. Impossibly red, purple, sensual as sex.

Good grief, no wonder he was fantasizing about red-headed women. Even the plant life around here was stirring him up. He needed to go home and look up Tina and get this out of his system.

At least the rain had stopped. Well, slowed down to a mist. "A soft day," as Colm was wont to call it. Easy to see how the Irish were noted for their way with a good euphemism, if you could by any stretch call this a soft day. A sloppy day. A mucky day. A drizzly, damp, mold-making day.

"Don't get your knickers in a twist, lad," Colm was saying as he popped out of the driver's door. "She's just a woman."

Zeke didn't even bother to tell his friend to shut up. He just followed him straight up the hill beyond the tiny lane onto a tinier rutted path through high grass, bristly fuchsia and barbed gorse. Ravens swooped overhead with raucous calls, and a cow or two lowed in the next pasture. There was evidence of sheep everywhere, and the fresh, thick smell of farmland.

And water. He heard it tumbling over unseen stones somewhere beyond the hedges. He saw it pool in untidy puddles in the road, in the fields, in the rocks. He shouldn't be stumbling over fairies, he thought. He should have met a mermaid.

He was just about to ask where they were going when he saw the backhoe, the pile of equipment and support beams that were going to be used when they began to pick their way through to the center of the cairn.

Zeke had, of course, seen cairns in pictures. He'd caught a distant glimpse of the legendary Maeve's Cairn atop Knocknarea, a distinct mound atop a smooth-topped mountain, where legend had it the ancient fairy queen slept. He'd never come face-to-face with a cairn, though. He did now. Picking his way over a crumbling stone wall and beyond a tangle of barbed wire, Zeke pushed aside another corner of hedge to come up short.

Stones. A million or so stones, piled by human hand

to a height of at least thirty feet. At least thirty feet around. Tantalizing, like the icing over a mystery cake. Carefully, lovingly, meticulously constructed to completely cover the massive boulders that made up the chamber beneath. All dead in the middle of what Zeke now realized was a ring fort, a circle of earth supported by stone. So ancient it was ragged and worn away, fringed with yew and hawthorn and oak like a tonsured head. Outside fortification of stone and earth, then a depression, and then a secondary inner fortification. Cairn. As if built to be protected, first by the original owners and then by the fairies who followed.

Zeke didn't believe in fairies. He'd never seen ghosts or heard spectral voices or met dead people in the road. But standing there, just beyond the site, he felt again that frisson skitter straight down his spine. Something old, deep. Something, he hated to admit, familiar.

"Yeah," Colm murmured without turning away himself. "It's somethin' altogether, isn't it?"

And Zeke, looking up at an edifice that hadn't been disturbed in at least three thousand years, could only, in the end, nod. "Thanks for inviting me, Colm."

Colm, for once, didn't laugh. "Thought you'd like it, boyo."

And then Zeke was struck by whimsy.

It was an impulse he couldn't seem to control. It wasn't a mountain. Not a bell tower from whose ramparts entire vistas could be viewed. Hell, it wasn't even a good steep climb. It was just a big pile of loose rocks. Even so, Zeke seemed to be suddenly afflicted by the age-old impulse to be King of the Hill. He wanted to stand on top.

"We should be gettin' back, now," Colm said, his pipe giving off a little curl of smoke. "There are a couple of wee little government men supposed to meet us down at the local for a pint."

"I'm going up," Zeke told Colm, fingering the smooth egg-shaped chunk of adventurine he'd pulled out of a nearby streambed. "Pay my respects."

It was said that everyone visiting Maeve on the top of her windswept hill had to leave a rock in obeisance. Zeke suddenly felt compelled to pay the same obeisance here.

"You be careful up there, boyo," Colm told him. "Even the fairies don't save you from a head injury, all right, and I've had more than one quasi-mountain goat come down on that very thing."

Zeke waved him off. "Ah, Colm, I've climbed rock faces a thousand feet up. This is child's play."

There was mist against his face. Salt in the air that crept in from the ocean. Zeke could hear the sheep in the next meadow. He could hear the ravens, always close by as if to keep a good eye on things. He could smell the sharp tang of Colm's tobacco and the darker, earthier hint of peat smoke on the wind. He climbed carefully, knowing that although the whole structure was solid, each rock was loose and an invitation to fall butt-first back to the ground.

Crunch. Crunch.

He was holding his breath. How odd. It was as if,

even with the sounds and smells and tastes around him, the world was holding absolutely still. Had stopped spinning on its daily axis just to watch Zeke Kendall climb a fairy hill.

He wished his family could see him. Especially his brother Jake. Zeke smiled. He could just see himself sitting at the kitchen table back in Wyoming, telling Jake how he thought stepping onto this hill was like stepping through a doorway into magic.

He reached the top just after the sun set. The western sky was a gaudy red that faded to the purple of fuchsia closer to the sea. He could see it from here, could see Maeve on her distant mountain, and knew about where the Carrowmore field was in between. He felt, some-how, as if he were standing on a matrix. As if, if he just looked more closely, he would be able to see perfectly well what the old inhabitants had wanted to say with their constructions.

If he just stood there a little longer, as the shadows collected in the glen and washed over the stones, he would see what they had seen.

Suddenly he caught sight of her again. A flash of color, a waterfall of laughter, a scent of cloves and gorse. Not even thinking where he was, only that he had to catch her this time, Zeke spun on his heel. He saw her skip into the deep shadow. He yelled out to her.

He thought she called back. "No!" was what he thought he heard. But that couldn't be right. So he called to her again.

He didn't realize that from below him, his cries

sounded like those of a man falling. He didn't hear
Colm curse and scramble toward him. His attention
caught by a flash of peacock green in the shadows,
Zeke lost his balance and went off the side of the cairn
headfirst. He bounced thirty feet straight down and then
further, into the seven-foot depression.

For a moment there was the startled cry of disturbed
birds, the crash and rumble of a body falling. The
sudden, stricken silence that inevitably followed.

But Zeke didn't know. He didn't know, because he
was looking up into the most beautiful green eyes
he'd ever seen.

"What happened?" he asked as he saw his friend
Colm, as if through a veil of water, bending over the lip
of the rath and calling down. He couldn't seem to care,
though. He couldn't take his gaze away from those
grass-sweet eyes. "Don't I know you?"

"You must get up, Zeke," she said, leaning over him,
her eyes anxious and her hands silk-soft as she patted
at his cheek. "You have to get away before the queen
sees you. It's your only chance."

"The queen?" he asked, smiling. Not feeling anything
at all but the brush of her satiny fingers against his face.

She reached under his shoulders, trying to push him
up. "The queen of fairies."

"Sounds fun."

Odd, how she shifted, her colors darkening, her eyes
growing almost wild. "No!" she begged, pushing him,
harrying him. "You don't know what you ask. She'll
destroy you."

But Zeke couldn't move. Odd how he didn't seem to mind. "I'd rather sleep, I think. And oh, I should probably tell you…" Already his eyes were closing against the gentlest pressure of those wonderful fingers. "I don't believe in fairies."

Her voice was so soft it was like a thought in his head. A thought so suddenly dark, he shivered, even lying in her silken arms. "It doesn't matter" came her voice, sounding suddenly wistful. "They believe in you."

Chapter 2

She'd been in love with him as long as she could remember. It was all Nuala could think as she sat in the soft grass with Zeke Kendall's head cradled in her lap.

She'd loved him since she could remember loving. Since that first day she'd looked in the gazing water and seen him, so far away, wreathed in the hard dust of a failing ranch, his thin legs chapped and bruised, his startling green eyes bright as new grass.

He had grown so well. So strong and sweet and funny. She hurt to see those merry green eyes closed and the bruise forming on his broad forehead.

She was older than he was, she supposed. At least in terms he would understand. She'd already been aware before he was born. But in so many other ways she was younger, less tested than he. Less alive, for all her magic. She'd lived her life untouched, unmoved, until that first moment she'd met Zeke's eyes across the scrying water. It had been like brushing against something elemental. Now she was able to actually touch him, to hear the soft susurrence of his breathing, and it overwhelmed her. She sat on a carpet of grass in the

eternal gloaming with his head in her lap and his cal-
losed hand in hers. She felt his life force hum with
energy, like bees swarming over a new hive. Nuala
drank colors she couldn't see and heard the music of
places she'd never been, throwing her twilight world
into sharp, sudden focus. It brought her to exquisite,
painful life.

Which was only right, since she'd waited her entire
life for this moment. Which was wrong, because she
could only borrow it before she had to give it back
again. Before the queen caught sight of Zeke and
seduced him into darkness. Or, worse, Orla sucked the
very soul from him and left him, like the others, nothing
but a breathing husk.

For now, though, for this little time, Nuala could
cherish him in silence. He was hers, after all. She'd
claimed him long since. Him and his family, the
Kendall children who'd been left alone to survive on a
dying farm. Four bright, sharp spirits who had clung to
each other as they'd fought their way to adulthood.

But it was Zeke who had always compelled her.
Zeke who called to her across an ocean and more, as
he'd sat alone by a campfire, the coyotes whimpering
in the distance and the moon a cold friend.

Nuala couldn't help but smile as she pushed a strand
of wayward hair off his forehead. Chestnut, thick and
ragged, silky as sprite wings. He'd stopped cutting it a
couple of years ago during one of his digs out at the
Four Corners Reservation, that place of browns and
reds and harsh sun. Now he wore it tied out of the way

with a leather thong one of his nephews had crafted in scouting.

His face was tanned and strong, the Irish heritage in him honed and focused by generations in America. His hands were elegantly shaped, callused from digging in hard dirt and rock and other people's memories.

His eyes were closed, but she knew those, too. Laughing, green as an Irish field, more often than not distracted as he considered the lives of people long dead. There were crow's feet at the corners from his wry smile, and twin furrows between his brow from concentrating against a high desert sun.

Nuala shook her head as she rubbed at one of those furrows with the pad of her thumb. Who could be happy in such a place, she wondered, where the wind scoured the earth away and the rain never fell? She wondered if Zeke knew that he'd made it his own purgatory.

If only she could be the one to bring him out of it. She didn't have time, though. She had to give him back.

"He's not yours, ya know."

Nuala didn't bother to look up at the soft male voice. "Yes he is, Michael. He's been mine from the moment the two of us were created."

"Maybe so, but herself won't be thinkin' so."

Nuala smiled up at her uncle. "Well, she's never been one to share, now, has she?"

A sly grin appeared on the weathered face. "It's her charm, *mo chroí*."

"It's her legend. And if she does nothing else, ah, sure, she knows how to spin a legend."

Bowlegged and leathery and sparkly-eyed, Michael commanded the white horses of faerie. It was a sad eye he turned on her now. "He's not goin' back, girl. You know that. Why not take him for yours? Sure, he'd make a fair consort when your time comes. It would protect him, anyway."

Nuala looked back down to Zeke's sleeping face. She stroked his cheek with her long fingers. "My consort is already chosen."

Michael shrugged. "There's no reason you can't practice first on one who pleases you. No reason you can't keep him, too."

"There's every reason, Michael. He doesn't belong here. His colors are too bright. He walks solid on the earth, leaving deep footprints in passing where we leave none. He needs the sun and the wind and the sky. Not the half-shadows we inhabit."

Zeke Kendall bit at life like a glutton, bathing himself in its colors and tastes and textures. Even in that high, sere desert of his. To doom him to a life of eternal dusk would suck the very soul from him.

"Besides," she said, as if it didn't matter, "he's already mine. Just because I have to give him back doesn't mean I have to give him up."

"But you wouldn't have the joy of his touch, *mo chroí*. You wouldn't have the chance to bear his child. To dance through the glens with him through all the days."

"Then I won't."

For a long moment her uncle was silent. Nuala still heard everything he wanted to tell her, though, every warning he'd made from the first moment she'd taken those Kendalls as her own.

She had no business trucking with mortals. It was against all rules of the fair folk for one of them to adopt an entire family, as if she were their guardian angel. But she didn't care. She'd come to love that hard-worn family, those quiet moments when those four orphan children had bonded together to survive what most adults couldn't have. She'd come to love Zeke, who'd suffered most of all from what had happened and showed it the least.

And now she held him, actually held him in her arms as if he belonged there. She had him heavy and whole in her hands, not elusive and shifting in the water. She could caress his chafed skin and smell the man on him. She could winnow her fingers through the glorious silk of his hair to her content. And for the moment, before she had to give way to her destiny, she could pretend that it would always be this way.

"Let me sit with him for a while," she begged. "It's all I ask."

"Then we'll talk to herself?"

She nodded. "Then we'll talk to herself. And with a lot of fairy luck, we'll be able to talk her into letting him go."

Still, Michael sounded sad. "It's going to take more than luck, all right, and you well know it."

That Nuala did. It would take something sacrificed. Well, she would be the one doing the sacrificing to her capricious queen. She would do anything to make Zeke happy. Even give him up.

Soon.

For now, though, she just wanted to sit and sup at his spirit. She wanted to taste him on her fingers and smell the sun on him. There were days when she saw it reflected in Zeke's eyes as he stood out there on those high plateaus, and she envied him its heat. She envied him the fact that he faced fierce weather.

The land here was always still, always muted and subtle and soft, even when darkness threatened. Nuala loved her world like a child her very mother, because so the earth was. But sometimes, oh, sometimes she wished she could see the hard-edged colors Zeke saw. She wished she could feel the wind cut at her like a saw. She wished…

Ah, but wishing was for children. Even fairy children. She had nothing to give Zeke but half-remembered dreams and the possibility of loss. She had no life but that which passed in twilight, in the nooks and crannies of the world. She had magic, and she had the sight, and she had the music. But those things were falling away in the world where Zeke made his life, and no one could use them anymore. No one except the fairy court she would soon inherit. The court that could be such a terrible danger to him.

So she sat and stroked the hard planes of his face and rubbed at the calluses on the pads of his fingers, and she ached for what was not possible.

"Well, now, isn't he a fine, braw specimen of a man?" Zeke heard a soft voice, low as magic, sensuous as silk. Dietrich and Bacall and Helen of Troy, all wrapped up in soft Irish vowels and a chuckle that was an invitation to sin. He stretched like a cat against the sound and found it much more compelling than the fact that he couldn't seem to move.

He'd fallen, hadn't he? Had he hurt himself?

He couldn't say he cared. He just wanted to wrap himself in that voice like black satin and think unspeakable thoughts.

"I'm thinkin' I should keep him, so." The voice came again, like a sudden brush of a hot wind against his face. It was temptation, that voice, unapologetically carnal. If he could have moved, Zeke would have been squirming with it. He would have crawled after it, if necessary.

"He doesn't belong here."

Wait. He was confused. Wasn't *that* the voice he'd followed down the cairn? Fairy music, his sister-in-law would have called it, like bells on a breeze. But different suddenly. Softer. Sadder. More worried, somehow.

It didn't need to be. How could anything be wrong with that other voice around? That other voice called to every lascivious fantasy Zeke had ever had.

"Oh, come now, little man," the first seductive whisper called, almost in his own head. "Aren't you after havin' too long a sleep? Wake to me, now. Wake to see what you've stumbled over."

Little man? Zeke wanted very much to laugh. If she thought he was little, she must hang around with the defensive line of the Green Bay Packers. There weren't four out of ten hotel beds that fit his long feet and longer legs. Zeke was six-five and still growing, according to his sisters, who were in charge of buying Christmas sweaters.

"Give him back," the other voice pleaded, there in his head. Making him smile and want to sigh. "Sure, you don't need another. You ask too much."

Well, whatever else was going on, he decided it was worth it to end up being fought over by two of the most seductive voices he'd ever heard in his life.

"I'll not, so," the first voice said and laughed, which made him smile.

"I'd rather you didn't," he said without opening his eyes.

More laughter, low, like woodwinds in a Ravel symphony.

"You wouldn't, would you, little man? Sure now, open your eyes to me, then."

Oddly enough, this time when he tried to open his eyes, Zeke didn't have any trouble. It didn't mean his problems were solved, of course. He had to blink a few times to focus, and even after that, he wasn't sure he was doing it right.

Something was wrong with the world, or with his optic nerves. There seemed to be a glistening feel to the light, like late evening sun reflected off the sea. Everything around him seemed brighter, yet somehow less distinct. Just a bit more beautiful and less real, a land caught beneath a shallow sea. And Zeke, who had spent much of his adult life in the wind-blasted desert of the Southwest, found himself mesmerized.

And then there was the face hovering above him.

Dear God, he thought. It must be his eyes. Or his head. No woman could look like that. Ageless, exquisite, with eyes like a cat and hair like aspen leaves in the fall.

And her smile. Zeke, who hadn't so much as read a poem since he'd had to recite them for punishment in high school, wanted to write odes to it. He wanted to lick it like a cat.

"Hello, little man," she greeted him, her smile widening, her long, delicate white hand lifting to brush his hair back.

Zeke knew that his smile was goofy and big and breathless. "Hello, yourself."

That was when the second face made itself known by letting go a very unladylike snort. Zeke blinked again, refocusing. His stomach had just done flip-flops, and his heart was in his throat.

It was she. The beautiful woman from the fairy glade. The one who laughed like wind chimes. The one who somehow looked familiar.

"Well, I ran hard enough to let you catch me," he said with an even goofier smile.

She didn't look amused. "I told you to be careful, then, didn't I?" she demanded, hands on sea green-clad hips.

She was wearing that dress again, a swath of peacock silk that lifted and swirled in a breeze Zeke couldn't feel. A breeze that tangled in her hair, making it dance, rubies and garnets and gold in the unseen sun.

"And yet here you are."

Odd, how she seemed to him brighter and sweeter in her peacock than the other woman did in her white. Odd, how even with that exquisite silken body next to her, it was the girl in peacock he couldn't take his eyes from.

He frowned again, plagued by an almost memory. "Don't I know you?"

"You warned him?" the other woman asked, her voice deceptively soft.

His siren faced the other woman head-on, even though Zeke could see that her hands were trembling there on her hips. Silver-ringed hands that had stroked his face in the sunlight.

Sunlight.

He'd fallen off that cairn at sunset in the rain, yet he could have sworn the sun had just been shining. The minute the siren spoke, though, the air seemed to darken around him. The trees shivered in a chill wind that unnerved him.

He tried to move again, with little improvement in the results. "Can you tell me what happened?" he asked. "I mean, I know it's a cliché, but where am I?"

"You're where you're meant to be," the first woman told him without looking away from the woman he'd followed. "My house."

He saw the wrinkles of a stream-carved landscape, and old, gnarled trees cloaked in an almost fluorescent moss. He saw boulders and heard water skittering over stones somewhere nearby. He saw clouds and distant mountains. He didn't see a house. He didn't remember being near a house. Just a...

"Oh, no."

"Just so," the ageless woman said with smoke in her

voice, still looking at the girl, the one he'd run after. "Didn't my little Nuala here decide she'd save you for herself? That's right, now, isn't it, Nuala?"

"It is," Nuala answered.

"Nuala?" he asked.

Neither of them bothered to look down at him. "It's my name," the girl answered, her hair trembling in that unseen wind. Red hair, copper hair, hair like a Colorado sunset.

Except he wasn't in Colorado. He was in Ireland. In that other woman's house. Except there wasn't a house.

"You may call me Mab, if you so choose, little man," she answered as if he'd asked. "But use it with caution. Its power is fearful. Most don't understand it." She gave another smile, more feline, reaching out to touch the other girl's cheek. "Some, though—" she sighed "—don't respect it as they should."

"I respect it," Nuala assured her dryly. "I'd be a fool not to, now, wouldn't I?"

"And unnatural."

"Aye. And unnatural."

"But you would challenge me for the little man here, would you?"

Zeke saw the younger woman, Nuala, pause. Gather herself, as if deliberately making herself smaller. More subservient. Instinctively, he wanted to protest. For some reason, though, his mouth wasn't working much better than his legs.

"And how could I ever challenge you, my queen?" she said. "I would ask. Plead. Sure, and don't you have your choice of consorts from the most beautiful of us?

You could choose any mortal who wishes to spend his days in the glade. This one, though, doesn't."

"And you know that for certain?"

"I do."

"What glade?" Zeke finally managed to ask. "Where are we?"

And don't I know you?

The woman who called herself Mab waved an elegant, silk-draped arm at him. White shimmering silk like samite over alabaster skin. A subtle dance of snow and shadows. "Patience, little man." As if that were all he deserved to hear.

Mab.

The name was an odd one, but he swore he'd heard it before. Someplace old. Somewhere in stories his sister-in-law had entertained her children with or included in the books she wrote on folklore. Someplace...

Oh, good God. Now he remembered. Mab. Queen of Fairies. It was a variant of the name Maeve. Maeve, who was supposed to be enjoying her eternal rest at the top of that nearby mountain underneath about fifty thousand tons of stone.

She turned on him as if she'd heard him, that woman with the impossibly yellow hair that seemed to wave gently in the stillness, golden seaweed against the tide. She smiled with eyes so ancient Zeke wondered if they'd seen the glory days of Rome. Smiled on young Grecian gods. Watched the birth and death of the ones who had laid down this very cairn.

"Ah, no," she answered him. "The one you're thinking of is another of us. Older, far wiser and more powerful." She and Nuala quickly bowed their heads, as if paying obeisance. Then she smiled again, sultry and sure. "But she has gone on now to the Land to the West. Where my court travels soon. You'll like it there, I'm thinking, in the land of eternal sun."

"You're leaving?"

How could a person feel so bereft at losing someone he'd just met? But Nuala, flame-haired Nuala, suddenly seemed vital to him. As if he'd waited his whole life just to stumble over her. Stumble, he guessed, being the operative word.

"Does it hurt you then to know that?" Mab asked, and seemed delighted. Her eyes, those cat eyes of yellow-green, seemed to gleam with anticipation. "It doesn't have to, now. Does it, Nuala?"

"Set him down, my lady," the red-headed beauty pleaded. "Sure, why don't you play with something else?"

Mab seemed to grow in size. Zeke blinked, wondering if he was getting worse. Hallucinating now. She seemed to glow, and it was with a dark light that cast an odd shadow over Nuala of the sunset hair. For a second, less than a second, Mab changed. Melted into a face that terrified, black-eyed and sharp-toothed, that golden hair undulating snakes. A nightmare, a sharp punch to the chest that made him want to close his eyes, to scuttle back.

And then, before he could believe what he'd seen,

gone. And the blonde beauty right where she'd been all along.

"I'll be thanking you not to try to assume your place before your time, my little Nuala," the queen suggested, and Zeke thought the sound of her purring voice was terrible.

He was afraid for the girl. Afraid, suddenly, of that exquisite, ageless woman. And yet he still couldn't take his eyes from her.

"Am I paralyzed?" he asked to fill the suddenly profound silence that even the birds didn't break.

That quickly, the darkness left the queen and she shone. Literally, as if the sun were reflecting off satin. "Now, why would I be doin' something so harsh to you?" she demanded with a flick of that lustrous hair. "A queen's consort has no business being imperfect." Again her mouth lifted; her eyes lit with predatory heat. "And I'm thinkin' there's nothing at all imperfect about you, little man."

At least Zeke knew he didn't have a head injury. He was able to pick up on the pertinent point. "Queen's consort?"

"A rare privilege, it is. If I choose you, you'll find yourself living with an eternity of pleasure and laughter and music." Her eyes grew dark, her pupils large. "And, of course, me."

Well, that sucked the air right out of Zeke's lungs. Just that last word conjured up visions of milky thighs and perfect breasts. Sinning and sensuality and slow seduction. He could actually see it in his head, him twined with her like a pair of vines, every inch meeting in heat and shadow and silken delight. Touch and taste and indescribable ecstasy. In seconds he was flushed and impatient and itching to move.

Toward her.

The queen with seduction in her eyes.

These people must be able to communicate without words, because Nuala snorted again, and Zeke had the most disconcerting feeling that she could see the same images he could. And, honest to God, he found himself blushing. And he hadn't blushed since his first look at Betty Williams' breasts back in seventh grade.

"It's not polite to eavesdrop," he told her, trying to smile.

She wasn't smiling back. She was staring at Mab with something like disappointment in her eyes. And, suddenly, without her saying a word, Zeke could see her even more clearly in his mind. Buttercream skin, a smattering of freckles over soft shoulders, a shape as sleek as a seal. He could actually feel the weight of her breasts in his hands and the silk of her hair against his face. He tasted unexpected joy and went rock hard in an instant.

"You can stop now," he growled, relieved as hell he was still in his jeans and workshirt. At least his wayward thoughts wouldn't be obvious to the world at large.

She looked down at him. "Stop what?"

"Putting those images in my head. I don't need any help, believe me."

He thought she might be the one to blush this time. Instead, she shot Mab a questioning look. "I did no such thing."

Mab actually frowned, which seemed to dim the sunlight around them and set the trees to dipping. "It wouldn't be to my amusement to do so, now, would it?"

Nuala looked back and forth for a minute. Zeke could see the dusting of freckles across her nose and found himself wanting to kiss them, one by one. To touch them with his tongue. He wanted to reach out and trace the contour of her collarbone. Just that, as if it were the key to every sensual excess in creation.

Well, he decided, if he was going to have a dream, it might as well be an erotic one.

"You aren't dreaming, little man," Mab informed him archly.

Zeke smiled in delight. "Of course I am. Can you think of any other reason I'd have two gorgeous women arguing over me?"

The two of them looked at him as if his hair had caught fire.

And then, oddly enough, Nuala gave him a wry smile. "No," she said, as if humoring a madman. "None at all."

He lifted a hand. "See? Now, if you'd just give me my legs back, I'd like to take a look around. Since I'm here anyway, maybe I can learn something about the real fairies who used to live here. I'm an anthropologist, you know. Besides, my sister-in-law would never forgive me if I passed up the chance. She collects stories about you people, ya know."

He didn't mention the fact that he wouldn't mind exploring some of those sexual fantasies the girls kept tossing around.

Nuala lifted an elegant eyebrow. "You don't believe in fairies."

"It's *my* dream," he reminded her. "I can believe in anything I want while I'm here."

"Just so," Mab assured him, her eyes conveying a far more complex meaning. It was as if the earth itself were calling, carnal and wise and ancient as life. It stirred him and shook him in ways he couldn't even begin to describe.

But, oddly enough, it didn't compel him. What compelled him seemed to be the sound of fairy bells on the wind. Nuala's voice, her scent, her soft green eyes.

"It's not your choice, little man."

Zeke smiled again. "My dream. My choice."

Mab wasn't amused. "It's not her choice either. She has responsibilities that don't include you."

Zeke frowned. "Fairies have responsibilities? Like what, mowing the pasture and milking the unicorns?"

"She will be Mab," the woman said, her voice soft and terrible. "She has no room for you."

"But you're Mab," he said, feeling stupid.

"Send him back," Nuala pleaded. "Please."

"No," the queen said. "I'm thinkin' I won't. Sure and don't I think I like the challenge."

As if those were magic words, suddenly Zeke had his legs back. He didn't waste a second, but climbed right to his feet to find that he towered over both women. Oddly, though, he still felt as if he were looking up at Mab.

At least he could stand. His head still hurt, though, sharp and insistent. And moving quickly made him a bit dizzy. You would think if you were dreaming you wouldn't notice those kinds of things.

"Thank you," he said with a bow, as if that were a normal thing. "I appreciate the return of my limbs. Now, have you seen my hat?"

Nuala smiled, even though she still had shadows in those pearlescent green eyes of hers. "I'm afraid you left it behind."

"Behind where? I had it on when I climbed that damn hill."

Mab frowned again. Again the light dimmed, and a cool breeze whispered against the back of Zeke's neck. "I'd be pleased if you didn't be disparaging my home, little man."

Zeke grinned at her. "My apologies, my…um, how does one address the presiding queen of the fairies?"

Her smile was slow and enticing. "Lover," she offered, the word setting off those images again.

God, she had long legs. Supple, strong long legs. And evidently, from the pictures that flashed in Zeke's mind, almost double-jointed.

"How 'bout something a little less personal?" he asked, suddenly able to smell honeysuckle and musk.

She sighed. "My lady will do, then. For now."

"My queen—" Nuala said, but the queen cut her off.

"What are you willing to offer?"

Nuala never hesitated. "Anything."

The queen's eyebrow lifted. Then she smiled, but it

was not a pleasant one. "Well, we'll have to think on that, won't we?"

Nuala seemed to shrink again. She had her hands clenched in those diaphanous skirts, as if holding herself together.

"If it would please you, my queen."

Mab stood there for a moment, contemplating. Her hair glowed eerily, drawing light and compelling the eye. The filmy white material of her dress pulled taut across her lush breasts, compelling Zeke to look, to see that an exquisite emerald hung deep in the valley between, a startling, mesmerizing stone in a mesmerizing place.

Mab saw the direction of his attention and smiled again. "Yes," she said on a perfect purr. "I'm in the mood for a challenge, all right. I'll consider your petition, Nuala. But you should be after thinking hard about what you are willing to offer in exchange for his freedom."

"Until then, he keeps his time," Nuala demanded.

Mab took a second to think. "It is only fair. So it will be."

Nuala seemed to simply deflate, as if all that had held her up had been her bravado.

"I thank you," she said with a graceful curtsy.

Mab lifted that imperial eyebrow again. "You thank me, what?"

Nuala bowed her head. "I thank you, mother."

Mab nodded, evidently satisfied. "Just so," she said. And then with no more fanfare than a sigh, she was gone.

Chapter 3

It was Zeke's turn to stare. *"Mother?"*

Nuala watched Mab glide away as if she had no feet at all. One day maybe she herself would have the ability to command such grace. One day, when she was queen. When she became Mab.

No, she wouldn't. Because no matter that she was her mother's daughter, she should never have been the heir. She didn't have the stature or the power or the ruthlessness that was demanded of the Mab. She preferred the insignificant tucks and folds of the land to the splendors of the court. She yearned for solitude rather than service.

It didn't matter. Her mother had finally made the decision to take her court from this glen to the Land of the West where the sun never set. When she went, those who stayed would turn to Nuala as their new queen, whether she was worthy or not.

Still, it was better than going. She wasn't ready yet. She wasn't sure she ever would be. Never to see this place of exquisite greens again. Never to listen for the ravens on the wing or the cows lowing in the pastures or the whisper of the breeze though the leaves.

Never to see the sun reflect off one man's eyes as he stood with his head thrown back to a desert sky.

"Nuala?"

She turned to him now and fought a fresh well of sadness. "Aye," she answered him. "She's my mother."

Zeke whistled through his teeth, his attention on the vanishing figure of Mab. "Must be like growing up with Marlene Dietrich."

Nuala frowned in confusion. "I'm not sure I know."

He grinned. "I guess you wouldn't. Marlene's movies probably don't play the Fairyland Rialto."

"I know John Wayne," she offered, thinking that Zeke was just as tall, but more handsome by far in his plaid shirt and faded jeans. "He was here once. A big man, he was, just like you. He was after making a movie with a wee, dear man who had pixies in his eyes."

Zeke nodded, evidently stunned. "Barry Fitzgerald. You were alive when *The Quiet Man* was filmed here? You *saw* it?"

Uncomfortable with the image Zeke must have of her, Nuala shrugged. "Time is…different here. I'm younger than I seem."

"You measure things in the reverse of dog years."

She frowned again, but Zeke waved her off. "Sorry. Human joke."

She smiled at that. "Mortal. We call you mortals. Not human. We're human ourselves, after all."

He looked surprised. "How can that be?"

She smiled. "Sure, we weren't always faerie. We were human, like you. Would you like the story?"

"I'm an anthropologist. Of course I'd like the story."

She nodded. "We'll be after visiting Ealga, then. She's the storyteller. She's one of the few left who remembers."

"I'd rather you tell me," he said, reaching out a hand.

"And whatever for?" she asked, taking hold, the callused warmth of him disconcerting her. "I don't have the music in my words. Sure, it's not my gift."

He smiled, and Nuala thought a woman could survive on no more nourishment than that smile. "What *is* your gift?"

"Harp," she managed. "I play the harp."

"I'd like to hear it."

He didn't need to, she thought. Its music was there in his voice. Oh, sweet Mother, how she was going to miss his voice.

"You will, so," she promised. "We'll have music tonight at the banquet."

"You have a banquet tonight?"

"We have a banquet every night. It is our way."

His smile grew into a big grin. "Hmmm. Wine, women and song. I think I'm gonna like this place."

"Well, don't," she cautioned, suddenly frightened. "Better men than you have been lost here and never found their way back. I don't want you to be one of them."

"Why not? Wouldn't you like it if I stayed with you?"

She was the one who saw it this time, his strong suntanned hands on her skin, his mouth covering hers, his thick mahogany hair twined around her fingers. Flesh against flesh, friction and fusion and fire. Heat, oh, such heat. Gasps and soft cries of wonder.

That flash of vision threatened to shatter her.

"You aren't meant for here" was all she could say. "It would destroy you. Sure, it would destroy your family."

He frowned. "What do you know about my family?"

She couldn't help it. She reached up and laid her hand against the soft sandpaper of his cheek, just as she had earlier, just as she'd wanted to do since he'd been a child and she'd seen him standing in that terrible cold barn where he'd found his father.

"Ah, well, I imagine you'd say it's another gift I have. I can look into the gazing water and see what is far away. I saw you there when I was a girl."

"You couldn't have. You were watching *The Quiet Man* being filmed."

"I told you," she said, pulling her hand back. "Time is different here altogether. A fairy's childhood is longer. I promise. We were children together, you and I."

"And you...*saw* my brother Jake, and Gen and Lee. And me."

"Oh, aye. I dreamed sometimes that you were my family. That I sat with you for meals around that big wooden table with the cloth of red and white checks in your kitchen. I would be eating with you and telling your brother Jake what I learned that day at school, and sure wouldn't I ask for second helpings? What was it you called it, now? Stew?"

He was staring now, the light in his eyes suddenly

brittle. "No, you wouldn't. You wouldn't have wanted to be cold and hungry and frightened every minute of your life."

She wanted to reach up to him again. But she didn't. He'd just erected that invisible barrier he sometimes employed to keep people away. To keep himself safe, when really there was no safe place, even in her world.

"Ah, I'm sorry, Zeke. Sorry for all of you that your parents died when you were so young. I'm desperate sorry you scraped at that land for so long before your brother found the magic in it. But you had him, sure. You had your sisters. You're lucky, Zeke. You truly are."

She wondered what he saw in her eyes, then, because he was the one to lift his hand. To lay that callused, strong palm against her cheek, as if he cherished her. And this time it was himself who smiled.

"You must be a fairy," he said. "No human woman would take me to task like that and get away with it."

"Mortal," she said, losing herself in the warm shelter of his hand, the sea of his eyes. The only way to extinguish a fairy life was to lose it in deep water. Nuala thought she risked that, sure, looking into Zeke's fathomless bright eyes. "I told you. We call you mortal."

"Which Ealga is going to tell me more about."

Barely, she was able to nod. "Aye."

He took her breath, she swore. He took her soul, just with the beguilement in his eyes. He was doing it now, looking on her as if he could scoop up the heart and core of her. As if he could reach in past all her magic and sense and will, and call her away.

He could, she knew. He could do it with nothing more than a flick of his fingers. With a smile, so his dimple peeped out and his teeth flashed. So his eyes, those mesmerizing spring green eyes, lost the wary edge he didn't realize they held.

But for now, he stood still. He kept from smiling, even as he reached out to her again, as if to touch her. To test her. To find out, she knew, whether she was real.

She was real. She was sore and anxious and hungry for the life in those eyes. For the memories in that fine, handsome head of his. For the strength and breadth and song of him.

"Do you…uh, would you be wanting to go now?" she asked, not even recognizing her own voice. Not acknowledging the fact that his hand still hovered near her cheek.

"No," he finally answered. "There's something I need to do first."

"Oh?"

He nodded. "I want to know about you." He shook his head, allowed his mouth to curve just a bit. "Don't I *know* you?"

His hand had fallen back to his side. Nuala saw him rub at his jeans leg, as if testing himself.

"Ah, well…" she managed, briefly looking into the shadows of the glen where tiny wee beings passed their lives among the bluebells and foxglove. "That'll take some explaining. Why don't we walk, then? By the time I'm finished, we'll be at Ealga's."

Zeke took a quick look around. "I guess that would be okay. I won't get lost, will I?"

"No more than you are now."

He flashed her another grin. "In that case, lead on."

She frowned, still anxious after that fall of his. "You're feelin' all right, then? Your head isn't bothering you? It was quite a tumble you took, you know."

"Yes, I do know. I can feel every rock I rolled over. But my head only hurts a little now, and the dizziness is better."

"And you're not feeling anything else? Anything troubling?"

"Other than a massive amount of confusion?"

This time Nuala smiled. "And why should you be, now? 'Tis all very simple. You climbed a hill to find the fairy queen, and so you did."

His expression was wry again. "Did I tell you I don't believe in fairies?"

"Did I not tell you that matters to no one here but you?"

He laughed, and Nuala felt her heart leap like a salmon. "As long as I know the ground rules." He shook his head again, a lock of hair escaping its confines and sweeping his forehead. "But it's going to take some getting used to."

Nuala tilted her head, savoring the sparkle of his wit, his words. "What?"

"This place. This dream. It's so real, but it's not real at all, which makes me think I can do anything here and not pay the consequences."

It wasn't his words that stunned her but his gaze. The sudden lightning that again sparked between them. The sweet music of passion a fairy understood well. In an instant there were poems said between them, promises, psalms. Nuala saw him again in her arms, his strong, sunkissed body enfolding hers, his eyes open and laughing and incandescent. She tasted the heady bouquet of his scent and wanted more. She wanted it all, just as she had every time she'd sneaked away to look into her scrying water.

Oh, she wanted to tell him not to believe. Not to give in to the sorcery of this place and assume that all was possible without cost. He would be gone soon, back to his family, and she would be left to lead her fractious, frivolous clan through the next millennium with a consort she hadn't chosen but had promised herself to. Zeke would be hurt. She would be shattered, never to be put back together again.

But she couldn't. Sure, she couldn't say so much as a word.

Selfishly, she wanted him to fall in love with her. She wanted, with a desperation that ached in her, for him to look to her every minute, to smile when he saw her, to laugh when they made love. She wanted to be the only woman in his eyes, even for the short time they had. Since she'd loved him that way for so long.

So she smiled, her decision made, and led him farther into the land of faerie.

If this was a dream, it was a damn gorgeous one. Not only was the earth they walked glistening and sweet and green, but the people who inhabited it, one and all, were beautiful. Some pale as snow, some dark as night, some terrible in a way he couldn't explain. All graceful and long-bodied and sloe-eyed.

Not that they came up and introduced themselves. Zeke only caught them out of the corner of his eye. Tucked in trees and inhabiting shadows. They watched him, though, the interloper in their magical world. They stayed so still that sometimes he thought he only imagined seeing them.

But they watched.

"Greetings to you, lady," Nuala called suddenly.

Zeke turned to see her bow to a tall, full oak tree, the kind that seemed to sweep its branches straight to the ground.

The tree dipped a bit, swayed, and damn if it didn't look like a curtsy. "And greetings back to you, child" came a voice at once old and impossibly young that made Zeke think of spring and winter and time.

"A friend of yours?" he asked, trying like hell to see who had answered. It couldn't have been the tree. Last he checked, he was in fairyland, not Oz.

"It is, so," Nuala said with a soft smile. "She is Ailish, the dryad who inhabits this tree."

"A dryad."

"Aye. You might want to be saying hello yourself. She'll remember you then, when you return, and listen for us for you. Dryads care for the sacred trees they inhabit. They're old and wise and whimsical."

Zeke could have sworn he heard a rustle of laughter from the tree. Firmly believing in the "when in Rome" rule, he smiled himself and bowed like a courtier. "My lady Ailish," he greeted the entity. "Your home is magnificent and must harbor a host of beautiful birds and animals."

"My," the voice crooned, the tree seeming to shake out its leaves a bit, like a woman flipping back her hair. "Isn't he the silver-tongued one, now?"

Nuala's smile was delighted and sweet. "Oh, aye, my lady. He's that and more." She walked on, stepping so elegantly the grass never bent beneath her feet. "She likes you," she said.

Zeke looked over to see the remnants of that magnificent smile. "She does, huh? What about the rest of them? Everybody who's watching and following us like we're a Mardi Gras parade?"

Nuala gave him a sharp look. "You can see them, then?"

"Shouldn't I?"

"Sure, not everyone does, even here. But don't let it worry you. They mean no harm."

"Not according to local legend."

She shook her head, sending that gem-hued hair trembling all the way down her back. "You are under the protection of the queen. At least now, until she says differently."

He saw the shadows collect in her eyes and frowned. "Yeah, that might be a point we should discuss."

"We will. But first, you should learn more about us."

He nodded, perfectly happy to walk alongside her. "Since I'm an anthropologist and all."

Her smile wasn't as bright as he would have liked.

It still gleamed and mesmerized, though, a potent drug. And he could smell those cloves again. And something more elusive. Iris? Alyssum?

"Since you're an anthropologist."

He smiled back with every tooth in his head. He couldn't take his eyes off her. She was so delicate, even though she came up to his shoulders. She was slant-eyed and high-cheeked and luscious of lips. Kissable lips. Lips a man couldn't stop wanting to plunder. Green eyes, forest eyes, eyes so deep and still and bright he couldn't look away from them. A body crafted to fit a man's hands, sleek and supple, but rounded in all the perfect places. Just watching the sway of her hips made his mouth water.

Whoever designed these fairy dresses should be rewarded for ingenuity. Crafted to float and slide and furrow over the most interesting places, they were everything a man could fantasize.

And just now, when Nuala shook her head, Jake saw her ears, and they were so perfect, he wanted to laugh. Small, close set ears with just the faintest suggestion of a tip at the top. Fairy ears, if he'd ever seen any.

Damn, could he come up with the perfect dream or what? Not only the answer to the puzzle he'd been sent to solve, but delivered by the most delicious woman he'd ever met. A woman who made him ache, certainly. But one he felt he knew better than he did, whom he wanted to know better yet. Whom he wanted to lie with and talk to and just sit beside. And he had never met a woman like that in his entire life.

One of these days he was going to have to figure out how to have a dream like this back in Utah.

"Zeke? Are you all right?"

Her voice sent skitters of pleasure down his spine. It was magical wind chimes again, where there wasn't any wind....

Good God, was he really thinking this way? The only time he'd ever used an adjective in his life was to describe the living conditions of dead Anasazis. He was about to break into sonnets, and he couldn't stop.

He blinked, as if trying to focus better. "I feel as if I don't want to leave you," he blurted out.

Her smile was even more enigmatic. "Sure, it's the magic of the place. See? The sun shines, even as the dark grows near."

He looked around and thought it really had to be a dream. Either that or he'd hit his head harder than he'd realized. The world around him was hazy and soft, with the gleam of light in it. He couldn't see the sun, but the landscape reflected it. Not bright, but subtle, mysterious as those shadows that collected in all the velvet corners and crevices of the earth. Seductive as the women who populated it.

"Don't they call this the gloaming?"

"If we were in the mortal world, they would, so."

"I don't recognize anything. There should be a farmhouse here, and at least a half dozen fairy mounds within a mile or two."

But there was just a soft forest, with oak and alder and hazel and blackthorn, bluebells carpeting hillsides and moss-clad stones littering the streambed. He could smell peat smoke and the clean wash of rain and the coconut tang of gorse on the breeze.

"Ah, well," she said, "you're not in that realm. Fairy is on a different plane altogether, something I've heard you mortals call dimensions. There are just places and times where it is easier to cross over."

"The veil is thinner here?"

She looked up, surprised. He grinned at her.

"Just because I chose to study North America doesn't mean I don't know the lore. After all, my family all came from here."

"Yes," she said with a peculiar inflection. "I know."

Zeke found himself smiling again. "My great-great-grandma was a powwow woman. A healer from Ireland. You might have known her."

Nuala's smile was delighted. "A bit before my time, I'm afraid. We'll be after asking Ealga."

He still had the feeling she was holding something back. Something she should be telling him but wasn't. He decided he didn't care. He had time. For the moment, he would just enjoy her company and see what came. He would bask in that sensual glow of her, the scent of earth and exotic flowers that surrounded her. He would fill himself with her laughter and revel in the mystery of her eyes. Her eyes that were the exact shade of the new leaves on the trees overhead.

The realization stopped Zeke in his tracks. The trees were indeed just bursting with leaf. New leaf.

He spun around to see that even in this odd half-light,

the grass was that sharp, saturated yellow-green that only appeared in the spring. Then he saw the rhododendrons and the wild yellow flags that filled the fields. And damn it, he'd seen those bluebells and not realized the meaning.

When he'd fallen, it had been late summer. That oak should have been drooping with leaves, the heather thick and the flags a spring memory.

"How long have I been here?" he demanded, suddenly panicked.

Lifting a gentle hand to his arm, Nuala smiled. "Sure, not that long. Our seasons are different altogether."

"There are foxglove growing in September."

She laughed. "Ah well, the foxgloves always grow here. How else would the wee ones have their hats?"

"Wee ones? Fairies have children?"

She stopped there in the grass, that filmy peacock dress wafting like smoke in the breeze, her impish smile like a light. "Sure and how else would we have adults?"

"But I thought that the little people...I mean..."

"Ah, I see. You'll be looking for leprechauns, then, won't you?" She shook her head. "One misplaced fairy and the whole world is after looking for a pot of gold. The leprechauns live east of here. And there aren't that many, I'll have you know. They're just more flashy with their wares."

Zeke was fast being left behind. "Uh-huh. So the other wee ones who aren't children...?"

She shrugged. "Aren't we just as varied as mortals?

Some clans are sprites who skim the water, and some live in the glades and dance on the flowers. Some are great and fierce and ride the wind. And the Tua, who are oldest and wisest, watch over them all. All but the dark faerie, of course. But it is not spoken of."

Zeke looked over to see her make an odd sign with her hands. It reminded him of somebody crossing themselves against evil.

"The dark faerie?"

"You'll be meeting none of them. Don't fesh on it."

Zeke nodded, uncertain what to say. "And the rest of the fairies? They'd be willing to talk to me?"

"If you're not after frightening or insulting them. Remember. We live at the edges of your sight, in the dusk and the far places. We stay here, now, woven into the earth because we find mortals too fond of fighting and taking and fury. They pillage the sacred places and pave over the magic. They walk away from what is beautiful, and then, when they refuse to believe, wonder why we leave."

As Nuala spoke, Zeke took another look around and saw, this time, small spirals of smoke from over the rise. Odd, small structures of wood and wattle that seemed to be houses. He saw animals and children and an immensely old woman seated at a loom in a yard. And just around the curve of the stream, he was sure he saw one of his brother Jake's prized horses, Grayghost himself, even though he'd been dead all these years.

He blinked, wondering where the hell they'd all come from, this whole community of pointy-eared people. The sight of them incited a fresh headache. He was having trouble enough keeping up with two women. The sudden crowd literally made him dizzy.

"Tell me something," he said, rubbing at his left temple. "Am I going to wake up gray-haired to find that all my friends and family are dead?"

For a second there was silence. Zeke turned to Nuala, surprised to see a look of anguish on her face. "Nay," she said, her voice so soft he almost lost it in the burble of the nearby stream. "The queen has made her promise."

"What is it you wanted to say?" he asked, seeing the ambivalence in her eyes.

She shook her head, her smile rueful and small. "You already know me too well, Zeke Kendall. I was going to ask if you would be after minding so much if you did. But it's not my question to ask, nor your offer to be making."

Again he was assailed by images, years and eons spent in Nuala's soft arms, tucked into these shadows and valleys, where wee creatures wore foxglove hats and all the women served up sexual fantasies.

Nuala must have known. She frowned, and the visions changed. Instead of savoring his time, he languished, fading year by year into nothing. Into something no longer human, a sun-starved wraith who couldn't find rest or passion. A moan on the wind, left alone and forgotten by the ones who loved him most.

It was his turn to shake his head. "I get it," he all but growled, the images leaving a bad aftertaste. His headache was intensifying, unsettling his stomach. "So what *will* happen?"

Nuala was watching him more closely, it seemed. "Until you make your decision, the two clocks will match themselves and you'll age no more than normal."

"My decision?"

"Ah, well, we'll talk about that later," she said. "After we see Ealga and learn your anthropologist answers."

He was rubbing at his temple again, the dizziness increasing. His stomach lurched, and he thought he could hear somebody calling him to wake up. Surely just the sight of a fairy village shouldn't be laying him low like this.

"Zeke?"

He kept rubbing his head, his focus wavering. "I don't think I feel well," he admitted, closing his eyes. Hoping like hell that everybody would still be there when he opened them. Or maybe that they wouldn't be. He didn't really know anymore.

"Look at me, Zeke."

Her voice was so peremptory. So strong. Her hands were on his face. Could she hold his sanity together with her hands? Could she make this dream make sense, or stop the feeling that he was slipping away somewhere? Hell, hadn't he already done that?

And then, suddenly, he found himself on his knees. The world spun, and his head seemed to split wide open. "Ah, God..."

"Zeke? What's wrong? Talk to me, Zeke. Please, now, open your eyes."

He heard her voice as if from a distance. He heard, suddenly, other voices, whispering, murmuring, anxious and hurried. But he couldn't make them out. His head hurt too damn much.

Then he felt her. She laid her hands back on him, cool, soft hands that calmed the panic. Soft, stroking hands that seemed to sap the pain away.

"Am I being punished?" he asked. After all, his thoughts hadn't been exactly altruistic. "I promise, whatever I did...I won't...do it again."

Could fairies do this? Could he survive it?

"Ah, no," she whispered next to him, around him, inside his splitting head. "It's all right. Just lie still and let me make you feel better."

He was lying down anyway, he thought. His eyes were open, he knew they were, but he couldn't see her. Couldn't see those hot green hills or the clouds that glowed with late sun. All he could see was a wavering light that blinded him until he had to close his eyes again.

"You're sure," he said, gritting his teeth.

"Rest," she said. "Just rest a bit. It will be better. Close your eyes now, close them soft, and all will be well."

Her voice was music: woodwinds and cellos and the most soulful flute, wrapping itself inside his head, around his head, around his arms and chest and heart. He strained to hear it, it was so soft, and in listening, he began to calm. He began to ease. He lay in her arms and let her stroke his face with those magic hands of hers, and he began to heal.

"It's better now," she declared on a melody. "Better

now, softer now, sweeter now. Better in the core and the heart of you, in the meat and marrow of you, in the light and sorrow of you, in the depths and delights of you…"

And it was. As if called to ease by her words, his heart slowed, his pain eased, his panic calmed, and he felt as if he could rest. Could rest in her arms in the new green grass.

"Now sleep," she called on that breeze of a voice. "Sleep and I'll be here to watch over you."

He tried. He courted sleep as the voices murmured his name and Nuala stroked his head and the pain dissipated like red mist. And then, he thought he felt a drop of rain fall on his cheek, soft warm rain. And as it struck it sapped the rest of the pain away and he slept.

Tucked into the crook of the largest oak in the wood, the queen rested naked against the chest of her latest consort, a beautiful, black-haired, blue-eyed fairy named Ardwen who kept the court's laws, even as he pleased his queen and she pleased him.

They were doing neither right now. Even though they lay naked and fit together with ease, their hands instinctively touching and soothing, they were watching Nuala as she sat cross-legged as a girl cradling the mortal's body in her arms.

"She's wasting her good fairy tears on him, I'm thinking," Ardwen mused, his handsome, full mouth pulled down in a frown.

Mab didn't move so much as an eyelash as she considered her daughter. "She's showing a new gift, *I'm* thinkin'. It cannot hurt the girl to come to healing if she's to be the queen. Her people will need that when I'm gone from here with the old ones."

"Is she healing because of a gift," he asked, his voice sounding a bit petulant, "or because she thinks she's after loving that waste of a mortal?"

"You question her decisions?" The queen's voice was soft, so soft that the tree above them shuddered. It was never a good thing to hear the queen go quiet.

"Ah sure, she's young yet," he hedged, his tilted blue eyes worried. He knew better than anyone that his position wasn't a secure one, and he worshipped his queen in ways a mortal couldn't understand. "She has to find a way beyond this infatuation, so."

Mab caressed her consort's arm with long-nailed fingers. "Just so, just so. And haven't I insured she's after learning even now?"

Ardwen stroked the sweet arch of her breast, his soft fingers savoring the silken skin of a fairy queen. "I still don't understand how you allowed her to bring him here."

The queen laughed, and the tree shuddered again. "You're thinking *she* brought him here?"

It took Ardwen a long moment to frame a reply, and not because he was distracted by the cool, sleek slope of that breast. "But why? Isn't this the time she should be focusing on what she is to be? She hasn't the luxury, sure, to be amusing herself so with a mortal."

"This is the time, my fainthearted consort, for her to be tested. She is to be queen, and this queen must know for sure what she's made of."

Ardwen wrapped his arms more tightly around his fairy queen, gently so she knew he cherished her, rather than constrained her. "She is your daughter," he reminded her with perilous valor.

Mab went very still. "She is to be queen."

And Ardwen, who knew his queen as well as a consort could, shuddered along with the tree. The girl who bent over that sleeping mortal was still sweet and open. It was time, it seemed, for her to get over that and find the dark rage that fueled a queen.

"Just so," his own queen answered. "Just so."

And, finished with her daughter, she turned once again to her lover.

Her lover of the moment. The queen had no intentions of giving up that delicious morsel on the ground to her daughter. She had to have some reward for carrying the load of the entire court on her milky white shoulders, after all. But for now, she would enjoy the attention of Ardwen of the Earth.

Farther out among the trees, two other fairies watched Nuala and her mortal. Each had a stake in young Nuala's future. Darragh, a pale silver-haired fairy with bewitching dark eyes and the power of thunder in his fingers, was to be Nuala's consort when she became queen. It had been decided long since, when he and Nuala still romped among the wildflowers and wove blankets from clover, that his role would support hers in the time to come. She with her wisdom and quiet strength, he with the power of storm and darkness.

Darragh was a jealous fairy, more of his position than his intended. He had grown up knowing what his place was to be, and he was not about to see it lost to a whim the queen had not seen fit to cure her daughter of. He had no truck with mortals and knew that his queen shouldn't, either. So he sat there against the roots of an alder tree, his body so still even the rabbits didn't recognize him, and he watched the fairy who would be his stroke the pain from that mortal as if she had a right to. He watched, the way her fingers skimmed his skin, her voice soothed his pain, her tears washed his face. He watched and he thought about what he would have to do, especially if Mab chose not to do anything.

But then, when he thought that, he smiled. He knew better than to think that Mab would pass up the chance at a handsome mortal. He would wait for Mab to set her daughter straight. And if she didn't, he would be more than willing to do it for her. After all, he was to be the queen's consort. It would be his right.

The other fairy who watched Nuala was Orla, one of the *leannan sidhe*. It was Orla who lured men to their misery, Orla who created slaves out of the mortal men who heard her siren call and followed her footsteps into the dusk.

Orla was also a daughter of the queen. Orla was a covetous daughter, though. It was she who should inherit the court, not her unworthy sibling. She knew it, and she thought Nuala knew it, too. Orla had the hunger for power. She had the ruthlessness and the sharp mind. She even had the rage that fueled a queen to battle, if necessary. After all, wasn't she the one who drew mortal men into her snare and then tossed them aside, to pine themselves to death? Wasn't it she who had helped fend off the last attack of the dark faerie with no more than her glance?

As sleek as a black cat, she stood in the shadows of the hazel tree, whose dryad watched in apprehension, and she thought how it was about time the queen recognized the fact that Nuala was unworthy. That it was Orla's time to reign.

No matter what it took, Orla would make it happen. It was, after all, for the good of her fairy clan. She couldn't help it that she might just enjoy the methods she had to employ. Especially, she thought, licking her red lips, if they included destroying that comely mortal Nuala thought was hers. At the thought of what that could mean, Orla smiled. As far as the eyes could see, trees trembled.

Chapter 4

Zeke opened his eyes to the ugliest creature he'd seen in his entire life. And in his life he'd faced everything from young rodents to old cowboys.

"Holy crap…"

He instinctively bolted back from the thing, hand out in defense. It was wrinkled and small and nut-colored, with the palest blue eyes he'd ever seen, and sharp, pointy teeth.

He thought it might be smiling. Or grimacing in pain. He wasn't sure. But it stood there at his feet, gnarled little hands on lumpy old hips, indeterminately colored hair frizzing around pointy ears and falling in its eyes like a badly groomed pony. Or donkey. Or rhinoceros. Something ugly. Really, *really* ugly.

"What the he—" He cleared his throat, remembering Nuala's warning about not insulting anybody.

At least he thought this was an anybody. It hadn't spoken yet, or moved, or made its character known. The last thing Zeke remembered was Nuala holding him in her arms. Well, that and another of those erotic dreamstates that involved Nuala *and* her mother. Definitely not something he was going to pursue right now. Probably, if he were smart, ever. Besides, he had bigger problems to worry about.

Where was Nuala? Zeke battled an instinctive flare of panic.

He hated that. He was sure there was a perfectly logical explanation—as logical as it got here. Nuala hadn't left. She hadn't...but that thought wasn't going to be finished. Zeke wasn't going to fall prey to old nightmares, even though he seemed to be caught in a place that fairly bred the damn things. He especially wasn't going to waste his energy on nothing more than a character in a lurid dream. He was going to wake up soon, anyway. He would move on, just like always.

"I'm sorry," he tried again, pulling himself to a seated position to find that he was on some kind of bed. A soft bed, with the whitest, best-smelling sheets he'd ever enjoyed. Hyatt could make a fortune putting these sheets on their beds. They really did smell like fresh air and flowers. Lavender and lilies. Something like that. The bed was even long enough, which was completely disorienting, since it was tucked under the eaves of what looked exactly like one of those odd hobbit houses.

Then he realized what he should have seen first off. He was naked. Stark, staring, hairy-legged naked, his legs protruding from under the far edge of the pristine white sheet that suddenly didn't seem big enough to cover his pertinent parts.

"Can you tell me where Nuala is, please?" he asked,

trying like hell to arrange the sheet for best coverage as he tried even harder to pull what had happened into focus. His head still hurt, and he fought a bit of residual dizziness. And that damn burn of old fear, right below his breastbone.

He looked up again, bracing himself for that ugly face. "Can you tell me what happened?"

He couldn't tell if the creature understood English. What did trolls speak? he wondered, just before he remembered that these people seemed to be able to hear thoughts.

"And don't you be forgettin'," the thing said in the most calm, sweet voice he'd ever heard in his entire life, a voice that promised warm biscuits and lemonade and a big, soft lap for hugs. "I can hear you just fine, all right. And don't be calling anybody a troll in this glen, if you don't mind."

"I'm sorry."

He seemed to be saying that a lot. And the sheet just got smaller. He could feel a distinct breeze against his backside.

"So you fell down a fairy hole, then, did you, mannie?" It shook its head, huffing a bit. "You're a clumsy lot, you mortals. Always tripping over perfectly good fairies and then not knowin' what to do with them."

Again he was mesmerized by that voice, by the certainty that he could smell those damn biscuits baking. If he could just close his eyes, he could drift away on that voice. Pretend it was his mother's, and he could barely remember a time when his mother hadn't sounded thin and frayed with pain. If she'd stayed healthy and strong, though, this was the voice she would have had. She would have smelled like sunshine and lavender, instead of medicine and decay.

He was sure, however, she would never have stripped him and given him nothing but a handkerchief to cover himself with.

"So, you're a...um, fairy?" Very carefully, both hands anchoring the perilously small bit of linen, he swung his legs off the long-enough bed and damn near smacked his knees on a little chest of drawers that sat against the wall.

The minute his legs were off the thing, the bed seemed to shrink to normal size...or rather, hobbit size. He focused on hanging on to the sheet, terrified it would disappear altogether.

"I'll thank you not to be calling me a hobbit, either," the thing snapped. "Hobbits are hairy, and they can't dance."

Zeke just about managed to blink his eyes. "You know hobbits?"

"Of course not!" it retorted, hands still clenched on those lumpy hips. "Hobbits aren't real!"

Zeke fought the most overwhelming urge to giggle like a schoolgirl.

"Oh, you're awake!" he heard from the doorway.

He didn't even need to look up to know it was Nuala. No matter how nice other voices were in this deranged place, they weren't hers. He looked up,

ashamed that he felt the urge to weep in relief just at
the sight of her. He looked down to see an expanse of
hairy chest and knees and decided he couldn't possibly
feel any more uncomfortable.

"Would *you* tell me what happened?" he begged.

Nuala tucked herself into the doorway and smiled at
him, bringing the sun in with her.

"He called me a hobbit, this one," the creature who
resided there complained, waving an impatient hand at
him.

Nuala laughed, and Zeke smiled, even though he
still felt fuzzy and a couple beats off rhythm. And naked.

"Ah, Bee, he can't help himself. Sure, he's never met
anything like us before." She leaned closer, her grin
impish. "He doesn't believe in us at all, don't you know?"

The Bee creature huffed again, hands back on hips.
"Then how does he explain sittin' on our bed and
insultin' us, I'm askin'?"

Zeke rubbed at the side of his head. "Even if I did
believe in... you know, I sincerely doubt I could explain
any of this."

"You'll be wanting to thank Bee," Nuala assured
him as she stepped around the little thing to stand within
inches of his bare toes. "She's our healer. Our own
bean tighe. I brought you to her when you...when you
weren't feeling well."

He still wasn't feeling completely well, and he was
hearing things again. Murmurs and whispers at the edge
of his thoughts. He swore he could hear his name, as if
somebody were calling—or commanding—him.

"You'll be after listenin' soon enough," little Bee told him with a grotesque smile and a pat on his cheek that felt like thistledown. "For now, go play with the girl. She's the one healed you, not these old hands."

Zeke looked up to see that Nuala was blushing. "No, Bee," she was protesting. "I just…"

Bee smacked her like a recalcitrant child. "I know it better than any, girl. It's time you did. Now, go play with the lad."

"The lad has no clothes," Zeke reminded them both with the barest civility. "At least give me my boots. I hate walking around barefoot. You never know how many fairies you're going to trample."

Nuala giggled like a waterfall. "Sure, and I think we ladies would much prefer you just as you are. Don't you think, Bee?"

The little fairy's face folded into a thousand creases. "Ah, and didn't it make *my* day?" Zeke thought it might be smiling.

He just closed his eyes. It was better that way. He could just see himself back at the university. *"So there I was, sitting naked in this fairy house…"*

"Ah, now, give the man some dignity," a new voice interrupted from behind Nuala. "We'd ask the same for ourselves, now, wouldn't we?"

Little Bee huffed in annoyance. "And doesn't she just take the joy out of everything with her perishin' thoughtfulness?"

Nuala chuckled and turned, and Zeke saw who she'd been hiding. Another fairy girl stood behind her, smaller, and slighter than Nuala. Slim as a reed, sharp-eyed, and capped with a nest of blonde curls. If she hadn't been in one of those amazing dresses, this one in a silvery blue color that seemed to ripple into lavender, he would have sworn he was looking at Peter Pan.

"Zeke Kendall," Nuala said, swinging her arm toward the girl, "I'd like you to meet the best friend a fairy ever had. Sorcha, the seamstress."

The blonde shot Nuala an impatient scowl. "Sorcha the seamstress who also just happens to be your sister."

Nuala leveled a beaming smile on her. "Ah, how could I be forgettin' that?" she demanded. "Weren't you the one stole the blankets when we were young?"

"And weren't you the one who stole my first spells?"

"They never would have worked, Sorcha. I couldn't just let you be mistakin' the words and turn our good farrier into a newt."

Sorcha's eyes got even brighter. "It would have been a great improvement on him."

"Well, you're after making a better magpie than a seamstress," Bee snapped. "Give the man his clothes, so."

Sorcha blushed. "He *would* have," she muttered, then stepped forward. For the first time Zeke saw that she was carrying his clothes, evidently cleaned and pressed and presentable.

"I was after trying to craft a good set of immortal clothing, like," she said, her face pursed as she looked on his folded and pressed jeans as if they were an alien growth, "but they refused the forming. It was Nuala finally convinced us we couldn't wait any longer to give you your things back. You understand, I was only using them for size, not takin' them away."

She wasn't close enough for Zeke to grab his pants, and he couldn't figure a way to reach over and snatch them without letting go of a vital piece of protective property. "Of course I do. Now…"

"But that's all right, you know," she said with a sudden sweet smile. "Sure, we'll figure it out. I have the size now, and you have the time, all right."

"No, he doesn't," Nuala insisted, grabbing the clothes out of Sorcha's hands. "The queen and I are about to have a talk."

She tossed Zeke's clothing to him, her attention still on her sister. Zeke grabbed the suddenly soft, suddenly fresh clothes and took in a good breath of them. They smelled like breezes and mist and meadows. Damn, he could get used to that. Usually his clothing smelled like sweat and dust and thousand-year-old remains.

"If you don't want him, can I have him, then?" Sorcha asked *sotto voce*. "Wouldn't he be just grand to wake up to of a morning?"

"Nobody's havin' him," Nuala insisted, then turned on Zeke as if it were his fault. "Come along, then. You've no more business here."

He just sat there. The fairies just stood there.

Finally he had to cough. "Um, I'm not sure how this works in your world, but in mine, a man is given a bit of privacy to dress."

The three of them grinned like wolves.

"You had none when we undressed you," Nuala reminded him with a wicked glint in her eye that suddenly called up those salacious dreams all over again.

Zeke prayed for anatomical restraint and frowned. "I wasn't conscious when you undressed me. For some odd reason, it makes a difference."

Bee laughed so hard, her little ears quivered. "Sure, and I hope he's not around for a festival. He'd be havin' seizures."

Zeke scowled.

Nuala grinned. "He's only a mortal, Bee. They're a much shyer lot than we are."

"*I* don't hide under flower petals," Zeke growled.

Nuala chuckled. "And I'm not usually after wearing so many clothes. Faith," she said, flicking at his jeans, "you could smother in this heavy business."

Zeke refused to be charmed. "This heavy business protects me from the brambles."

"Sure, we'll have to at least keep him for Samhain," Sorcha insisted with another of those knowing grins. "I'd be willin' to bet I'm not the only one would offer pure gold to see him dance around the bonfire as the good mother made him."

"That'll be enough of that," Zeke chastised, holding his clothes closer, since the sheet had shrunk again. "And you can stop playing with the covers, if you don't mind."

That quickly, the sheet was full-sized and his knees warmed considerably. Not to mention his rump.

"Now. If you'd give me a minute," he said with a quick flip of his hand in the direction of the door, "I'll be glad to be up and about."

"Ah well, we might as well give in," Nuala sighed, shepherding the others out the door. "Sure, as hard as it was to get those blue things off his legs, imagine how hard it is to get them back on."

"And what about those loose things he's after wearin' *underneath?*" Bee demanded. "Whatever are those for?"

"I've heard they're called boxers, Bee," Sorcha said. "It seems to be a question mortals are obsessed with altogether. Boxers or briefs."

Fortunately for Zeke, the door closed at that point and he was free to contort himself sufficiently to get his clothes back on. Truth be told, he'd never thought that much about clothing. It was just something that kept you warm in winter and out of police stations in summer. But he had to admit that faced with these people...or whatever, he appreciated the barrier that a good pair of jeans offered. Not to mention the camouflage. For a minute there, he'd been thinking about how little Nuala did wear, and truth be told, that sheet just wasn't going to be enough to prevent major embarrassment.

After quickly tying his shoelaces, he got to his feet, head bent like a dowager to avoid banging it on the ceiling, and took the three steps necessary to open the front door. Evidently there had been quite a gathering around Bee's house to see the mortal. The minute he opened the door, they scattered like leaves in a wind.

Literally.

Zeke couldn't help staring. He'd seen people run away when threatened, but he'd never seen them fly. Or flit. Or disappear altogether. Only Nuala, Bee and Sorcha remained.

"People come and go so quickly here," he muttered to himself.

"They were after worryin' over you," Nuala assured him, that sly grin still tucking up the corners of her mouth.

"They were after being curious about the big strapping mortal in their midst," he disagreed.

"Ah, well, that, too."

"All right, then," Bee said with a flick of her hands, as if brushing them away. "Off with ya. No reason to be in a healer's house when the business is finished."

Zeke smiled, and bent way over and bussed the tiny healer on her leathery cheek. "Thank you for your help," he said, realizing that he'd grown quite fond of the old girl.

She gave him another cuff, but he could have sworn she blushed. "Now *that's* the way to be thankin' a person," she informed Sorcha.

"I wouldn't know," the sweet blonde said, her tilted blue eyes suspiciously bright, even for the pout on a face it didn't fit. "And here was I after spending my whole afternoon on his clothes and all. My *whole* afternoon..."

So of course Zeke had to buss her just as firmly. "Thank you for cleaning up my clothes. They haven't smelled this nice ever. And it was a nice gesture to try to put me in the local uniform. But I have a feeling I'm just not made for it."

"Isn't that just what I was trying to tell them?" Nuala demanded.

Sorcha was still blushing rosily from Zeke's kiss. "Whiskers," she said with a giggle. "Now there's somethin' I could get used to altogether. Are you sure we can't keep him, Nuala?"

"Play with somebody else's mortal, Sorcha. This one's goin' home."

Sorcha made a point of sighing. "Ah well, then. I'd be fierce grateful if you'd muck yourself up again, mortal. I figure every time I clean you up again, I get another taste, which I'm thinkin' I'd enjoy prodigiously."

Zeke couldn't remember when he'd last been more delighted. "You really spend your time cutting cloth and wielding a needle?" he asked.

"Oh, it's much more complicated than that," Nuala assured him, smiling on her sister. "Our garments and gemstones reflect us, our talents and strengths and spirits. It's Sorcha who sees how. The color, the material, the structure. She attends every birth, every coming of age. She is Keeper of the Stones."

"She can speak quite well for herself," Sorcha said, hands on slim hips.

"But she never says enough about herself. Does she, Bee?"

"None of the good ones do, girl."

Zeke was still a couple of statements back. "And you see Nuala in peacock blue?"

A huge smile broke over Sorcha's pixie face. "Oh, aye, cannot you see it? Our Nuala is such a rare spirit, sure her raiment could be no less bright. It is the color of her sight, her sharp mind, her music. Especially her music."

"Then why in God's name is the Queen in white?" Zeke demanded. "No offense, I'm sure, but I don't think I've ever met anybody who belongs in that color less."

"Ah, well, white is the royal color hereabouts, the measure of her place. Not her personality."

"So she changed clothes with the job?"

Sorcha smiled and nodded. "Most of us are born to our colors, our stones. See the rings we wear? Each has different power stones that reflect the wearer's strengths. But the queen, now, sure she doesn't know she'll have the job till later. 'Til the old queen leaves."

"And what was Mab's color before?"

Even Nuala was grinning now. "Scarlet."

Zeke nodded. "Well, that puts my universe a little more in order. What color am I?" he asked.

Sorcha tilted her small head again and sighed. "Well now, isn't that the problem? I think you're the very material you're wearing, and it isn't fairy material at all."

"Yeah," Zeke agreed. "I'd probably be pretty hard on cobwebs and moonbeams."

Sorcha laughed, again sounding like birdcall, bright and chirpy. "Well, then, I'll be after seein' you both tonight, will I?"

Nuala kissed her sister's cheek. "Oh, we'll be there, all right. Right alongside herself, if I'm a judge of anything."

Sorcha nodded briskly. "Then I'd better prepare, shouldn't I? There'll not be an empty seat, I'm thinking, and there's a particular seat I'm wantin'."

Nuala smiled at her sister, but Zeke saw that there was sadness in both their eyes, the language of history and kinship.

He kept his place as the interloper and waited until Sorcha tripped off down the path before returning his attention to Nuala. "Now what?"

She smiled and began walking. "Now we find a place for you to rest 'til the banquet."

"I did rest."

"And a good job you did of it, too. But I doubt you'd suffer from a little more."

Not knowing what else to do, Zeke followed her. It was then that he took his first good look around since stepping outside the clever little house. That quickly, he came back to a complete stop, astounded. They stood amid the cluster of houses he'd noticed before, all with smoke curling from their chimneys, and flowers running riot over fences and doorways. There were people tending gardens, and cattle and sheep scattered over the fields. He thought he'd imagined it before, especially since there should have been no chance it really existed.

"It's a village," Zeke announced, as if Nuala didn't already know as much.

"Of course it's a village," she said with another

musical laugh. "Where do you think we live, then? Out in the rain?"

Zeke stopped a moment in the middle of a well-trod street. "Well, yeah. I guess I did. You know, on the petals of flowers, that kind of thing."

"Ah, well now, there are those who do just that. Flower fairies, they are, and they don't mind a bit of mist and bother. But we like our comforts about us like anyone else."

Zeke stayed right there in the middle of the path, distracted by the creatures around him. "Oh," seemed all he could manage. He was rubbing at his temple again, trying to get all this to make sense.

"Are you feeling all right?" Nuala asked, watching him.

He turned to see that she was frowning at him. He suddenly couldn't bear to see the twin furrows between her eyebrows and felt compelled to rub them away with his thumb. He didn't, though. He at least maintained that much restraint.

"I'm fine," he assured her, although his head still throbbed a bit, and he could hear those voices again in the distance, fading in and out like a radio somebody had left on. "How did I end up in Bee's house?"

Her frown eased only a fraction. "Ah, well, you did hit yourself a great whack comin' down that hill and all. You said it yourself. You just needed a bit more time to be restin', is all."

"And how long did I do that? Rest, I mean?"

She smiled then, at once rueful and shy. "Well, now,

we don't really feel the need to be measurin' time like you do in your world. It was early when you came to us. It's closin' in on night now. They'll be preparing the banquet."

He looked around to gauge the light, trying to more accurately measure the passing of time. It was impossible in this place, though. If you couldn't see the sun, how could you measure its trajectory? All he could tell right now was that the light that seemed to permeate this place had softened, become more dispersed. It was harder to see all the denizens, although he did notice that like kids everywhere, fairy children were cramming in their play until the very last minute of the day.

For a second they distracted him, those fairy children. Bright as pennies, they had wise, sly eyes and enchanting giggles. Red hair and blonde hair and blue-black hair like ravens' wings. And all with those faint points on their ears. All watching him as if he were the latest thing in video games. Also like children everywhere, it took only a moment for their attention to wander.

All except one. A small child, with copper hair that seemed to fluoresce in the half-light and the darkest, gravest eyes he'd ever seen. For a minute the child just stood there, clad in some kind of tunic top and leggings and soft slippers on his feet, all in forest greens and royal blues. He stood so still that for a moment Zeke wondered if he was really there. His eyes were dark, and so old in that young face. They frowned, as if the boy were trying to decipher something. And then, like a shaft of light, he smiled. Nodded. And then just turned away.

Zeke was stunned to hear Nuala gasp beside him.

"What?" he asked, turning to see that she, too, was watching after the now-gamboling boy.

She shook her head a bit. "Nothing…"

"You're not looking like it's nothing. Who was that?"

Still watching the children, Nuala smiled. "That is Kieran," she said. "We get to borrow him sometimes, from over to Castle Matrix."

"Borrow him?" Zeke asked. "What do you mean? Isn't he a fairy?"

"Oh, aye," she said, still caught in some kind of spell. "A throwback from two mortals who didn't know they had the blood."

Now Zeke watched the boy and thought how, once seen, it was near impossible to take one's eyes from him. "Kind of like a recessive trait, huh? Who knew?"

"He will be our next seer," she said in tones of reverence.

"Your what?"

Nuala lifted a hand, as if the explanation encompassed more than words. "Every so often, when it is most needed, the faerie are blessed with a seer. A great gift altogether, but a heavy burden. Sure we haven't had one since you mortals strung up the electricity the first time. You can't know what that does to a fairy's spirit. Well, now, the time has come again. And our first glance at Kieran, didn't we know he was the one? He was only three, and there he was, seein' us right in the middle of the day. So his parents agreed to share him, for us to teach him what he must know. But it must be his choice to stay or leave."

"A seer. And what does he see?"

"The past. The future. The pattern."

"The pattern?"

Again that lift of the hand. "Where it all fits together, this world and yours and all the others."

Zeke couldn't help lifting an eyebrow. "The *others?*"

That quickly, Nuala's attention was back on him again. She smiled and patted at him, just as she had at Bee, although Zeke bet Bee hadn't had the reaction to Nuala's touch he always did.

"Ah well, that might be something you may not be ready for just yet. First, why don't you let us entertain you with our food and our music and our ways? After, sure, you can ask all the questions you want."

"After you tell me why he nodded at me."

Nuala tilted her head, much as her friend the seer had done. "Ah well, that's simple. He's been away from basketball now this long while. He'll be wanting to ask you scores and such, and about a team named the Knicks."

Zeke lifted an eyebrow. "Basketball?"

Nuala smiled. "Mad for it. But he'll find you when he wishes."

There was more she wasn't saying. Zeke very much wanted to ask, but one look at her suddenly serene face decided him. It wouldn't do any good. Inscrutable, these fairies.

Besides, she'd started walking again among those

quaint houses and old, majestic trees, that gossamer dress drifting about her like a nimbus.

"And should I eat any of the fairy food?" he asked instead as he followed along. "I have heard that it's a bad idea. For mortals, anyway."

Nuala nodded, her hair trembling again, catching fire in distant light. "In the usual course of things, I wouldn't want you to be eatin' here. But the queen has given her protection." Her smile reappeared, literally stabbing Zeke in the heart with its purity. "Sure, you should enjoy it. Few mortals get to taste such a meal and come back to tell the tale of it."

Zeke couldn't take his eyes off her. He couldn't imagine how he was going to keep his hands off her. Her skin glowed in the waning light, as if lit from within. Her eyes were deep and mysterious, a cool glade at dusk. Her hair... God, her hair. He wanted to touch it, to winnow it through his fingers and wrap it around them both like a curtain no one could penetrate.

He wanted her in every way he could think of. And standing there in the middle of Main Street in Fairyville, he suddenly couldn't figure out why he couldn't have her.

Zeke loved women. All women. Any women. He loved the mystery of them, the illogic of them, the smell and the taste of them. Never before had he questioned an attraction. And he knew from long experience that nothing increased the pleasure of them more than patience. Well, he could certainly be patient with his fairy princess, if it meant he could spend more time with her. If he could dally at her feet.

If, in the end, he could claim her.

"And you?" he asked. "What do you like? What is your story, Nuala? I believe I was going to ask before, but we got sidetracked."

"So you were," she said, not meeting his gaze. Instead, she smiled at the children and nodded to those who passed. "Ah, I don't have much of a story, now. I've lived here all my life, then, haven't I? I learned the harp from Agheam himself, who is master harper to the *Tua*, and I've learned scrying…well, that on my own. And… and, well, I've prepared for the time when Mab leaves these shores and doesn't return."

"She really is going, huh?"

Nuala looked up at him with those fathomless green eyes, suddenly vulnerable and hesitant. "Aye. She will leave in her time, and take the old ones with her."

"How many does that leave here?"

She shrugged. "Oh, still too many to count quickly. Enough to tetch at your poor mortals for a few years to come."

Zeke looked around again at the dimpled earth that cradled these delightful little houses, at the swift-footed men and graceful women who drifted about their day, and the children who scampered through the woods. He thought of all the magic he'd lost in the hard glare of the reservation, where dreams couldn't hide. Of the mists and enchantments forfeited to technology and science. He thought of all the tales his sister-in-law had saved from his great-great-grandmother, the powwow woman.

"I'm glad," he said, because it didn't cost him anything in a dream to believe in this. "I'm glad there are some staying. It would be a sad old world without a little magic."

Nuala seemed to feel the same way he did. "Aye," she whispered, as if it were a burden. "It would that."

Around them the bees hummed, and evening birds chittered and swooped. The other fairies were slipping into their houses, leaving the path empty for Nuala and her mortal. Fairy lights flickered among the trees, and a deer paused at the edge of the field.

The world was perfect, colored and scented and sounding of peace. Soft and sensuous and soothing. Zeke couldn't help being drawn to it, even the drip of water from the leaves, the shadows that pooled along in the lane. He wanted to stay here, and he wasn't sure whether it was because of the gentle fading of light around him or the beautiful woman at his side.

"There is darkness here, too," she said, her voice hushed. "It isn't wise to idealize any place or person."

Zeke looked over to see that she was gazing into the deepening evening around her. He saw the shudder of fairy light limn her face and thought he'd never seen anything more beautiful in his life.

He wanted so much to touch her. To hold her and search out every nook and cranny, to incite smiles and sighs of repletion. He wanted to explore those visions he'd had of her breasts and thighs and tongue.

She turned to him, and the images returned.

Her hair a waterfall against his chest as she leaned

over him, her peach-tipped breasts brushing against his
skin, her eyes glowing and her voice breathy with
desire. He swore he could feel her fingers on him, could
smell the musk of desire on her. He stood there not
even touching her, and he knew he could taste the honey
on her lips.

And he knew, seeing her standing there as still as a
deer that sensed danger, that she could taste it, too. Her
eyes grew large and dark, and her hands fluttered up,
but only briefly, as if trying to capture the lightning that
sparked between them. Her breasts lifted with her
quickening breaths.

"What are you doing to me?" he asked, amazed at
how flushed his poor battered body felt.

She couldn't seem to take her gaze from him as she
shook her head, the fire in her hair licking against the
night. "I was going to ask *you*, so. I've never…"

He couldn't help lift an eyebrow. "Never?"

This time the wave of her hands was impatient.
"Like this. I've never seen…never tasted…"

Zeke nodded his head, as if he understood. "Then
this isn't normal courting practice for fairies?"

He startled a laugh out of her. "Ah, no. I can't say
that it is."

Zeke nodded, never taking his gaze from hers. Never
chancing the loss of the sweet fire in those eyes. "I
have to kiss you," he said in wonder.

She only nodded. "Yes."

He leaned forward, seeing her eyes dilate, her
nostrils flare. He heard the sharp intake of her breath

and felt the silk slide over her arms as he wrapped his hands around her. He saw her eyes close, and he kissed her.

Gently, no more than a whisper. A greeting, a grace. Knowing that if he took more, he would be lost.

He was lost even so. Once, when he'd been up on a mesa out in the middle of nowhere, he'd been caught in a lightning storm. There had been no rain to defuse it. The Four Corners was usually too dry for that. The air had crackled all around him, skittering along his nerve endings and standing his hair on end.

It felt just like that right now. As if, if he opened his eyes, he would see a lacework of lightning shatter the sky. It shattered him, stunned him. Sent him reeling.

He heard a small whimper and knew it was Nuala, and he held on more tightly, wrapping his hands around her back. He eased her mouth open beneath his and got his first real taste of her.

He knew there would be honey, and there was, honey and smoke and the tang of cloves. There was mystery, and there was madness, and he didn't care. He *couldn't* care. If he cared, he would have to let her go.

And he couldn't let her go.

"Excuse me," a massive voice said.

Nuala stiffened. For a second Zeke held on, not willing to break this incredible connection.

"Nuala!"

Nuala elbowed him hard. Zeke pulled away, still thinking that it would only be a moment. No, it would be a lifetime, but he could wait until the interruption was past.

"Darragh," Nuala said, and she sounded stricken.

That got Zeke's eyes open to find a man-fairy standing before him. He had silver hair and dark, dark eyes, and a tunic the color of smoke or rainclouds. The thunder in his face matched it perfectly.

"Can we help you?" Zeke finally asked.

"No, but maybe I can be helpin' you," he said, his voice too deep a rumble for such a slight being.

"Darragh, leave him be."

The fairy faced her then, and seemed to grow even darker. It felt as if the air seethed and crackled with his anger. "Are you after havin' another consort, then, Nuala? That you'd display yourself so in the middle of the street?"

"It's not like that," she protested, graceful hand out to him. "He'll be leaving soon. Herself will see to it."

"She'd better," he said with a scowl. "It would be a trial, now, to have to break the laddie here."

Zeke bristled. "The laddie…?"

But Nuala put a hand on his arm to stop him. "Go now, Darragh. Find your place on the seat of the council and remember who you are."

"I remember just fine. It's you who seem to have forgotten."

And with no more than that, he turned and stalked off.

"Pleasant guy," Zeke said, still distracted by the residual lightning that flickered along his arms. "Who is he?"

Nuala shook her head. "Well, in human terms," she said with a sigh, "I imagine he's my husband."

* * *

Young Kieran O'Driscoll stood before the queen of the fairies without trepidation, because he was the only one but the bard who would dare to give the queen the truth.

"Have your say, then, little boy," she said, standing tall and regal in the *Tua* crown. "You've come back to tell me about Nuala's guest, you say."

"His coming may well spell doom for the *Tua*, my lady," the boy said, his own posture regal. "He brings the *Dubhlainn Sidhe*."

It was a sentence that should have sent the queen trembling to her knees. Nothing was more feared than the *Dubhlainn Sidhe*, who rode the wind and sowed strife behind them.

"A dire warning," she said, sounding oddly unconcerned. "Do you suggest we send him back?"

"It's already too late. All was set in motion the minute you brought him through." The boy took a breath, truly troubled. "He may well be the catalyst for a great Fairy War."

The queen lifted an imperious eyebrow. "You expect me to simply accept this?"

For a long moment the boy just looked at his queen, his expression grave. "I expect that you must, since you have long known this would be the inevitable outcome when you failed to help the *Dubhlainn Sidhe* recover the Dearann stone when it was first lost so you might have reestablished balance."

It seemed a dark wind suddenly blew, swirling

around the little boy in a sound of whispers, of moans and sighs of despair. It seemed the queen grew in stature, her eyes glowing as bloodred as the ruby in her crown. "You wouldn't be thinking to chastise the Queen of Faerie, now," she said, very softly.

He never flinched, looking oddly her equal, even for the disparity of their sizes. "I'm thinking to fulfill my duties. The time has come, my lady, as I'm sure you knew it would. The court of the *Tua* is in great peril."

"From the *Dubhlainn Sidhe*."

"They *will* ride."

"And I cannot stop them?"

The little boy looked grave. "Maybe by calling truce. Working with them to restore order."

"They don't want order," the queen snapped. "They want my power."

The boy simply kept his silence. The queen looked out over the verdant hills, as if she could see the *Dubhlainn Sidhe* approach on their fire-eyed steeds. She stood so still, it seemed she had been cast there. Finally, though, she simply looked hard on the seer who stood no higher than her waist.

"It will be considered," she said.

"Soon," he begged, finally looking like a frightened boy. "Please."

Chapter 5

Nuala ushered Zeke into the banquet hall just as the first notes of music drifted out into the dim air. She knew they would be the last ones arriving and all, but she thought the less time Zeke had to deal with all the curiosity, the better. It was going to be enough just to have to face the queen. Especially after Nuala had spent the last long while trying to explain to Zeke what her life was to be.

"He's your *what?*" he'd demanded out on the path, as Darragh had stomped off and the night settled.

Nuala ached at the anger she saw in his eyes. "He was chosen for me," she tried to explain. "When we were first named. He will be the consort when I am Mab."

His hands were up in the air, as if squaring a wall between them. "I don't play around with married women," he accused, looking betrayed.

She knew that. As frivolous as Zeke could be with his affections, he'd never sought to hurt or trespass. It was his own particular code of honor.

"It's not like your world, Zeke," she'd tried to

explain. "We...Darragh had no call to accuse you, so. He has no place until Mab leaves."

"You said he was your husband."

She sighed. "It was the closest thing I could think of to describe it. A queen must have a consort. The first is chosen for her. But she chooses any others she wishes—"

"At the same *time*?"

"—and until the time of her ascension, she is free to learn and celebrate as she chooses, just as any of the faerie may."

She'd thought the concept would appeal to Zeke. After all, it hadn't just been the ranch she'd seen in her gazing water. When on a dig, Zeke was a hermit. But in between, he'd long enjoyed the favors of women. Beautiful women, shy women, sweet women, clever women, all blossoming under his admiring smile and clever hands. All left behind in his ceaseless flight.

She'd thought he would understand.

"So you're just practicing until the big day?" he asked, sounding much too surly.

And she snapped at him, "I thought you'd enjoy an interlude, Zeke. After all, there's no woman you've stayed with, is there?"

He looked at her as if she'd just stripped him naked again. "What does that have to do with anything?"

"Do you ask the mortal women you court if they plan to marry somebody else? If they might even have someone certain they're committed to?"

He sputtered. He actually sputtered. "Are you saying you just want a one-night stand?"

She frowned. "A—"

"A short relationship."

It was a good thing he couldn't hear the howl of despair that seemed to lodge in her throat. "A short time is all we'll be given, Zeke. You will go back, and I will be queen."

For a moment he just stood there glaring at her, his hands jammed in his jeans pockets, his shoulders hunched, as if defending himself from something. Then, at once troubled and amazed, he shook his head. "I have to think about that, Nuala."

Nuala nodded right back, because she knew that once he considered it, he would realize it was *just* what he wanted. What he'd always wanted. And even though she'd have wanted more from him, she was selfish enough to settle for this.

"It's all I ask," she said. "In the meantime, wouldn't it be lovely to enjoy the banquet?"

And before he'd been able to say another word, she walked him right into the hall.

Every day of her life, Nuala had walked into this hall right about this same time of the day, as light faded and the mystery took hold. She knew it like her name. But she saw Zeke's eyes widen at the sight of it and saw it anew. And she had to admit that it was certainly worth gaping over.

The hall was large and long and breathtakingly high, an arching palace woven of live trees, the leaves and needles plaited into thatch, the branches and roots the walls. Yew and hazel and oak and alder, each tree blessed and blessing, their histories humming in them. Firelight and moonlight glowed on the faces inside and reflected in the mirrors that lined the walls. Flowers rioted over the long tables, and the soft strains of music lifted into the dim recesses of the ceiling. The floor, the most beautiful Kerry crystal, glittered and glowed with the light of the fairies who passed over it.

Ah, the fairies. Not all of them, of course, for they would never fit all at once, nor wish to be there, having halls of their own. Only those favored by the queen, which meant the company could change on a whim.

The *Tua de Danann*, of course, tall and stately and elegant in Sorcha's robes as befitted the royalty of any race. The sprites and the woodland fairies, the *Daoine Sidhe* and the Seelie Court itself, which would march in solemn procession through the hills so the mortals could hear them. Goldsmithing elves and tinkering gnomes. Boggarts and brownies and woodland sprites, some still tumbling about the rafters on rainbow-hued dragonfly wings, some dancing, hummingbirds in flight, some bowing in the regal dance of discourse. The room rang with the clink of crystal, the waterfall of laughter, the drifting refrain of the woodland pipes.

Nuala loved this hall that lived in itself, and imbued the inhabitants with wisdom and age and grace. She loved all the ranks of faerie who collected here, no matter how noisy or contentious. She loved the food and the glimmering light and the music and dancing. She even loved the awesome sight of Mab, where she sat at the high table in her samite robes and her starlit crown, with the burgundy-clad Ardwen alongside as her consort.

Of Mab odes had been written. Plays and epics and symphonies. None had ever matched her grace or her beauty or her timeless allure. No mortal or fairy could withstand her rage or conquer her heart. Mab was queen. She was all that man had ever imagined her to be and far more.

And there she sat, as straight as an ash, her hair gleaming a thousand shades of gold, her gown shimmering snow, and the royal jewels on her hands and neck and wrists throwing off rainbows as she moved. Emerald and iolite and moonstone. Those were the personal gems of the queen. Those and the state gem that graced the very apex of her crown. The great stone, Coilin the Virile, which gleamed like blood in her hair.

Next to Mab sat Sorcha, her silver-blue dress sheathed in a silver-sheened mantle, in her blonde curls a coronet of spidersilk woven in webs, her jewels the sharp red of spinel and gentle glow of opal. She waved at Nuala and motioned to seats on her side, far down the main table from Mab. Nuala considered it, even though Darragh sat like a thundercloud nearby.

But she knew Mab would never allow it. Mab had a new toy to play with, and she would never let him alone. Besides, Nuala's other sister waited beyond those two empty seats, and right now Nuala didn't have the patience for Orla's sarcasm and resentment.

Black-haired, crimson-and-gold-clad, with diamonds

in her hair and smoky quartz and citrine for her jewels, Orla watched Nuala like a lioness did a herd of gazelle, just waiting for the first moment of weakness that would enable her to claim the throne that had been promised to her sister. What Orla didn't understand was that Nuala would gladly give the queen's seat to her. She dreaded the day Mab's ship sailed.

What Nuala couldn't tell any of them was that as much as she loved this place and these lives and this magic, she didn't belong here. She never had, being not as much of them and too much for them. She could smell the peat in the soil beyond their realm. She could hear the rustle of life within the earth and taste the substance of it on the breeze. She had been given fairy cloth as fine as gossamer to wear, yet yearned for the abrasive friction of Zeke's heavy denim. The coarse weight and solid certainty of it. The roughness of Zeke himself.

She'd seen it on him, of course, in her water over the years. That dusting of golden hair on his chest and arms that had more often than not glistened with sweat as he'd worked those hard digs. The calluses on his fingers and bare feet. The scars that nicked fingers and elbows. She'd known such a craving in her own fingers to explore them all, to run her tongue over him like a forbidden treat.

Fairy men were beautiful, all right. They had all the same parts a human did. Darragh, her chosen consort, had a face and form that could ensorcel women of any race. But fairy men were smooth and silky. Like their world, they were otherworldly. They weren't made to create friction.

When she'd helped strip Zeke that day, Nuala had been struck silent by the sight of him. The size of him. The tang of sweat on him. As tentatively as a breath, she'd reached out. Her fingers trembling as if stricken with the ague, she had trespassed across the hard sculpted planes of his chest, letting her fingers savor the alien spring of that hair, the unyielding strength of his muscles. The solid warmth of his skin. She'd tested callus and scar and been besotted.

She didn't belong here. How could she, when she lusted for things that weren't for her?

But it wasn't her decision to make. It wasn't Orla's. The queen and the seer and the council spoke for the world of faerie. And from the day Nuala had been given her stones, her future had been cast.

But there Orla sat, watching the door for the moment Nuala walked in. Watching for a second of weakness, a chance at Nuala's seat. When she caught sight of Zeke, Orla smiled, a terrible predator's smile, all teeth and heat. Licking glistening red lips, she raked her cat's eyes over Zeke as if sizing him up for a meal. And while Nuala might have ignored Orla all these years, this time she simply could not. She bristled with outrage. She just didn't let Orla know, for oh, then, wouldn't her sister pounce?

"Quite a place you have here," Zeke said beside her in hushed tones.

Nuala's smile was as much relief as delight. "Ah well, we like to call it home."

"It makes all the legends pale in comparison."

"Well, now, shouldn't a queen have a grand place to play?"

"If the size of that ruby in her crown is any indication, I'd say she could afford any kind of place she wanted."

"The stone is not hers," Nuala said with a small courtly bow of reverence. "It is Coilin, the ruling stone of the earth faeries. It is one of three that maintain harmony in the world."

His anthropologist's gleam lit his eyes. "And those are?"

"They are Donelle, Ruler of the World, who keeps to the Land of the West where it might not be forfeit in a whim. Coilin, the male stone, which you see the matriarchal *Tua* hold, and Daireann, the female stone, which was the power for the patriarchal *Dubhlainn Sidhe*. The Faeries of the Dark Sword. The stones kept the balance."

"Kept? Past tense?"

"Dearann was lost," she said, her voice hushed, as if the *Dubhlainn Sidhe* could overhear her.

"Not a good thing?"

Nuala actually felt the urge to look over her shoulder. "It has cost the *Dubhlainn Sidhe* their gentler light."

Zeke took a considering look at the room around them. "And given the female *Tua* strength and power."

Nuala laid a hand on his arm. "Softly, Zeke."

He smiled down at her. "And what will be your legacy when the stone is in your crown?"

Nuala had no answer. How did she admit in the presence of her mother that she would feel stronger with her own stones, her amethyst, peridot and chalce-

dony, her green gown and the tiny diadem of snow-
flakes that appeared in her hair whenever she stepped
through the formal doors of ritual and ceremony?

Coilin frightened her. Coilin's very name meant
"virile." It was the stone that made Mab terrible. Nuala
did not want to be terrible.

"I will hope to wear it with grace and wisdom," she
said, then deliberately stepped away from the topic. "I
hope you like to dance," she teased. "There'll be a great
lot of dancing tonight, along with the music. There's not
much fairies like to do better than dance. Especially,
you'll find, herself the queen."

Zeke took a considered look toward the ceiling, where
fairies still scampered among the trees. "Yeah. I got that
impression already. Anything else I should know?"

"Ah, I'm sure we'll come to it when we need to."

He was still looking around. "Now might be good.
Have you noticed that we're the center of attention?"

"Oh, aye. It's not often we get visitors dressed like
you," she said. "Sure, they're all just curious how you
can move about in all that bother."

"All that bother has saved me from more than one
gorse bush, I'll have you know."

Nuala chuckled. "Well, sure and you're safe from
their like here."

Zeke seemed to consider that. "Maybe so. I have a
feeling there are other dangers here, though."

He was right. There *were* dangers. The hall bristled
with tension. The minute they'd walked in the music
had faltered and the conversation dimmed. Even the

fairies who had been doing acrobatics up by the ceiling had stopped to hover, their eyes on their guest. Some thrummed with curiosity, some with nervousness, some the hot glare of resentment.

Nuala could feel it, the anger that this mortal could disrupt their paradise. The worry that he had the power to upend the course of their future. They'd seen her with him. They would have known, no matter how hard she might have tried to hide it, how attached she was to him. They would wonder what that would mean. So they watched her, and they watched him, and they watched the queen. They even watched Orla, who had a cat-in-the-cream smile on her full red lips as she lounged in her chair, stroking her golden goblet with long-nailed fingers.

And the queen, who loved nothing more than a bit of drama for her dinner, let them all stew in their worry, drawing out the suspense until the very walls of the hall vibrated with it. Nuala could do no more than stand there along with all the others and wait for her mother's pronouncement. She knew perfectly well that if she tried to take her seat before her mother had spoken, she would be called to account in the most dramatic way. She was not yet, after all, queen.

"I don't suppose we could catch the next show," Zeke muttered alongside her.

"Courage," she muttered back, the hot attention of a thousand eyes setting her nerves on end. "They don't bite, after all." She couldn't help it. She grinned. "Well, at least not the ones here tonight."

Zeke shot her a look of alarm, which made her want

to giggle all over again. "Don't be forgettin' that you're bigger than anyone here," she advised.

"Bigger, yes," he admitted. "But I sincerely doubt I'm as powerful."

Well, that she had to give him.

"Well then, little Nuala," the queen finally spoke, and Nuala could actually hear a collective whoosh of released breath from the gathered throng, "I see you've brought us a gift."

Nuala pulled together every ounce of courage she had and accorded her mother a courtly bow. "It's a guest I've brought, lady, one who came to us through no fault of his own."

"No fault?" the queen asked, one eyebrow lifting as she lounged by her consort. "And wasn't he the one was after digging around my home like a garden pest?"

"Would you not have the rest of the world know you?" Zeke asked before Nuala could say anything, his posture strong and tall and as regal as his hostess, even in scruffy denim and frayed wool. "Your beauty and accomplishments and life?"

"The stories are there," Mab drawled, as if none of this interested her. "The songs, the poems. No one questions the might and beauty of the queen of faerie."

"But those are old stories," he protested. "Old poems. An older Mab, I think. Would you have no one know *you?*"

"You won't be finding me beneath that hill of rocks, little man."

"Not even a hint? Nothing you'd like us mortals to

know? We've heard the stories, and we're curious. Surely you've been curious yourself about a race other than yours. Don't you want to know about mortals?"

She waved her hand in dismissal, her emerald ring flashing. "I know mortals, all right. Petty and proud and foolish, every one of them."

"Oh, I'm not sure I'd call them all petty," Orla crooned, her gaze fixed below Zeke's waist with a salacious smile.

A rustle of laughter lifted from the tables. To his credit, after a moment of widened eyes, Zeke offered a wry smile. "You weren't in that house when they undressed me, too, were you?"

Orla made a *moue*. "No, and I'd like to know why. It bein' my favorite sport and all."

"Stripping helpless men?"

Her eyes almost glowed. "Oh, aye. The more helpless the better."

Again to his credit, Zeke laughed. The hall of faerie, breathlessly watching the whole interchange, gaped in surprise. Even Mab took note. Nuala, her heart caught in her throat at the peril Zeke faced, fought to hide her own smile. Nobody toyed with Orla. No man had withstood her. For that matter, Nuala couldn't remember the last time a mortal had faced the queen herself with anything other than terror and trembling. It was a fierce proud man she had for herself. At least while he was here.

"And wouldn't you like to introduce the two of them, Nuala?" the queen commanded with a feline smile. "Let himself know whom he spurns."

Nuala hated being played with like this. When she was queen, it would not be tolerated.

"When you are queen, little Nuala," Mab reminded her with that terrible soft voice, "you will enjoy the same pleasures as every Mab has before you. Now favor me with your obedience."

Nuala bowed once more, her cheeks flushed. "As you wish, my queen," she said in her most official voice as she straightened. "Zeke Kendall, it would please me to introduce you to my sister, Orla, also daughter of Mab."

Zeke betrayed himself with no more than another lift of the eyebrow. "Another sister, and as beautiful as the last. My pleasure, ma'am."

"It will be," Orla promised.

His grin was brash and unapologetic. Nuala saw it, recognized it as his banner of attraction, for didn't he love all the women, and wasn't she shamed by her own jealousy?

He is mine, she wanted to shout from the depths of her very soul. *Mine!*

She did not. She was being watched far too closely as it was. She was just lucky none of them were listening in on her and heard such a pitiful cry.

"And what is it *you* do?" Zeke asked Orla, his smile still wide and knowing, his stance perfectly easy.

Orla lifted an eyebrow, and Nuala could all but smell the arousal on her.

"What do I *do?*" she asked, her voice low and sultry as she drew a finger down her long white throat.

Zeke nodded. "Sure. Bee is a healer, and Sorcha is

a seamstress, and the queen is…the queen. What is your specialty?"

Orla's smile grew positively feral. "Dissension," she purred. "Chaos."

For a second the entire hall held its breath. Nuala could see that Zeke's pupils dilated. His nostrils flared, just the slightest bit. She went as still as death, terrified. But he didn't move. He didn't offer any fuel for Orla's fire. "Well, good," he said with a wry nod, confounding them all. "Everybody should have a skill."

Nuala couldn't help it. She let loose a bark of laughter. Even the queen looked a bit nonplussed. Orla looked more thunderous than Darragh. And the hall rustled with its own reaction, the anxious sprites freed to flight.

"Come sit by your mother and your sister," the queen said to Nuala, "and tell us while we dine why we should allow your friend to escape."

"You will let me speak?" Nuala asked.

"And me?" Orla added, steel showing beneath her velvet.

Nuala swung on her sister, suddenly afraid again. Orla's smile bordered on triumphant.

"I will allow any arguments," Mab said with a terrifying smile, and waved a languid hand. "Until it is time to decide. But first, let the little man enjoy our food."

For a moment Nuala couldn't even seem to move. One step the wrong way and all was lost. She knew it. Everyone in the vast hall knew it. But Nuala saw the immutable force of the queen and knew that for now she was caught. So she led her Zeke into the lioness's

den to have him watched by every fairy and sprite in
the hall as he tasted the food and drink of faerie, as he
savored the pristine linen tablecloths, and the gleam and
glitter of golden tablewear and crystal plates. As the
queen watched him with shrewd eyes and Orla smiled
in suspicious triumph as she nibbled on fruit and sipped
from her jeweled cup.

"This is supper, huh?" Zeke asked, looking down the
table to the procession of platters filled with fruits and
cheeses and meats and all the produce from the faerie
gardens. "It's a wonder you fairies don't get too fat to
fly."

Nuala couldn't help but stare a bit. He seemed
completely unaffected by the women who sought to
seduce him. She couldn't believe it. She couldn't
help it. She giggled.

"I hear we have a high metabolism," she assured
him and took a nibble of cheese.

Zeke took a peek at the younger fairies who still flitted
up near the rafters. "Yeah. I can see that. They ever roost?"

"Oh, aye. When they sleep."

He nodded, as if hoarding the information away.
"It's sure something my sister-in-law didn't know in her
stories of the fairies."

"Ah, sure, it's there. Mortal children know. It's they
can see us best in the gloaming. The twinkle of the
lights attracts them."

"Twinkling lights attract anybody. But there are…
well, lots of different *types* of fairies, aren't there?"

"As many types as there are mortal types, I imagine."

"Oh, I don't think we're quite as varied as this bunch."

"Well," Nuala had to admit with a grin, "I'll admit I haven't seen any of you mortals fly, now."

"Not without at least one engine and a lot of metal around them. Do *you?*"

"Do I what?"

"Fly."

She shook her head. "Ah, no. I've a great fondness for the two good feet the holy mother gave me."

He looked over at her, those handsome, long-lashed green eyes twinkling more than the fairies in the rafters. "You afraid?"

"To fly?" She straightened, donning her robe of dignity. "Sure it's never that. It's just that I never enjoyed the times I tried."

"Nuala gets the nosebleeds," Sorcha said from farther down the table.

"Well, *you* flew into a tree," Nuala retorted, both of them suddenly grinning like girls. "Broke two branches and your front tooth."

Sorcha shook her head with a show of sadness. "And wasn't I executing a brilliant tumbling maneuver and didn't see the thing in the way? It's jealous you are, girl, and you should admit it."

"I'll admit no such thing. And you weren't tumbling," Nuala laughed. "You sneezed and lost your concentration."

"A vile rumor," Sorcha said with a giggle, "spread by my detractors."

"By your flight instructor," one of the flying fairies called down from the roof.

"Ah, and isn't there a critic in every crowd?" Sorcha called back. "Sure and if you're born in the air, I'd think it would be a wee bit hard to keep from flyin' about. We earthbound fairies have a bit more work to do to get up there."

"But get up there she did," Nuala agreed with pride. It had been a grand day altogether, with Sorcha giggling and shrieking like a girl as she'd swooped down to frighten the sheep in the meadow before roosting in the trees with the smiling dryads.

"How?" Zeke asked. "How do you fly?"

All eyes turned to him with a quizzical confusion. How could you *not* fly? Nuala thought a second how to explain to this earthbound man what a fairy took for granted.

"Peter Pan," she finally said.

He frowned a bit. "You saw that movie being made, too?"

"Ah, no. But sure, we've heard of it. We hear of most of what goes on outside."

"So you all fly like Peter Pan?"

"Fairy dust."

Zeke laughed. "Oh, come on."

Nuala wanted to laugh back. "Sure you can see the fairies flying, now, can't you?"

He acquiesced with grace. "A point well made. So it could make *me* fly?"

This time the laughter was uproarious. Even Nuala

could hardly keep a straight face as she pretended to consider it. "Ah well, now, I'm not sure it's *that* simple."

"Why not?"

She let her eyes go wide. "Well, now, Peter's a boy, isn't he?"

Zeke seemed affronted. "*I'm* a boy."

"A statement I'd like to be verifying myself," Orla purred.

"A statement I *have* verified, I'll have you know," came Bee's voice from a nearby table. "And I can tell you that that lad hasn't been a boy for a good long while now."

Even Zeke smiled now. "Oh. You mean young. Not…"

"I mean small," Bee chortled. "And trust the *bean tighe*. Small describes you nowhere, mannie."

Now all the faerie were enjoying the repartee. Nuala found herself smiling, proud of her mortal. Proprietary of his smile and his laugh and his wit. She so wanted to stay here forever, seated next to him in the great hall and hearing him spar with her friends and confound her family.

But at the same time she could barely stay still. It was torture being seated next to him, conversing like friends, their bodies touching ever so slightly as they moved. A brush of a hand, a nudge from a hip. The most fleeting hint of his scent on the air: earth and sun and man. Nuala could hardly keep her attention on her food, much less her mother and sister, who were simply waiting until their best moment to attack.

She should keep her wits about her. But it was so hard, when all she wanted to do was drink in the feel and smell and sight of Zeke, like one of those sad animals she'd seen wanting for water in his desert. When just the sight of him sent her pulse skyrocketing.

As she savored those moments, Nuala forgot to mark the passing of time. But inevitably, the food was eaten and the fairy mead drunk. The tables were cleared and the music begun. It was her turn to play, one of the most precious tasks she performed for her world.

After all, little captured the passions of faerie like music. They had been known to kidnap great players and hold them, just for the privilege of succumbing to the spell of a sweet fiddle or pipe. It was the only thing to quiet them when surly, and the only thing to rouse them when sad.

"Show your mortal what you do for us, then, Nuala," Sorcha begged, eyes bright with anticipation. "Play for us."

"Play for us," the rest of the hall chanted along, the words whispered and murmured to the ceiling and back.

"That's right," Zeke said. "You play the harp."

"She does not," her mother snarled, "*play the harp*. She makes it sing, so. She makes it weep and laugh and court. It is a gift to us, her music."

What good was it to be faerie if she could still blush like a silly girl? Nuala wanted to know. She was doing so now, suddenly anxious and uncertain, when the only thing she never questioned in her world was her music.

But then Zeke smiled at her, his dimple peeking out,

and she lost her discomfort. "Play for us," he echoed the whispers around the room.

So she stood up and stepped from the high table. Her lovely *Ceo Sidhe* waited for her. As she approached, she heard the strings begin to hum, calling to her, anticipating her touch. She felt the music grow between them, lightning caught between clouds. She smiled, because here she was as powerful as her mother, as her sisters, as her clan. Here she could court Zeke Kendall with all her heart and not a word spoken to him.

Here, before she had to give him back.

If her mother let her.

Because if her mother didn't, if she chose to enslave this proud, strong man, Nuala thought she would never want to play her music again.

Lifting her harp in her arms, Nuala settled into the high-backed oaken chair and bent to listen. The music waited. The hall paused, every breath held for the first note her enchanted *Ceo Sidhe* would sing. And into that breathless hush came the voice of her mother.

"And after you play, Nuala," she crooned, "then we will settle your little man."

That quickly the magic vanished. The music fell away, and the glittering horde of faerie seemed to growl. The queen had stepped too far. She had sullied a sacrament, and every fairy in the hall knew it. Nuala struggled to banish the end of the night. She closed her eyes to keep her mother from her and bent over her dearest friend, nestling her against her shoulder, wrapping tender arms around her as if to protect her from capricious queens, just as she wished she could protect her mortal.

She would think of him later. Now, there was just the music. And maybe, if she played with grace and truth, she could charm a capricious queen and save the man she'd loved ever since she remembered.

Gently, tenderly, her touch a reverent request, Nuala plucked the first strings.

"In the darkest days of the past," her voice rang out, the melody as old as time, the words painted in every fairy heart, the anthem calling them to greatness and immortality, "in the golden dawn of time, walked the great ones, the wild ones, the terrible, thundering wise ones...."

Zeke couldn't breathe. He couldn't move, stunned to immobility by the liquid cascade of music that echoed and resonated through this impossible place. He'd had trouble enough getting used to this building...tree house...whatever. After all, how many places had he been that had been lit by fairy power? The ceiling soared straight into the night, a cathedral of trees decorated in starlight and populated by a collection of mythical creatures he couldn't possibly have imagined all on his own.

Then he'd found himself facing off not just with the queen but with that third daughter of hers, the black-eyed siren who made the other girls in the family pale in comparison. Just the sound of her voice was enough to make a man sweat.

But, oddly enough, even as his body had reacted like a randy teen, his mind had been completely dissociated. He'd been fascinated at the same time his unruly anatomy had been testing the stitching of his jeans.

And then Nuala had sat down and picked up that harp, and everything else had fled. Zeke had heard that listening to beautiful music could transport you straight to heaven. He'd never believed it—until this very moment.

Zeke had never been one for music. It had always been the dry silence of the desert that had drawn him, where even a thought threw an echo. But he'd been wrong. He'd never heard anything like this. Good God, his entire body sang with every pure, delicious note. His skin tingled, and his eyes burned as if he wanted to cry. And he hadn't cried since the day he'd stumbled over his father in the barn when he was six years old.

And even weirder, every other being in the room looked the same way. Surely fairies heard good music. Hell, they were legendary for it. But every eye was moist, every mouth open just a little, as if the owner was so mesmerized they'd forgotten basic muscle control. Every heart was on every sleeve. Even the queen's.

She listened with her eyes closed, her hand clasped in her consort's, a small, private smile on her lips. She swayed to the movement of the music, as if she were ingesting it like opium.

Fairy music.

Now Zeke understood what his sister-in-law meant when she talked about how people pined to death for the sound of it. He could pine to death.

But it wasn't just the music. It was Nuala. The smile on her face. The impossibly delicate dance of her fingers. The glow that seemed to pulse around her as her fingers flew over those strings. The sweet, pure joy on her exquisite face.

Zeke had a niece who was a musician. Elizabeth. She was a good musician, would one day be a great pianist. He'd seen that same preoccupation on her features, the way she disappeared into the notes that poured from her piano as if they were air and water and prayer. He understood her passion and applauded her gift.

But this…this was something altogether beyond that. This was…

Oh, hell. This was magic.

Orla couldn't breathe. She was enraged. Frantic. Frightened.

He had laughed at her.

Her.

No man laughed at her. No man refused her.

Neither would this one. Especially since it seemed that he intended to choose her sister over her.

Orla had thought to wait. She'd thought to give the queen time to wreak her revenge for her by choosing the man for herself, since all Orla really needed was his ruin and Nuala's misery. But now, watching his taut attention as he looked on her puling excuse for a sister, she knew it wouldn't be enough.

Stupid, worthless mortal. He deserved no better than to waste away until all that was left was the skin on his bones and eyes that burned with the fever for her. It was her gift.

It was her *right*.

But she couldn't betray her intent. Not yet, anyway. Not until the moment when it would hurt him the worst. So she held herself very still, her hand clenched around the cup that was hers, a gold cup engraved with *ogham* that spoke her powers and gleamed with the smoke of her stones. She smiled, an inscrutable smile even her mother couldn't pierce, and she waited.

She waited through that caterwauling her sister called music, the clink and clank of notes that did no more than give her heartburn and obviously struck up some kind of allergy, since she had to wipe at her eyes.

She fought hard not to sneer. She would show her sister who had the power. Who should be queen. She would steal her mortal and then throw his husk on the pile with the others.

She couldn't wait.

And then, in the space of a heartbeat, everything changed. From one note to another, Nuala's music changed, and Orla's plans right along with it. For the first time all evening, she found herself smiling for the pure pleasure of it.

Nuala didn't notice the change herself. She'd spiraled too deeply into the music, submerged in song and melody and verse. She'd dived deep into the wellspring where the melodies rose, where the fairy lore lived, where the heart and soul of her swelled with truth, with joy and passion. Closing her eyes, she sank into the pool of beauty and let it pour over the room.

And as she sang, as she played so that *Ceo Sidhe's* notes cascaded like sunlight glittering off a waterfall, she lost herself. She lost her place and her past. She lost the awareness of her audience. All she knew was the river of music that flowed through her. All she heard was her beautiful *Ceo Sidhe's* voice. All she felt was the resonance of her instrument and her voice and the millennia of musicians who had come before her.

She didn't hear when her song changed. She didn't realize that her music, usually so bright and strong and life-giving, began to resonate with yearning and love and loss.

She didn't open her eyes until the last note dissolved amid the shadows of the trees, and when she did, all she knew was that, as always, her heart was full. Her skin tingled with it, her head echoed with it; her chest hummed with it.

She knew how the faerie court felt about her music. She knew that most nights she scattered light and laughter amid the shadows here. Tonight, she thought, she'd sewn wonder. So when she turned to her audience, she smiled, giddy and delighted.

It was only then that she realized the atmosphere wasn't normal. Usually the faeries greeted her music with a reverent hush. Tonight, the silence was stricken. Strained. Awful.

Nuala almost dropped her harp as she looked around to see not joy in the eyes of her fairies but stark desolation. Tears. She began to tremble. It was wrong. It shouldn't be like this. And then she saw the queen.

Her mother was usually proud of her in that self-congratulatory way queens had. Nuala depended on it. Tonight, however, instead of seeing approbation in her mother's golden-green eyes, she saw fury. White-lipped and rigid, the queen slowly rose to her feet. Nuala followed to hers.

"I have changed my mind," the queen said, her voice terrible. Did Nuala see tears glistening in those legendary eyes? "Tonight is not for settling the mortal after all. Michael?"

"Here as always, my queen."

"Take the little man with you. Sorcha, see to your sister. And now, my court, I bid you good eve."

Nuala stood frozen in place as Mab swept from the hall like the last light of day, her high court following. She realized that the rest still hadn't moved and was shattered. Court protocol demanded Mab receive obeisance when she departed. Instead, the faerie court remained frozen in stunned silence, their stricken eyes not on their queen but on Nuala.

Well, she thought, feeling sick and shaken, it seemed she'd answered one question for them, to be certain. And sure it was the last answer any of them wanted.

Chapter 6

"I guess this means we're not going to dance," Zeke said to no one in particular.

A gnarled and bandy-legged little man stepped up to take his arm. "Not tonight, laddie. Not tonight."

Zeke took a quick look at him, but found his attention back on Nuala where she stood alone holding on to her harp as if it were the last real thing in the universe. "What the hell happened?" he asked.

He'd been so overwhelmed by her music, so completely absorbed, that he hadn't even realized he'd already wiped his cheeks by the time she sent that last note spinning into the crowd like fireworks.

It was when he'd seen the queen's face that he realized something had gone wrong. He'd turned to the rest of the room and discovered that every other soul in the place knew it, too, and what was more, seemed to know what it meant.

He didn't, that was for damn sure. He saw Nuala's smile crumble to ashes and wanted to jump up and defend her. But the queen had beaten him to it, rising in that imperial way she had and stalking out as if Nuala had personally insulted her.

Zeke didn't understand. He just knew that Nuala had given him music that was too beautiful to bear and then seemed to be punished for it.

"What happened?" he repeated, not seeing the fairies disappear into the darkness or hearing the anxious whispers that followed them. He only saw Nuala alone and trembling, her head bowed.

He took a step toward her, but the little guy beside him held him back. "Ah no, lad. You'll need to wait on seein' the girl 'til tomorrow. The queen has said it, and in my long and perilous experience with herself, I'd say you wouldn't want to push her right now. Trust me, she'll calm by sunrise."

Finally Zeke looked down into the brightest blue eyes he'd ever seen. A dead ringer for a leprechaun, all crow's feet and nut-brown skin in brown leather and a squashed little hat. Zeke couldn't help but think in passing that *this* was what fairies were supposed to look like. Like Colm O'Roarke. Not like Nuala.

God, not like Nuala.

"But what did she do?" he asked the little man who came no higher than his collarbone.

The little guy sighed and looked over to where Nuala's nice sister was talking to her. "Ah, well now, lad, she committed a terrible crime in front of the queen, so. She told the truth."

Jake frowned. "What do you mean? She played the harp. She sang. She mostly sang old folk songs, and a couple that sounded like the begats out of the Bible."

"The history," the little man said with a consi-

dered nod. "The girl was after singin' her family tree
for you."

"And for that she gets this kind of treatment?"

"No, but I'm afraid that's not somethin' I can figure
out how to explain before dawn. Now then, come along
wit' ya. I have a feeling you aren't ready for our late
hours yet, especially after that knock you took on the
head. As for meself, I'm of a mind to think my services
will be needed before this night is through."

"Your services?" Zeke asked, letting the little man
lead him toward the door.

The little guy shot him a big shiny smile. "Ah sure,
shouldn't I have introduced myself, then? Nuala's Uncle
Michael. Uncle Mick, some call me. I'm the master of
the horse hereabouts. But I'd appreciate it, now, if you
didn't tell the horses that." He leaned in, chuckling. "Sure
they refuse to acknowledge any master but themselves."

Zeke took a look around at the dark and near-empty
hall. "And what makes you think you're going to be
working?"

Michael shook his head. "Oh, there's a feeling in the
air, lad. If I were a betting fairy—and, truth to tell, I am
just that—I'd lay wagers that tonight the queen will ride."

"Ride? Where?"

Another smile, mysterious and sly. "Where you
mortals can catch a glimpse of her and create more
myths."

"What did I do?" Nuala groaned as her sister led her
back out into the deep night.

The last thing Nuala expected was laughter. But laugh Sorcha did, although it sounded a bit sore. "Ah, girl, how long have you been playing that harp of yours?"

Nuala blinked, a bit bemused. "Since I opened my eyes to that first spring, which you know perfectly well, since you were the one to put it in my hands."

Sorcha nodded. "And in all this time, why is it you're the last to know that you can't escape the truth in your music?"

"What truth?"

"Whatever truth you speak to, of course. The past, the future, the perilous state of wonder, the magic of small places. All of it, any moment of it. We rely on that honesty, your audience. We feed off of it like honey and milk."

"But what happened tonight?"

Sorcha reached over and swept a tear from her sister's cheek. "Tonight, best of my sisters, you fell in love. And could you have done it with a fairy lad, we wouldn't be standin' here in the dark trying to figure out how to avoid herself the queen for a few hours. No, you had to be beguiled by a mortal. And you've known since the moment you snuck your scrying water into that dip in the forest where you thought she couldn't see you, just what she'd think of that silliness."

"But *we* have mortal in us," Nuala protested. "After all these millennia, *all* faerie do. Even herself."

Sorcha rolled her eyes with all the drama of her race. "Ah Nuala, do us all a favor and don't be after remindin' herself of that. Won't you incite a storm even Darragh couldn't conjure?"

Nuala snorted. "If she rules the faerie, shouldn't she have the courage to look the truth in the eye and name it?"

And didn't Sorcha laugh again. "Oh, girl, save me from the cost of your courage. Come along now. I think we're needin' some sleep so we can better plan for tomorrow. Let herself ride the pique out of her, and then, when the sun shines, she'll see this for the joke it is."

"It's no joke, Sorcha. I think it was his chance for escape I just lost in there."

Sorcha looked out to the darkness that had just swallowed Nuala's mortal. "It was your heart you lost, *mo chroí*. Sure and hasn't every fairy alive done that at least a hundred times during the wax of the moon? The problem with you is that the power of it flies to your fingers when you play that harp of yours, so no one can mistake it. Play her a happy tune tomorrow, a tune of the queen, and she'll not find such fear in the man."

For a very long moment Nuala stood staring off into the darkness where the fairy lights flickered fitfully and the night breezes fingered her hair. Then, her shoulders slumped just a little, she nodded. "Aye, Sorcha. You have the right of it. I'm tired now, and think I'd do best to be in my bed."

Even so, it was a long time before she closed her eyes.

The Queen of Faerie rode that night. Deep into the darkness where legends curled around campfires and the old ones listened for the sounds of magic, where babies laughed in their sleep and parents gazed fretfully out the window at the sounds that didn't belong in the modern world; she set her horses and her court into the hills to remind the sleeping world how much more it was than it seemed.

A procession of proud horses passed, their silver bridles jingling with the bells that hung from them, their riders tall and severe and regal. A thundering from a cloudless sky. A wave of prescience that swept the sleep before it. The moon that soared over the spare western moors cast silver shadows that suddenly took shape as a cavalry, as a royal court on tour. As a tantalizing taste of enchantment on a late summer's night.

The queen rode, and mortals remembered their folklore. The young ones discounted it. After all, they had technology, and they had progress, roads laid over sacred ground and televisions to displace the poetry of old with game shows and commercials. The young ones discounted it, but they slept badly, hearing hoofbeats in their dreams.

The old ones, knowing better, kept their eyes open and their doors protected with rowan. The queen was riding on a night that wasn't All Hallows Eve. None had the courage to step outside and discover what that meant.

Orla had just about had enough.

The evening had started out well enough. After all, her precious sister was in disgrace, and nothing whetted her appetite better. Then, while the queen had waited for the horses to ready themselves, Orla had taken her delight out on a human who'd happened to wander over the wrong hill. She could still feel the lust rising in him like sweat as she'd pulled him down. When he woke the next morning—*if* he woke the next morning—he would be smiling like an idiot and full of a story nobody would believe.

Yes, quite a nice way to spend an evening.

But then, by all the gold in the fairy halls, hadn't the queen decided that there was nothing for it but to rile up the humans a little? And since Orla was part of the high court, she'd had to ride, too. Not her sisters. Goddess, no. Those two puling infants had been excused for bad behavior. They hadn't had to spend the rest of the hours till dawn pounding across the sleeping earth like a circus troupe.

Orla hated to ride with the queen. She hated the pomp, especially since it gave no benefit to her. She hated the obeisance, the ritual. But most of all, she hated the horses.

Who in all the kingdoms thought it was necessary for faerie to make that awful connection with those temperamental beasts? Who had considered it a good idea to terrify humans with horses? You want to terrify somebody, send wolves. Bears. *Dubhlainn Sidhe.*

Now there was an idea. An impulse kept so ruthlessly pushed down that most days she could convince herself that she wasn't attracted to the idea.

Set the Fairies of the Dark Sword loose on the realm. Orla couldn't help smiling as she thought of the terror and chaos they could sow in their wake, a maelstrom that would overshadow the worst of Darragh's storms. Even the storm he was brewing tonight over Nuala's straying. With the warriors at her back, Orla could be overlooked no more.

Or maybe just one warrior. Just a dip of the toe into her world so the queen couldn't ignore the eddies. So she could see which daughter it was who could command enough power to control the Dark Sword.

The situation wasn't dire enough yet to risk the severe penance that would have to be paid for such a crime. Not yet. But if her mother kept up this nonsense, Orla might just be the one to lose her patience. Especially if she had to get on another horse.

By the time she handed the prickly beast off to one of Uncle Michael's minions, Orla was sore, smelly and thoroughly disgruntled. She needed another mortal.

Or some mischief.

"Well, what are you doin' here, lad?" Michael asked without bothering to look up from his work. "It's not even come to dawn."

"The storm woke me." Zeke looked up to see the clouds shredding with the wind. "Impressive."

Michael shrugged where he was unsaddling a horse. "Darragh was in a temper, so."

"The guy who's gonna be Nuala's…whatever?"

"He has lightning in his fingers, that one. The wind rises at his call. And, faith, he was callin' last night."

Zeke nodded, distracted, his hands shoved in his

pockets against the early morning chill, the collar of his flannel shirt buttoned and flipped up. The sun struggled above the horizon, its light faint beyond the trees. There was no breeze, no breaking of the wet chill of early morning. The air was so still, he swore he could hear an occasional cough from the little houses at the other end of the glen.

When he had decided he couldn't sleep any longer, he'd dressed and walked outside Michael's little hobbit house to find another small, bandy-legged guy to ask directions of. He'd been led to this glen at the edge of the small town, where more of the bandy-legged creatures were helping Michael as he unsaddled a herd of horses in the rising mist. A herd of pale, pale gray horses who looked disturbingly familiar. A herd of ghostly gray horses who all seemed to be watching him for something.

"Those are Diamond K horses," he blurted out without thinking. "From our ranch."

Several of the proud heads rose, shaking spectral manes at him. Michael didn't even hesitate as he continued to unbuckle the mounts.

"No," Zeke disagreed with himself after closer examination. "They're not quarter horses. But they... what are they?"

"Fairy horses, of course. And it would be a kindness not to be talking of them as if they're not here, lad. Give your hellos, if you will."

Zeke stared at the little man as if his hair were on fire. "Pardon me?"

A sleek silver handkerchief of a saddle in his arms, Michael nodded to the herd that had clustered even more closely, as if an audience to a play.

"You don't want to be insultin' them, then, lad. Say hello." He leaned in a bit, his eyes twinkling. "It wouldn't hurt to mention how handsome they are, now, would it?"

It took Zeke a moment for this all to sink in, at least as much as it ever would. It was still almost dark, the mist curling up from the grass, the sky a pearly pink that tinted the silvery horses the color of seashells. He could hear them rustle impatiently around him. He could smell them, the comforting scent of his favorite animal, the quick connection to his brother Jake and those strong arms that had controlled these fierce animals as gently as they had his recalcitrant siblings.

Zeke spent a long moment just savoring that sensation. Then, because he didn't know what else to do, he gave a formal bow. "I give you greeting," he addressed the horse closest to him, an exquisite stallion with liquid black eyes and the muzzle of an Arabian. "I was…uh, over-whelmed by the sight of you. We have horses much like you in Wyoming, you see." Several of the horses jostled a bit, as if in protest. "But not nearly as magnificent. If it had been lighter out, I could have told right away."

Did horses smile? These seemed to suddenly look satisfied. Then, after a quick dip of their heads, one by one they turned to amble back into the glen towards the sound of a nearby stream.

"Well done, lad," Michael approved with a tilt of his own head that looked suspiciously identical to the

Dangerous Temptation

horses. "I don't suppose you might like to help out here, would you? Give you something to do besides moon over my niece and upset the queen."

Zeke couldn't take his eyes off the horses. "I guess. Why do they look so much like Jake's horses?"

Michael had just handed off the last saddle to one of his minions. "And who's Jake, then?"

Zeke watched the horses wander off like a group of friends heading for a swim. "My brother. He raises the best cutting horses in the States."

Michael nodded. "Ah, the one who raised Grayghost. A magnificent beast, that."

Zeke looked down at the little man in surprise. "How do you know?"

Michael's smile was as old as the land. "Did you not notice his color? Such a pale gray as to be almost white? So it seemed he could slip into the shadows and disappear?"

Just like this herd of horses had just done. The mist rose higher, and the horses were gone.

"You're telling me my brother raises fairy horses?"

"Ah, no. He raises cutting horses. Can he help it if he's bright enough to spot a fairy animal?"

Now Zeke was staring at Michael. "You're insane."

Michael chuckled. "Sad to say to your own cousin, boyo."

That brought him to a complete halt. "What?"

The little man tilted his head again, his smile brash and impish. "You think it's a mistake you bein' here and all? A coincidence?"

Zeke waved him off like a used-car salesman. "Every folk tale ever written involves you people trucking with humans."

Pulling a pipe from his crumpled leather jacket, Michael nodded. "Aye, true. But we'd much rather truck with our own."

For a long, long moment nothing broke the silence in the glen but early birdsong.

"You're telling me I'm a...fairy?"

"We prefer the term *tua. Tua de danann.*"

Zeke couldn't help it. He let out a bark of laughter that startled a few birds into flight. "Of course I am," he said, laughing even harder. "When I'm not climbing rock canyons in Utah, I'm perched on a flower petal playing my tin whistle."

Michael just lifted one of his gray, bristled eyebrows at him. "I see it might take a bit for you to believe."

Zeke couldn't stop laughing. "Michael, we don't have...*tua* in Wyoming. Hell, we don't even have Hare Krishnas."

Now Michael laughed. Zeke hadn't noticed that he'd begun to follow the little man as he walked back toward his house.

"Well, you didn't spring full-stirruped in Wyoming, now did you?"

"Of course I did. I was born right there. As were my father and grandfather before me. And trust me, not one of them ever lived in a fairy fort under the hill."

"Of course not, lad. What business would Wyoming have with fairy forts, I ask you? But your family?

Didn't that brilliant author Amanda Marlow write a lovely book based on your great-great-gran who was a witchy woman? Well, lad, where do you think that lovely lass came from?"

Zeke stopped, suddenly not nearly so amused. "How could you know that? Did Nuala tell you? Did she see it?"

Michael's smile was older than patience. "Nuala would never betray a confidence. Sure, we always keep a certain contact with our own, no matter how diluted the blood. And with those bright green eyes of yours, you can't deny us that." He tilted his head a bit, considering. "You might not believe we exist, but sure you've heard us."

Zeke froze in his tracks, appalled. Suddenly, inexplicably afraid. "What do you mean?"

But Michael didn't answer right away. He stood there as if debating something. Then he gave his head a quick shake and his hand a wave in the direction of a fallen log that just happened to be situated by the side of the path.

"Sit down, do, lad."

Zeke didn't move. "I don't think so."

Michael gave him a push that surprised him into landing smack onto the log. And before Zeke could collect himself to bolt upright, Michael delivered the leveler.

"You've heard the banshee, Zeke."

Zeke's knees simply collapsed.

"Don't be absurd, old man. Banshees are no more real than…"

Michael didn't so much as smile. "Me?"

Zeke jabbed a finger at him. "This is a dream, damn it."

"Ah, no, lad. It's not. Nor is the banshee."

"There *was* no banshee." But he was sweating.

"When you found your da in the barn that morning, you were searching for him to see if he'd heard her. If anybody else had heard that high, keening voice that seemed to fly on the wind."

Zeke swore his heart was just going to fall out in the dirt. He could hear it in his ears. "You don't know…"

"The banshee follow clans, Zeke. Especially clans with fairy blood. She followed yours. If you'd read that grand book your sister-in-law wrote about your family, you'd know that. You weren't even the first in your family to hear her."

"Jake didn't."

"Jake did. He just wouldn't tell you. A man like Jake finds it hard to believe in what he cannot touch."

"Well, it's something we both share."

"I'm not thinking so. Jake is a fine, braw man, but he doesn't have the spirit to hold an old arrowhead in his hands and see those who shaped it, right there in his head. He can't imagine long-dead civilizations like you can. But he heard her that day, so. As did Gen. Even little Lee. Wasn't she already crying when you came out of that barn?"

"I don't know. I don't remember."

He did, though. He remembered it all. That frantic flight to the barn, where he knew his father would be, because for some reason that high, thin voice scared him. Scared him into running. He remembered crashing through the door from harsh noon straight into shadows. He remembered yelling.

"Dad! Dad, you gotta come here!"

He remembered tripping right over his father's feet. Stretched out there on the hard-packed dirt, a hole in the sole of his boot, his threadbare flannel shirt lying open in the heat. Zeke remembered the sweatstains on his father's undershirt. The flat stare of his green eyes. The slack sag of his jaw. And that high, keening voice wailing on and on just out of sight, as if it were the wind working at a loose window.

But there had been no wind that day. Only sunlight and shadow. And his father dead on the barn floor.

Zeke had been six years old.

"There is no such thing as a banshee," he grated, sweating as hard as his father had that hot summer noon when his heart had failed him.

"You heard her again when your mother, Goddess rest her soul, died two years later."

He'd run so far that day, all the way to the original settler's cabin up in the high meadow where they all went when they wanted to be alone, his chest heaving, his heart thundering. He had stood there, alone but for the aspen and the hawks and the sharp shoulders of the mountains at the edge of the meadow. And the sound of that voice that had climbed right up the mountain with him.

"No."

Michael put a hand on Zeke's shoulder. "Ah, it's not

such a bad thing to own, lad. After all, she gives a great service. A chance to prepare."

Zeke bolted up off that log as if he'd been burned. "Why are you doing this?"

For a long moment Michael just looked up at him, his hands on his hips, his eyes at once sad and wise. "For you to understand what you stumbled over here, lad. For you to know that if you can't make it home, you belong just as much here as there."

Zeke didn't even bother to look around to see the lazy beginning of the day in this place. The curls of smoke that rose from the little chimneys, the rosy glow of distant sunlight, the animals scratching and pacing for their food.

"Well, there you're wrong," he said. "I don't belong here. I would never belong here. And I'd never stay."

"Even for Nuala?"

His heart was racing again. But he shook his head. "Even for Nuala."

He didn't walk away. He ran, never noticing the glint of auburn in the hair of the woman who watched from the edge of the trees.

Chapter 7

Nuala found him hours later, down by the brook.

"Michael should never have spoken," she said, not knowing what else to do.

He was just sitting there, his feet planted on the bank as if bracing himself against something, his arms crossed atop his knees, his eyes blank in a way that made her grieve. Nuala had seen that look before. It was a look Zeke had perfected. His protection, his barrier, his refuge against the truth. Against the pain of a childhood filled with abandonment and loss.

If only she could give him the words that would tell him how very lucky he was. What she would give to have those wonderful siblings waiting for him on the other side. If only she could once and for all break down that terrible wall that kept him running from the sights Michael had called back today.

Nuala hadn't been kind to her uncle when she'd found out what he'd done. Michael was a good soul. But he was still a fairy, and fairies simply didn't understand grief or guilt. Michael had only wanted to help, not having a clue he could be making things so much worse.

Nuala had had eons of time since then to consider what she could do for Zeke. What she could do for them both. It had taken her this long to step up to it.

"I'm sorry, Zeke." "Sorry" was a word the faerie were simply not acquainted with. If her mother heard her say it, she would be paying penance until she went to the West herself.

Finally, as if just hearing her, Zeke looked up. That quickly, he was on his feet, his hands around her arms.

"Are you all right?" he asked, bent over her.

Nuala looked up into those anxious green eyes and wondered how she could possibly fall further in love with this mortal. Here he'd been dragged back through the worst moments of his life, and he was worried for her.

So she smiled. "I'm grand, thank you. I was worried for you, though. Michael had no right."

For a second she thought he wouldn't answer. Then, that barrier still up in his sweet emerald eyes, he shrugged. "I'm sure it's important for him to think I'm a fairy, too. Kind of like wanting all your friends to like the same sports team. It bonds, I guess."

Well, wouldn't this be the worst time to tell him that Michael hadn't stretched the truth even a little? Zeke was mostly mortal, but those eyes…Oh, those eyes. They betrayed the truth no fairy could miss. Green was the color of fairy eyes.

"And were you impressed by the horses of faerie?" she asked, allowing him his escape.

His smile was genuine and wide. "They're magnificent. But I get the idea I shouldn't let them know that."

She chuckled. "Faith, they're hard enough to live with as it is. Don't go givin' them ideas, please."

His smile didn't ease, but his eyes searched hers. "What happened last night?" he asked. "It seemed as if everybody was mad at you. And you were..." He stopped, shook his head, never letting loose of her. "I've never heard anything like it."

Well, there just wasn't any way to not be preening with that kind of praise. Still she tried not to. "It was fairy music, Zeke. Have you not heard that it is enough all of itself to ensorcel any mortal who hears it?"

"The way you play it, I can believe it. Is everybody else that good?"

"Of course. You'll hear them later."

"What about your mother? Is she still upset?"

Nuala's smile was gentle. "Oh, she's come around a bit. I played her a bit of breakfast music that involved lavish praise for the faerie queen, and it quite took the edge off her anger."

"But why was she upset?"

Nuala drew a breath and looked around. They were alone, tucked down into the brook's hollow, where only the birds could see them. Well, and her mother. But she'd left her mother chastising one of the trooping fairies who'd broken a blackthorn tree, and that would absorb her attention for a while.

Maybe they had time. The time while the sun still shone, anyway. Mab had told her that morning that Zeke's judgment had only been postponed a night. And if that were so, Nuala was left with only a little while with him, because once the decision was made, she prayed—for his sake—he could go.

Before he did, though, they both deserved to be able to celebrate their attraction.

Attraction. Faith, wasn't that just a pale word? Nuala loved Zeke like water, like the dance of a breeze through spring leaves. She loved him like light and air and life itself. And she had so little time to show him. To leave him something small to remember, if he was allowed to remember at all when he went back to his family.

So she took hold of one of his hands and led him to a small square of level grass. "Why don't we sit a bit? There's still a lot we haven't sorted out yet."

And, just like that, Zeke sat. Nuala followed, her skirt floating around her as she settled on the cool damp grass next to him. Close enough that she could smell that fresh air on him. She could see those little flashes of gold in his green, green eyes. She could all but hear the steady throb of his heartbeat. She was distracted by it. By the anticipation and terror of what she was about to do.

"I thought after last night Mab would never let you near me again," Zeke admitted, evidently not noticing her agitation. "I thought you'd be punished."

Nuala smiled, her heart picking up speed. What she wanted was perilous. Foolish. It didn't matter. She'd waited her whole life for it, and the only way she wouldn't go forth, was if Zeke turned her down.

Oh, Goddess, don't let him turn me down.

Just once, she wanted to taste what those mortal women had tasted. She wanted to see those hot green eyes sharpen with longing. She wanted…

She *wanted*….

"This is a complicated place," she began, reaching over to brush Zeke's hair out of his eyes, just to touch him. To inhale the potent scent of him. "Any place is when royalty's involved. Suffice it to say that the queen was a bit upset when I played, because in doing so I betrayed the relationship I'd formed with you and your family."

Zeke frowned. "Relationship? Just by looking at us in the water?"

She struggled to keep her smile bright. He could never imagine how lonely it could be in this magical world. "It was a relationship I'd wished for, though I am who I am. A family who took care of each other." Who never tried to poison other people's minds or drinks. "I guess you could say that the court heard the…well, the yearning for something that wasn't faerie in my music. It's what set them all off, I'm afraid."

They'd heard something else, as well. Something she felt now. The crackle of electricity. The hot flush of fascination. The instinctive need to lose oneself completely in another. The deep wish that just for once she could hand herself completely to someone, to surrender, knowing she was completely safe.

She could already feel the sleek slope of his shoulders beneath her hands, the rough texture of his tongue against her nipples. She could hear the stutter of his breathing as she set her hands on him.

Abruptly, Zeke straightened. "Did you…?"

Nuala yanked her thoughts back under control. "Oh, I'm, uh, I'm sorry."

His pupils had grown huge. There was a sudden sheen of sweat on his upper lip. He'd seen the very same images she had. He'd felt her hand skimming his naked flesh, though he was sitting there in respectable flannel and jeans.

She'd forgotten how very sensitive he was to that kind of errant thought.

"I didn't mean…" She hadn't meant for it to happen so soon. She couldn't say that, though.

"That's *you* sending those thoughts?" He sounded incredulous. "I thought I was just getting out of control."

Nuala couldn't help giggling. "And have you looked at yourself in a mirror lately? If you'd stayed at Bee's any longer, you would have heard her even better. Every lady fairy in the glen is imagining you without those impregnable pants."

An eyebrow went up. "Even you?"

Nuala took a deep breath. "Especially me. But I think you knew that perfectly well. You're just after teasin' me, now."

"No," he said, his eyes suddenly grave as he brushed the backs of his knuckles against her cheek. "Believe me."

He leaned closer, the shadows collecting along the sharp planes of his face, the sultry wind winnowing through his hair. Now Nuala could smell the tang of sweat on him, and something else, a hint of something uniquely him, and it set her heart to skidding.

"Nothing's changed since last night, has it?" he asked, his lips only a few inches from hers. "You're still married?"

She shook her head by millimeters. "I'm not married at all. Darragh will be my consort after the Mab leaves these shores. It's kind of after bein' a political appointment."

"With rights to produce heirs to the kingdom?"

Nuala blushed. Fairies never blushed, especially in matters of amorous behavior. But suddenly she wanted to reassure Zeke that she would be true to him, even after he left, long after he'd raised his own tribe of heirs with some pale, thin mortal woman who would never think to break through that wall of isolation.

"It's not a job you'd want, Zeke," she said instead. "You have no place being no more than a consort."

"But if it's to you, I'd sure be tempted."

Nuala didn't remind him of his words of that morning. She didn't warn him that he'd been right then, that he couldn't stay. Even for her. She kept her silence, held her breath, kept her gaze on his.

He leaned closer, his hand straying along her throat to where her pulse had begun to race. Her skin was suddenly so sensitive, as if it could anticipate him. She was humming with want, hungry for the approach of those callused fingers on her breasts, her belly, the soft white skin of her back. She craved the enchantment of his hands on her, his mouth, his skin. She wanted to take her own fill of him in return, to trace the contours of his throat with her tongue, to taste the salt of sweat on his skin. She wanted to fill her hands with him and revel in the sweet sorcery of his eyes. She wanted to explore him like a new country and stake her exclusive claim on him.

"This is a bad idea," he murmured, leaning closer.

Nuala bent toward him until her lips were a breath from his. "A very bad idea."

She felt him slide the neck of her dress down over one shoulder. Felt his fingers testing the shape of her arm and following it down. She saw the dark desire bloom in his eyes and shared the images in his head. She saw herself on her back in the grass, her dress gone, her knees up, waiting for him, reaching out to his sweat-sheened body as if seeking sustenance. She heard her cries when she was still silent and felt the moan he tried to suppress.

They hadn't so much as moved, lips so close Nuala could have consumed him without effort. Zeke smiled, a smile of welcome, of possession, of beguilement. Nuala couldn't take her eyes from him, from the hot spring of life in his eyes, the dimple that punctuated his smile. She couldn't breathe. He slipped his hand into her hair, tangling himself in her so that she couldn't move, so that shivers of delight cascaded through her, and finally, finally, he closed the distance to her mouth.

A very bad idea, she thought, even as her eyes closed. As she opened her mouth and gave him entry. His lips were silk, his breath as warm and alive as a summer breeze, his tongue delicious as he teased her, just a caress, a taste of his lips, a stroke against her tongue. He dipped and fled and dipped again, until she thought she would die for want of air, for want of more.

Just when she thought he would retreat, he invaded. Deep thrusts, parries, explorations. He mated with her, deep and delicious as his tongue danced with hers, as he claimed all of her, every corner and crevice, every breath and sigh, all his, commanded by his clever mouth until their breath was one, their bodies met and molded on the grass.

She was a fairy. She didn't know how to remove mortal clothing. She certainly had no experience with such thick, unwieldy material. It didn't seem to matter. It was as if she had magic in her fingers, or perhaps only urgency in her pursuit. She found buttons and unbound them. She pulled and arched and shoved, all the while giving in to her need to touch him. She needed to claim him, to trespass over those shadow-sculpted planes with impunity.

She knew he had already taken her dress. It was no great feat, as fairy dresses were no more than gossamer and hue. The grass was just a bit damp against her back, the breeze cool against her heated skin. She could smell the bluebells that littered the lawn. She could hear the birds chattering somewhere, and the whisper of the dryads as they linked arms to protect the lovers from spies.

Nuala had been naked on the earth before, but it had never felt so delicious, every nerve ending awake, every inch of her so stirred that she had to move. She had to arch against the urgent progress of Zeke's hands and float in the sea of grass that cushioned her. She had to wind around him, pulling him so close that even sunlight could not come between them.

Ah, there. His shirt was off. What she'd fantasized for so long was now hers. His chest. Oh, she wanted to consume his chest. Run her hands up and down that fine, curling hair, tease at his nipples, measure his shoulders and explore the contours of his arms. She wanted to trace every muscle in his flat, hard belly and trace that arrow of hair that disappeared beneath his jeans. And then she would figure out a way to get those jeans off.

She shouldn't do this. She would live for eternity knowing that it would never come again. That her future would be eons and ages with only the memory of Zeke's body, of the exquisite touch of his hands, the benediction of his mouth.

She shouldn't.

She would.

After Zeke left, she would devote herself to her clan. She would send her mother to the West with a brave heart and a head held high. She would take her place as queen. But before she did, she would be selfish enough to fill herself just once with this man. Just once.

Oh, his hands. Nuala moaned with them, shuddered with the unfamiliar abrasion against her most sensitive skin. Elegant hands, clever, quick hands, hands that had seen toil and injury. Hands she wanted to kiss, to fondle and comfort. Hands that worshipped her with rough grace, until she could barely breathe, couldn't even think past the brush of his fingers across her breasts.

"Since we shouldn't do this," he murmured, dropping kisses along her collarbone, his hands sweeping along her hips and thighs, "should I really be wicked?"

Nuala arched against him, desperate for his touch, for the bliss of his lips against her. "How should you...do that?"

"I could—" his mouth lowered, his hand slid up her side, his thumb tracing the curve of her breast "—feast on this breast. I want to put my mouth on you and suckle."

Just the words sent Nuala spiraling. Her nipples were hard as pebbles, her breasts swollen and heavy, her belly aching. "That's not wicked," she sighed, feeling his breath against her damp skin.

"It's not? Hmm. Maybe you don't want me to do it."

Nuala didn't answer. She just grabbed the back of his head and pulled him against her. He was smiling, she could feel it, as he dropped a quick kiss on her breast, as he returned to lick it with that raspy tongue of his that set off explosions of light in her. She groaned; she writhed; she clutched at him, knowing she was about to fall. Begging for the privilege. And when, finally, he took her breast in his mouth, when he laved it and teased it, and finally, when he suckled, his fingers slipping down toward the triangle of copper hair at the junction of her legs, she melted. She wept. She took her own possession of him, his arms, his back, the smooth slope of his bottom. She claimed him as her territory, as her conquest. As her own.

She thought she couldn't feel more. She was wrong. He dipped his fingers into her and set off a lightning storm. Nuala cried out, her head back, her hands barely able to hold on.

"Is this wicked enough?" he asked, teasing the slippery core of her, finding the hottest spot on her and making it incandescent. His fingers, oh, those rough fingers that made music on her body. She couldn't bear them. She couldn't hold still, her legs opening for him, inviting him, begging him to come to her.

"No," she managed on a gasp, "not quite wicked enough."

And then she triumphed over those jeans. Fumbling for sure, her fingers slick and trembling as she set herself against that stud and zipper, as she helped him pull the unwieldy material over his legs and follow with those boxers, until he was free. Until she could lay hands on him. Curl her fingers around the hot velvet of him, celebrate the size and strength of him, incite his own groans as he buried his head in her neck and gasped for air.

He was so perfect, so diamond bright and work-roughened. So real in a way Nuala had never known. He was the scent of the sun, the sound of a storm, the strength of the earth. Nuala measured him and teased him and tasted the drop of moisture that proclaimed his need, and she found herself laughing as if she were learning to fly all over again.

"Nuala," he ground out, his hold on her taut, his voice gravelly. "You're killing me."

She laughed again, surprised at her own power, at his patience, at the sense of coming home she felt as he settled himself between her thighs.

He kissed her, easing her mouth open and worshipping it as he opened her, as he settled the tip of himself against her, as he tormented her with it; in, out, in, out, until she was mad with it. Until she wrapped her arms around his back and wrapped her legs around him and called him home.

He slid deep into her, so deep that she couldn't believe they would fit, so deep she knew no other would ever claim her, would find that place in her so close to her fairy heart. Tears gathered in her eyes, and he kissed them away, his hands entwined in her hair, his mouth feasting on hers, his chest damp with the sweat of control. They found their rhythm, as old as the earth that cushioned them. They murmured, eyes open, drinking of each other, holding on to each other as he thrust into her, deeper, deeper, so that her desire gathered, sharpened, spiraled into a cyclone of need. Until she threw back her head, her voice keening like the wind that swirled through her. Until she shattered into shards of light and Zeke cried out, his voice a growl of surprise. Until he emptied himself in her with a sob. Until they both collapsed, spent and sated, into each other's arms, to be watched over by the birds and the dryads, who smiled in the nearby trees.

* * *

"You're crying," Zeke accused.

Nuala didn't move from where she lay nestled in his arms. "I always cry over beautiful things."

And his chest *was* beautiful. She was fingering that delicious hair again where it curled right along his breastbone. She was thinking of how good it felt to chafe herself against a man's beard. She was thinking that she never wanted to move.

The queen's court would convene soon. The birds were already warning of it. Still, she didn't want to leave the false security she had found in Zeke's arms. She didn't want to admit that this would undoubtedly be the only time they made love.

He still stroked her, long, lazy caresses that spun out silken shivers. Nuala found she craved that touch, so different from any she'd known, so sure and soft, so certainly Zeke.

"I don't suppose we could blow off the banquet," he murmured into her hair. "Stay here and be wicked again."

Nuala knew he didn't realize how much his words hurt her. "I'm afraid not," she said, struggling for control. "I've already worn the queen's patience too much. We must appear for her decision."

Zeke quieted. "I don't want to. I want to lie here and pretend we have forever, just the two of us."

Nuala raised herself on her elbow so she could face him with the truth. So he couldn't escape. "Believe me when I tell you that I would love nothing more, Zeke. But it cannot be. I pray to the goddess who made us that the queen will show some sense and send you home."

And when she did, Nuala would ask the queen to take Zeke's memory of his time with her. Otherwise Nuala would only hurt him more, perpetuating his belief that everyone who loved him left. She had to leave. She had no choice. The last thing she wanted was for him to suffer for it. Even though, in the most selfish corners of her heart, she wished that he could care for her enough to do just that.

If he remembered. Which she would make sure he wouldn't.

"You're sure you want me to go?" he asked, tucking a strand of hair behind her ear.

Nuala prayed he didn't see the sharp distress his words set off in her. "I'm sure you belong with Jake and Gen and Lee. You have all suffered enough. They couldn't bear to lose you."

"What if *I* can't bear to lose *you*?"

She actually had to close her eyes. "I'm sorry for it. But there is no other way." Opening her eyes, she faced him down. "Promise me, Zeke. Promise on your family that if the queen asks if you wish to stay, you will say no. You'll never get another chance, if you don't."

"You're sure?"

She laid her palm against his cheek and battled new tears. "Aye. I'm sure."

He didn't answer. Nuala couldn't force him, not without giving herself away.

* * *

"No. Thank you."

He stood before the queen this time, where she sat on her high throne, a sleek seat of the same Kerry crystal that lit the floor, so that it cast the softest of glows to reflect in her hair and off the spectacular ruby that graced that filigree gold crown she wore, the chair back rising like a beam of light towards the flickering fairies of the ceiling. All in all, perfectly designed to intimidate the supplicant, which he certainly was.

"You don't wish to stay here?" Mab asked, her voice that soft, disconcerting purr. She held a gold goblet in one hand and a branch of oak in the other. "With me?"

"Even with you, your highness. I'm sorry."

Nuala stood alongside her mother, straight and stately in her snowflake crown and peacock cloak. She was not allowed to look at Zeke, though. The queen wanted no influence from her daughter. To the other side stood that little boy, Kieran, with his wise eyes and grave countenance. If he really was the seer, Zeke wanted to ask what he thought. But the child just stood there, solemn and silent.

For a long moment the queen kept her own counsel. Then, turning to no one for assistance, she lifted the oak branch a bit. "Ah," she said, "but I am not finished with you, little man. You are no sport to me if you simply leave. And a queen on the verge of diminishment needs her sport, so."

Zeke saw Nuala flinch, go pale. He saw the little boy frown. Out of the corner of his eye, he caught Orla's suddenly feral smile and Darragh's nod of satisfaction. Seemed that the opposition was looking for a little blood.

"Have you heard of the story of Tam Lin?" the queen asked, snapping his attention back to where it needed to be.

"Tam Lin?" he echoed. "I think so. My sister-in-law collects those stories. Isn't he the guy who was kidnapped by...? Oh."

The queen's smile was cool. "Just so. Kidnapped by the queen of fairies herself. Saved by the young lady who loved him. Three tests she was given. Three times she had to keep her hold of him, even as the queen turned him into beasts that could have killed her. She had to prove her courage, her loyalty, her purity. If she couldn't hold on, then Tam Lin would be the queen's forever. But she did, so, right through it all. Stayed true to the boy through the fiercest, most frightening tests. Are you willing to survive tests such as that?"

He was a bit confused. "Who do you want me to hold on to?"

The queen's smile grew. "Why, didn't I tell you? Nuala, of course. You must cleave yourself to her, and her only, through the tests that come. If you stay as true as that girl did to our lost Tam Lin, then you are free. If not, then you belong to me. And, little man, I don't give my toys back."

"Do I have a choice?"

She shrugged, a move so elegant as to be dreamlike. "You could stay."

Zeke looked over to Nuala, but she still stood like a Marine at the Tomb of the Unknown Soldier, unblinking, unmoving. Pale as death at her mother's challenge.

"And do I get to take her back with me, like Tam Lin?"

The queen was still delighted. "Well, now, maybe that's one of the tests. What say you?"

Zeke nodded. "Well, I've faced my share of wild beasts in my day. Challenge away."

Her smile grew positively predatory. "Ah, but you may not recognize these beasts."

"My lady," the boy Kieran protested in a soft voice.

"No," she said. "It is done. You are the seer, child. Not the queen. You said yourself it wouldn't make a difference."

He opened his mouth, seemed to think a moment, and then simply nodded. "Yes, my lady."

The queen nodded back with absolute satisfaction. "Grand," she said. "Grand. Don't you think so, Orla?"

Suddenly Nuala came to startling life. "No!"

Mab turned on her. "He agreed."

"Please…"

"This is after being your test, too, Nuala. Face it or fade into nothing."

Zeke could see the torment in his Nuala's eyes. His instinct was to jump up there and protect her, not even knowing what from. It was the little boy who prevented him. Turning those dark eyes on Zeke, he simply shook his head. Zeke remained where he was.

The silence stretched into discomfort. Orla stepped out from the shadows, the gold of her gown glistening in the soft light, the citrines in her leafy crown glowing, the raven black of her hair swallowing the light.

"I am here, my lady," she said, even though her gaze was on Zeke.

"All right, then." The queen rose to her feet, the picture of grace and power. "Tomorrow, I think. After the midday meal. After all, we have faerie business to attend to in the morning."

"Tomorrow what?" Zeke asked.

The queen's smile looked suspiciously like her dark daughter's. "Tomorrow is the beginning. And only you will know the end, little man. Only you."

Chapter 8

Zeke wished somebody would tell him what the hell was going on. Hands in jeans pockets, he stared up at the velvety sky. The queen had long since retired and taken her daughters with her. Many of the court had followed Zeke to Michael's house, where he was supposed to check in for the night. The queen had made it a point to remind Zeke where his sleeping quarters were.

Well, he was standing at Michael's front door, but he just couldn't make himself go inside. So much had happened so quickly, he needed to restore his equilibrium.

Was this place real? Was Nuala? He could still hear the music of her sighs as he slipped into her. He could feel the silk of her hair in his fingers, the pillowy comfort of her breasts. He swore he could hear her breathing, when it was only the breeze.

He knew he should think about what this big Tam Lin test was he had to pass, but he would rather find Nuala and that secluded little stream bank. He ached like fire to be inside her again. To smell the flowers in her hair. To sate himself with the exquisite silk of her skin. God, he was as hard as stone just imagining it.

He wasn't a monk. Anybody who knew him would be happy to verify that. But if he had the courage, he would admit that he'd never felt like this. Like a minute away from her was too long. Like he wanted to dig in beneath those moss green eyes of hers and excavate her secrets. Hell, he just wanted to be with her.

He looked off into the darkness, wondering if he could pick out her house on instinct. Wondering if he had the guts to try. He was sure the queen wouldn't be thrilled if he did. He was even more sure the fairy horde who'd followed him would bar his way.

He just wasn't sure there really was a fairy horde, much less a queen. He wasn't sure he wasn't tucked up in bed back at Mrs. O'Brien's, dreaming this whole thing up. But for the first time, he hated that idea. He didn't want to think that Nuala wasn't real. He didn't want to believe that her bright, whimsical smile was no more than fantasy, that the feeling of homecoming he felt whenever he was with her was nothing but wishful thinking.

Which was probably why he should hope like hell he was dreaming, he thought as he rubbed at his aching forehead. The last thing he wanted was to get attached to somebody as fine as Nuala. He had places to go, dead people to dig up. He had no time for somebody who wanted to tag along.

"Excuse me," he heard behind him.

It was the boy, Kieran, his smile tentative.

Zeke turned to him. "Isn't it late for you to be up?"

The young face dissolved into a widetoothed grin,

and Zeke saw the little boy instead of the prophet. "Not here. I don't even have to do homework."

Zeke was surprised into a small grin. "That's because you have all that prognosticating to do, huh?" Taking another look around, he sighed. "Do *you* know what's going on?"

"Of course," Kieran said with a chortle. "It's my job."

"Well, can you tell *me?*"

The light left the little boy's eyes. "Ah, no. I'm afraid not. Rules, you know."

"No, I don't know. They forgot to hand out the *Fairy Handbook* when I arrived."

"Well, if we'd known you were coming…" He grinned again.

Zeke wished he could have had the time to properly know this kid. He thought he would like him a lot. "You want to walk around a little with me?" he asked. "I'm sure my babysitters want to go home, and I'm not ready for bed yet."

Kieran flashed another of those surprising smiles. "If you'll talk to me about basketball."

The fairies faded into the night, and Kieran followed Zeke down a faint path.

"What, you can't find any Shaq fans here?"

"Not so much." He shrugged. "They're all more into music and stuff."

"And you?"

"If I had a wish, it would be to grow taller. So I could play." His eyes alight, Kieran finally looked like normal kid, one who, no matter his powers, was just a little out of place here. Zeke was a small piece of home. "I have dreams of stuffing the ball, just like Yao or Michael Jordan. Of playing for the New York Knicks. I got to go to a game once when I was in America visiting relatives. And we get it on the satellite at the castle."

Zeke had to grin. Ah, the twenty-first century. "You mean you don't get a feed here?"

"Oh, no. It interferes with the fairy senses. If they want to see the outside world, they slip over."

Zeke couldn't manage much more than a shake of his head.

"So you...what?" he asked, peering down at the boy. "Commute?"

"Something like that. I'm due back in school after the holiday. History test."

"Holiday?"

"All Saints Day. The day after Samhain...Halloween. Which is in three days."

Zeke nodded, still distracted. "And you don't feel just a wee bit disoriented?"

Kieran shrugged. "I know no other way."

Zeke shook his head. "'You're a better man than I am, Gunga Din.'"

They walked on, their steps hushed in the deep gloaming, where the tiniest fairies lit the hedges like fireflies and the horses dreamed. "What did the queen mean, that it wouldn't make any difference?"

For a moment Kieran kept his silence, his coppery head down, his steps slow. Zeke saw that, like every other fairy, he kept his feet bare. "She meant that you must see to yourself, Mr. Kendall. The rest is fairy business."

Zeke was sure he didn't like this. "What do you mean, 'fairy business'? Nuala is a fairy. Isn't she my business?"

"No," the boy said, looking up at him like a martyr facing the fire. "Not really. She has said it, hasn't she? She must stay, and you must leave. The rest shouldn't concern you. There's nothing, after all, you can do to affect it."

Zeke came to a dead stop in the middle of the path. The boy had said nothing untoward, but Zeke knew something was wrong. Something too awful for a small boy to bear.

"What aren't you telling me?"

Kieran just looked up at him, his grave little face sending warning skitters down Zeke's spine.

"Are you in danger?" Zeke demanded. "Is Nuala?"

He got a solemn shake of the head. "It is not my place, Mr. Kendall."

Zeke bent closer, so close he could see the conflict in the little boy's eyes. "It's not mine, either, evidently. But I think I'm going to make it mine."

"No." Kieran straightened, took a quick look over Zeke's shoulder. Shook his head again, his eyes intent and anxious. "Please. The best you can do is go."

"And if I suddenly don't want to? If I decide I should just blow my exams?"

That seemed to frighten the boy even more. "If you fail these tests, you will be the property of the queen. You cannot help anything that way. You must be free."

"But what can I help if I leave?"

Again Kieran looked around, as if making sure they weren't overheard. "I can't tell you. I see the patterns, the possible outcomes, not the paths to the outcomes. I don't know what will help and what will hurt. I only know that you help no one by remaining as an unwilling consort. Please, you must believe me. I belong here. You do not. Nuala is right."

"And you won't tell me why this is so important?"

He got another anxious shake of the head, and Zeke had to remind himself that he was, after all, dealing with a little boy.

"Thank you," he said, laying a hand on the boy's thin shoulder. "I have a feeling you put yourself in the way of the queen to say that."

"Stay true to yourself, and you'll pass," Kieran said. "That's all I can tell you. But remember it every moment."

"I will. And someday, when we meet in the real world, you'll have to tell me what you couldn't tonight."

Finally he earned another smile. "We'll have a drink and trade baby pictures," the little boy said, and Zeke knew for a fact that they would. If the disaster that still haunted those young eyes didn't come to pass, anyway.

And then, just like the rest of his kin, the boy was simply gone. Zeke heaved a sigh, getting kind of tired of that trick. But when he took a moment to look around him, he realized they'd walked right to the door of another of the small houses, this one looking more like a cottage from Beatrix Potter, with flowers running riot over the door and a picket fence surrounding it.

Zeke didn't know how he'd done it, but he'd found Nuala's house. Not only that, but she was standing in the doorway. Zeke didn't hesitate to reach for the gate.

"No," she said, her voice quiet, her eyes lost in the deep shadows. "You have to go back to Michael's."

Zeke stood there for a minute, his hand on the gate. "You can't really mean you want me to leave."

He thought he saw her smile. "Don't be absurd. Wanting has nothing to do with it. You cannot be here now. Kieran should have known it and taken you another way. Now, go, Zeke. Please."

He didn't move. Instead, he began to weave fantasies in his mind. In his mind he walked up that pathway, his gaze never leaving hers, his body taut with anticipation. He gained her small porch, reached out with trembling hands to touch her. Just to touch her, his fingers racing over her forehead, the sides of her sweet face, her throat. Her breasts, her sweet, full breasts that were suddenly bare to him, milk white in the moonlight, trembling and warm in the moonlight, her aureoles pure peach, succulent and sweet in the moonlight.

He could taste them against his tongue as they pebbled for him. He could smell her, cloves and honeysuckle, could feel the cascade of her hair against his hands. He could hear the stutter and rasp of her breathing as he loved her. As he filled his hands with her, as he hauled her up against him, tormenting himself with the hollow of her against his erection. Hot, damp, mysterious...

"Stop!" she cried, and he found himself suddenly

back at the fence, his hands curled around the wood like claws. It looked as if she had tears in her eyes.

"Please," she begged, her voice breathy and frantic. "Don't. I can't tolerate it."

He was gasping for air, hurting so hard for her that he thought he would shatter. But he saw the pain in her eyes, and he knew she was right.

"I'm sorry."

He turned to go. He was already far down the path before he heard her. "I'm sorry, too."

"My patience runs thin, Nuala," the queen said from the bower of her bed. "It is not even moonset."

Nuala held her place at the base of the sacred oak. "The seer has been walking, my queen. He is troubled, and it is not simply the matter of my guest."

Mab considered her daughter, her eyes the hard, assessing eyes of a queen. "And you believe I know why?"

"It is why he returned so soon, isn't it?"

"It is a queen's business, Nuala."

"And I am to be queen."

"But not queen yet."

"I smell something on the wind," Nuala insisted. "Something that smells of sulphur and menace. Something that concerns more than the queen."

"But which only the queen can ordain. Know that I am in control of my court, Nuala. Know that all is in place for eventualities. Know that your place is still to learn, my daughter. Not yet to rule."

Nuala still stood before her mother, torn by the persistent sense of disaster, of disruption, that had plagued her since she'd seen Kieran standing at the bottom of her garden with Zeke. The seer was troubled, and Nuala couldn't put that from her mind.

"I would hope, then, Mother, that your decisions are wise."

Her mother refused to answer. There was nothing Nuala could do but bow and leave. But she couldn't relieve herself of the sense of impending disaster.

The dawn was still young when Zeke walked out of Michael's house. It was time to tend the horses of the faerie, which Zeke found he liked. After all, a horse was a horse, be it magical or not, and the sounds and smells gave him comfort. It was as close to home as he could hope to get for a while. It was a link to his family and the ranch where he'd grown up.

Michael had already left for the pasture by the time Zeke had risen, so he swallowed the ale, bread and honey set out for him and followed, figuring he would get in a good morning's work before facing the queen's test.

The mist rose once again, pearly and diaphanous as a princess's gown. The sun had already gone golden, dappling the ground and warming his face. The morning birds chattered, and the morning fairies feasted on flowers. Zeke could like it here.

He was whistling, hands in jean pockets, head up to the morning, when he damn near stumbled over a pretty big obstruction in the path.

"Oh," he said, stepping back. "Sorry."

She'd appeared out of nowhere, he was sure. The mist eddied around her, and the early light gleamed off her raven's-wing hair. Orla smiled, a gentle, sweet smile that sent *frissons* down his spine.

"You like the early morning," she said, nodding. "A wonderful time of day, isn't it? A time of beginnings. A time for—" she seemed to soften, as if dissolving a bit into the mist, the new shape so compelling that Zeke couldn't look away "—anticipation."

Her eyes were mesmerizing, a cat's eyes, an houri's eyes, smiling, inviting and acquiescing at once. Zeke blinked. He had the strangest feeling he'd disappeared from the path.

"Good morning," he greeted her.

"Good morning. May I walk with you?"

Zeke shrugged. "Sure. I'm going to groom the horses."

For a second Orla seemed to sharpen, a disconcerting feeling. "Ah," she said, shifting again, softening. "Magnificent beasts, horses. I have a preference for horses, you know." Sliding her hands just a bit over her hips, she pulled her gold fairy dress tighter against her lush curves. "Especially," she breathed, "stallions."

Her smile grew. Her posture changed, subtly, sinuously, until it seemed she'd wrapped herself around him even as she stood two feet away. Zeke felt the first tendrils of enticement attach themselves; he saw the flicker of decadent images bloom in his mind.

"Yes," she whispered, smiling, eyes hooded and sly. "Yes. Just like that, my lovely mortal. Sink into it, so.

Slide yourself into me like a warm bath, like the most delicious bed. Come with me now and know what ecstasy could be…."

Zeke couldn't feel the earth beneath his feet. He couldn't hear the birds anymore. He only heard her voice. It was like a ribbon winding around him, her voice. Like smoke and shadow and sin. It was the score to the gathering images in his head, to the pounding arousal in his body. Why didn't he trust it? Why couldn't he simply follow wherever it led? He wasn't sure, but something held him back.

She had long red-nailed fingers that stroked fire. She had a clever mouth that could sap a man's strength, that sought out his weaknesses and consumed them. She had a siren's voice, a Lorelei calling him to the rocks. She had such heat, such indescribable, silken skin, and she showed it to him in his head. Lush, pouty breasts with copper nipples, narrow waist, full hips, long, long legs that looked to have the power to break a man. She offered it all, from the lush red of her lips to the honeyed depths hidden beyond that dark triangle at the apex of her thighs. She offered surcease and satiation. She offered dreams darker than Zeke had ever dreamed.

He saw it all, that quickly. Even as she stood before him clad in gold and a harlot's smile, he heard the gasping surprise of climax, smelled the musk of sex. He felt her voice wrap itself around him like a spider trapping an unwilling victim.

He knew it all in seconds and found himself amazed.

Because, as legendary as he was sure her skill was, as shattering as the sex she promised, he was untouched, unaffected.

Suddenly he was standing on the path again, the dust of it clinging to his workboots, his flannel shirt chafing his wrists, his cock gone completely dormant.

For a minute, he wondered why. After all, Orla was offering everything he'd ever wanted from sex. Mindless, athletic, exhaustive rutting. She offered the most spectacular body he'd ever had the privilege to view. She offered the lure of dark dreams, guilt-free fantasy. She offered addictive lust in its purest, least complicated form.

And he didn't want it.

It wasn't that he didn't realize how tempting the offer was. After all, she was still romping around without inhibition in his head, and any other day of his life, he would have literally leapt for the chance to participate. But this wasn't any other day of his life. It was the day after he'd made love to Nuala.

And that, he realized with a sick shock, was the difference. He would have had sex with Orla. Great sex, probably legendary sex. But he'd made love with Nuala. And there was simply no comparison.

He found himself smiling a bit ruefully. "Thank you for the invitation," he said, struggling to ignore the new panic in his chest. "But I'm afraid I'm not interested."

Like a bubble, the images burst. Her eyes widened; her nostrils flared. Then, just as suddenly, a new image swamped him.

Good God, she was on her knees right there in the dirt, and she had her mouth on him. Bent over, her long dark hair sweeping the ground as she pleasured him. As she cupped his balls in her hand and raked that long-nailed finger down his naked thigh. She all but sucked the life from him, and he should have been fractured by it.

"No" was all he said, stepping back.

The image disappeared so fast that he almost stumbled, to find that Orla still stood before him, her expression blank, her nails fisted into her palms.

"I'm sorry," he said, because at an atavistic level, he was. Seriously sorry. God, how he wished he could still be satisfied with what she offered. Basic, primal, animal sex. Pure pleasure for no other purpose than to keep your brain quiet and your cock busy. Instead, he took a step, then another, until he was past her. Until he didn't smell the musk of her scent anymore. Until his heart rate slowed a little and he could think of the horses.

Behind him, Orla stood stunned into silence. Suddenly her own heart raced. Her palms grew damp, and she felt the first *frissons* of fear race down her spine.

He'd refused her. *Her*, the legendary *leannan sidhe*. He'd tasted every sin she could think to offer and then simply walked away. And when he had, he had condemned her. For if a *leannan sidhe* could not enslave the mortal she tempted, he enslaved her.

She felt it creep through her, a sinuous mist of something so unfamiliar that at first she couldn't name it. Something sharp as glass and heavy as night. Something that hurt. Hurt hard, right there in her chest. Something she suddenly knew for what it was.

Yearning. Need. The aching, sweating fire of frustration.

She was so close to turning after him. To abasing herself before him. To begging. No. She would strip herself naked and flay herself before she begged. She knew she would. She thought she would. But the need grew, like a fire kindled under her skin, and it ate at her.

"It was your test, Mab," she snapped, knowing it was at least partly untrue, her head back because suddenly she couldn't breathe. "You cannot make your daughter suffer the consequence."

She'd never wept, not in all her years. She'd always considered tears the tools of a weak woman. But she felt them now, swelling in her throat, a sour taste in her mouth, an acid in her eyes. She gasped. She shuddered. She clawed her long nails at her chest, as if she could rip the tears away.

"Do not do this to me," she demanded, and was mortified at the needy whine of her voice.

She couldn't bear it. She, who had reigned over her little realm with impunity, fought the shattering of her soul. She was the *leannan sidhe*. But she hurt so badly, a searing, penetrating hurt, that she almost turned. She almost ran after him, pulled him from those horses she hated, scrabbled at him like a small child pleading for a sign. One pathetic sign that he noticed her.

"Mab!"

She couldn't stand. She couldn't hold still. She couldn't survive this. She was being crushed beneath the weight of it.

"You're right, of course," she heard her mother's calm voice in her head. "You should not have to pay the price. Be free of it, Orla. I so declare it."

And that fast, it disappeared so suddenly that Orla found herself on her knees, as if Mab had cut her marionette's strings. She curled up there, her fingers in unacquainted dirt, her hair drooping into it, her nose filled with the smell of it. She couldn't rid herself of the memory of what had just happened. That terrible, crippling need that had consumed her. She couldn't ignore it or forget it, as if it had branded her in some way.

And how could she be the *leannan sidhe* if she knew what it was like to suffer the slavery of unrequited yearning? How could she be herself if she empathized with the ones upon whom she preyed as her right, as her legacy?

She was the *leannan sidhe!* And yet the sound of it suddenly tasted like the dust beneath her.

She'd thought she'd been terrified before. It was nothing to what she felt now. How did she survive? What did she do? How did she go on, with this blight on her future?

Slowly, Orla lifted her head. She had known all along, of course. She should be queen. Now, more than ever, she knew it. Nuala would never have the strength for it. If Nuala had suffered this sickness of the soul, she would have shattered and forfeited her focus. Her priorities. She would have been swamped by the need for something she could never have, unfit to be queen.

Orla had to make sure that happened. She had to make sure Zeke Kendall failed. If he didn't, Orla was afraid Mab would give Nuala her choice. Keep him or let him go. And even if Nuala let him go, she would still inherit the throne on the strength of her martyrdom. She would be queen, but unable to rule as she should.

But if Zeke Kendall lost, he would always be within her reach but out of touch. No matter how strong Nuala was, she was not strong enough for that. She wouldn't be able to overcome the idea that not only could she not have him, but her mother could. Did. And Orla knew her own mother well enough to know that if Mab won the mortal, she would never let him go.

On the other hand, after the deeds of this morning, Orla knew herself to have gained the full complement of powers needed to be queen. She had not just the magic and the legendary beauty, even the ruthlessness. Those had never been in question. But today, without realizing it, the queen had instilled in her the thing she felt most beneficial. Orla now knew the rage a queen needed to vanquish those who opposed her.

Orla would be more than happy to do just that. For a long moment she stayed where she was, there in the dirt, her alabaster brow furrowed, her body so perfectly still that the rest of the world held its own breath. She fingered through every option she had at hand to gain the throne. She considered the ones she didn't. She gathered her strength to her, her power and she made the decision she knew was preordained. Then, slowly, as gracefully as a dark swan, she rose. She gained her elegant feet and swept the remains of the earth from her golden dress.

She had to return to her home and change. There were stains on the front of her gown that would betray what had happened to her these last few minutes, and no self-respecting queen would ever expose herself so. Then she must collect her resources to put into motion her plan to win the throne.

It was time to contact the *Dubhlainn Sidhe*.

Chapter 9

Nuala would have had no trouble recognizing the odd feelings that plagued her sister. After all, Zeke had ensorceled Nuala so long ago that she couldn't remember a time when she *hadn't* wanted him. She'd carried the pain of yearning with her as merely another color in her display, the dark twin to her joy. She couldn't imagine ever being free of it.

She never did fall asleep during the long night, especially after she'd seen Zeke standing at her fence like the answer to a dream…or the worst temptation she'd ever suffer.

She knew that a queen had to be tested for her merit. Though she'd had her doubts, she'd never truly realized that she might not be worthy. Because caught in the primal darkness of the night, she had found herself beset with doubt. Could she really devote herself to her people once she lost Zeke? Could she be faithful to what she was when she knew she would spend the rest of her time on this plane pining for another?

She honestly didn't know. So she did what made sense. She fulfilled her duties. When her mother forbade her access to Zeke until after his first test, she took herself off to help Sorcha teach the children fairy history.

Today they were supposed to be reviewing the coming of the Milesians, the iron workers who had harried the bronze-wielding *Tua* into the earth. But it was a beautiful day, and fairy children were no more immune to the delights of truancy than any other. By the time Nuala arrived, Sorcha already looked frazzled.

"I'll have you know," the petite blonde complained, "there are days I'm after wishin' I shod horses. Wouldn't it be less effort all 'round?"

Nuala looked out over the gamboling children and smiled. "Ah, now, Sorcha, sure didn't we have our off days, as well?"

Sorcha chuckled. "You're not after makin' me feel sorry for old Mother Moira, are you? Goddess, a greater troll never lived. I still quail at the whistle of a willow switch."

"Undoubtedly because you always deserved it."

"'Tis a sore burden to bear more wisdom than a jealous teacher, now," her sister said with an impish grin. "Isn't it?"

But Nuala didn't answer. She knew that when Sorcha turned to her, it was to see a frown.

"You've lost your color, *mo chroí*. Is it worried ya are?"

Nuala pulled a face. "And how can I not be? I'm forbidden to interfere. And he needs me."

Goddess, she was afraid. She had no idea what her mother had in mind for Zeke's test, but she did know how devious her mother was and how rapacious her sister. Worse, Zeke was honorable. Could he beat them at their own game? Could he triumph and set himself free?

Did she really want him to?

Sorcha sighed, her attention wandering out across the meadows. "Aye. So he does. And doesn't it gnaw at a woman to know such a thing?"

It was Nuala's turn to stare. "Sorcha?"

Sorcha shook her head. "Did you know that Darragh's been followin' ya? In the shadows, where you can't see him."

Nuala didn't want to hear that either. "He has no reason."

"He's jealous, Nuala. And with every right."

"But not jealous of me. Jealous for his position. He'll have it, no matter what." She saw her sister's instinctive flinch and sighed. "You can't know how sorry I am that the court chose him for me."

Sorcha's smile was sad. "I can."

"He's not a good enough man for you, Sorcha. You deserve better than one who is forever petulant and resentful."

When Sorcha turned, it was with tears in her eyes. "Don't you think I know it? Don't you think a hundred times a day I'm wishing I could choose another to lay my heart on? One who would be stronger than I?"

Nuala had thought she couldn't feel worse. She'd been wrong. Reaching out, she gently took her sister's tears on the tips of her fingers. "Ah now, we could show them. You be queen instead of me, and you can have him."

But just as Nuala knew she would, Sorcha shuddered. "Even for Darragh, I wouldn't want that curse. I happily cede it to you, big sister. You've the heart and stomach for it."

But Nuala didn't answer her. Because not for the first time, she questioned whether that was true.

"Ah, wouldn't it have been grand if we'd loved where we should?" Sorcha asked wistfully. "You could love Darragh, and I could love...oh, I don't know. Tearsigh over there. He's a braw lad. And there's none look better than an elf in battle chain."

Nuala had been so caught up in Sorcha's regret that she almost missed the import of her words. Tearsigh? In battle chain? Nuala whipped around to find that, indeed, Tearsigh was passing with a troop of guardians at his heels. Suddenly, her heart was in her throat.

"Tearsigh?" she addressed the captain, a tall, black-eyed elf with broad shoulders and legendary skill. "Are you prepared?"

He stopped, saluted and dipped his helmeted head in obeisance. "Aye, lady. The queen so ordains it, and we obey."

"Good," she responded, as if she knew what he was talking about. "Good. Does she give you any sort of deadline?"

"No. Only the increased alert."

So her mother hadn't lied. She had been preparing. For what Nuala didn't know, but as her mother had said, it was the queen's decision. Nuala could only watch and worry. And wonder what it all had to do with Zeke's tests.

"Thank you, Tearsigh," she said with a nod. "You are our most loyal captain. Carry on."

The captain snapped out a command, and the column marched on, passing the gaggle of children who now marched alongside carrying birch branches over their shoulders like halberds.

"Nuala?" Sorcha asked, her voice low. "What do you know?"

Nuala shook her head. "Nothing." Nothing but the fact that she had been wrong to even think Zeke could stay. There was something in the wind, and no mere mortal could stand it. "Nothing except that it's time for Zeke to go."

Zeke worked horses all morning, first grooming them to a spectral gleam, then testing their paces over the long meadows and hills of the world of faerie. He pushed them as hard as they would allow, letting the wind whip away all the troubling thoughts that had been circling in his head like crows.

He could have imagined himself at home, if it hadn't been for the fact that no sharp-toothed mountains ringed these gentle hills, or the fact that fairies had bridled the magnificent horses he was riding into the ground so he could escape what had happened earlier.

Not Orla's attempted seduction. He'd survived worse. All right, he'd enjoyed it more than he'd survived it. He couldn't think of a thing he relished more than that light of sexual attraction in a woman's eyes. It colored the day and gave mystery to the night. It provided the perfect spice to life.

It hadn't been the seduction. It had been his reaction. He hadn't spurned Orla because of exhaustion or disinterest. He'd done it because of Nuala. Because of what they'd shared. Not just bodies, but something more. Something perilously good. Something he wanted more of. All of. Something that made him loathe to leave, and in his entire life, no woman had ever made him feel that.

What the hell had he been thinking to tell Kieran that he might want to stay? He wanted to get the hell out. He would crawl on his hands and knees if he needed to. If he didn't, he just might do something really idiotic and ruin his life completely. Something monumentally stupid like falling in love.

Beneath him, the sleek gray horse stretched out to take the hills like a sailing ship, so smooth he could imagine the animal wasn't even running. It was the third horse he'd taken out, and it seemed they all knew what he needed and were willing to offer it. But no matter his problems, Zeke had never willingly injured a horse in his life. So, sweating and tired, he pulled the beast back to a trot and turned towards home, his own sides heaving as much as the horse's.

"Sorry, fella," he apologized, stroking the powerful neck. "I didn't mean to take it all out on you."

The horse shook his mane, as if in acknowledgment.

"It'd just be nice to feel like I knew what was going

on," Zeke muttered. "Nuala disappears, the queen won't see me, and I'm left to take my troubles out on dumb animals."

The horse obviously wasn't quite *that* dumb. So quickly Zeke damn near came to grief, the horse skidded to a four-point stop. Head down, hooves up, spinning in place like a circus horse, he did his best to unseat his rider.

He wasn't any more pleased when Zeke just laughed. "You'll have to try harder than that," he said, easily keeping his seat. "I learned to ride when you were a scabby colt."

The horse came to a stop, and Zeke hopped off to face him. "I didn't mean to insult you," he said, stroking its velvet muzzle. "It's just..." But he shook his head, too overwhelmed by it all to be able to verbalize it.

"It's just that you seek to steal our Nuala."

Zeke snapped to attention. "Was that you?" he demanded of the horse. "Of course it was. Why talk to me now?"

One liquid eye focused on him. The horse's mouth didn't open, but Zeke heard the words anyway. "You turned down the princess," the animal said in a soft, deep voice.

"I did?"

"Orla."

"Oh." Zeke shrugged, disconcerted. "She's not to my taste."

The horse's mouth actually sagged, as if in surprise. "Then I'm right. It is our Lady Nuala."

Zeke scowled. "That's not open for discussion."

For a moment the horse seemed to consider that. Then he shook his head, the sleek mane shuddering beneath Zeke's fingers. "We give you welcome, mortal."

It was Zeke's turn for consideration. "Why?"

"Because you saw the truth."

"I turned down a woman looking for a roll in the hay, that's all."

"You are the first."

"First what?"

"The first mortal to refuse her. The first to know the difference between gold and dross." The horse dipped his head. "I am called Cadhla. While you are here, I will bear you on."

"Cadhla?"

He could have sworn the damn animal preened. "Handsome."

"Of course. Well, I'm honored."

"Yes. You are. And you are called?"

Zeke couldn't help but smile. "Most mortals call me Zeke. But the Hopi call me Muuyaw. It's their word for moon, but what it really means is 'Foolish Man Who Runs Around with No Home.'"

"And that name fits you better?"

Looking out over the mist-wreathed landscape, Zeke sighed. "I'm beginning to think so."

The horse nodded. "Mount now. The queen seeks you."

Zeke looked around to make sure a messenger

hadn't just topped the hill. Oh well, who was he to argue? Fairy horses undoubtedly had special channels of communication.

"Time for that test, huh?" Zeke asked, remounting. "Any advice?"

"Stay true to yourself."

Zeke sighed. "Yeah. I've heard that."

Still, he couldn't ignore the anxiety that had started to eat at his gut as he urged Cadhla into flight. The horse was right. The seer was right. He had to win this damn thing so he could get the hell out of here. So he let his mount carry him so fast he couldn't even see the hills pass.

"Good morning, my lady," Zeke greeted Mab a few minutes later as he slid from Cadhla's bare back. "We ready for the first challenge?"

"Thank you for bringing the mortal, Cadhla" was all the queen said.

She was seated in the crook of a great gnarled rowan tree, her posture magnificent, her raiment gleaming in the noon light, the ruby glowing like a dark sun. Her consort stood at her side, and many of the court had gathered in the shade of the trees. Birds chattered in the branches, and at least two rabbits were nibbling on clover. The sky, as ever, was a robin's egg blue decorated in wispy white clouds, and spring flowers littered the grass. Not a throne room most humans would recognize.

"Do you remember what the nature of the tests is?" Mab asked, her eyes intense.

"Something about fighting beasts."

"And would you recognize them if you saw them?"

He was paying attention now. The queen looked just a bit disconcerted. The court was dead still, as if holding their breath for his answer. He looked around but couldn't find the one face he sought.

"Where is Nuala?" he asked. "How can I cleave to her if she's not here?"

"She need not be present."

Which made him suddenly nervous. "Yes," he said, standing his ground. "I think she does."

The queen deliberated for a moment and then lazily lifted an alabaster arm. There wasn't quite a puff of smoke, but suddenly Nuala stood by the tree, blinking a bit as if she'd just woken up. She saw Zeke and then anxiously scanned the crowd.

"Is it time?" she asked. "Where is Orla?"

Then, oddly enough, the queen sighed. "Licking her wounds. She has been vanquished."

Zeke had thought the place was quiet before. That brought it to a dead stop. Even Cadhla, still standing beside him, seemed flummoxed.

Nuala had literally turned ashen. "Vanquished?" Her voice was a rasp. *"Orla?"*

Zeke looked from mother to daughter. One looked thunderstruck, the other irritated as hell.

"You're kidding," he said, the truth dawning. *"She* was my first beast?"

"You have passed the first test," the queen admitted. "You enslaved a *leannan sidhe.*"

A hiss of surprise escaped from the gathering. A rising babble. Cadhla nudged Zeke's shoulder in a way that made Zeke think of a classic "attaboy" between guys. The queen lifted her hand again, her expression thunderous, and silence fell.

Zeke looked around, not understanding. So what if he'd walked away from Nuala's sister? Admittedly, she was drop-dead sexy in an overblown Angelina Jolie kind of way, but that didn't change the basic laws of attraction. He hadn't been attracted.

"Impossible," the queen said as if to herself, her voice suddenly sounding resigned. "No mortal male has refused a *leannan sidhe* in my memory."

"I really am the first?" he asked, confused.

"The *leannan sidhe* has the power to enslave any mortal male. Orla is the greatest of her generation."

"How did you do it?" Nuala asked him, sincerely stunned.

It was Zeke's turn to freeze. He couldn't tell her the truth. After all, how could he admit that all Orla had offered was sex, when Nuala had offered herself? How could he admit, even to himself, how the two simply hadn't compared?

So he shrugged. "She just didn't appeal to me."

That didn't seem to compute any better. He swore every fairy in the glen stood there slack-jawed. Yeah, well, they probably weren't any more disconcerted than he was.

Nuala turned on her mother. "Then Orla...?"

"No. The test was not hers. She is whole." The

queen's smile grew enigmatic. "Maybe more so. We will see. Now, go, mortal. I weary of this. We will meet again tomorrow at the same time."

Zeke stared at her. "That's it? No trumpet fanfare? No laurel wreath?"

The queen was not amused. "It was one test. You still face two more."

"And if I win?"

"You may go."

"And if I don't want to?"

He couldn't believe he'd just said that. He wanted to call it back. Especially when he heard the cry of distress from Nuala.

"You wish to stay?" the queen asked, her attention caught.

"Do I have that choice?"

She nodded. "You do."

"No!" Nuala cried out. "Forbid him. I beg you!"

Zeke wanted to shut his eyes. "I'm just investigating my options here, Nuala."

"There are no options!" For some reason, Zeke no longer heard perfect certainty in her voice. He had a feeling that she really wasn't sure she wanted him to leave anymore. Well, that was something he was afraid he understood.

"Why don't we talk about it?" he asked, turning to her.

Another round of stark silence, all eyes riveted on the two of them. Nuala was so pale that Zeke thought she might faint. Damn it, he wanted to comfort her. He wanted to protect her, especially from whatever he'd seen in Kieran's eyes the night before. He wanted to claim that right. He wanted to claim all rights to her, and that was something he just wasn't ready for. Hell, it wasn't something he would ever be ready for.

"Please," he said, trying like hell not to snap at her.

Nuala looked to the queen. Amazingly, after another one of those pauses, she nodded. The gathered throng melted away, and the queen simply disappeared from her rowan throne.

"We can go to my house," Nuala said and stalked off.

Zeke had no choice but to follow. At least he had the sense not to speak again until she had ushered him through the front door.

"Please tell me you were joking," she said, shutting the door behind them.

But Zeke was suddenly too distracted to answer. He wasn't sure what he'd expected her house to be, but he hadn't expected this. It wasn't a fairy house, like Michael's, with homey pewterware, and furniture that looked as if it had been made from toadstools. No, Nuala's furniture gave Zeke a distinct feeling of déjà vu.

"Where did you get this?" he asked, turning to take it in.

For a long second, Nuala was silent. "I had it made." She sounded defensive and frightened at the same time.

Zeke finished his tour to see the flush on her face. "It looks like the ranch," he said, wondering suddenly if she had a patchwork quilt on the bed like the one his great-great-grandma had made. He was bit afraid he would see a forest of family photos on the bedroom wall, just like in Jake's room. The sight of the hand-hewn wood furniture made him uneasy.

He couldn't help it. Before Nuala could stop him, he walked through the door to the bedroom to make sure.

One look inside her bedroom left him breathing a sigh of relief. She might have been a bit envious, but she wasn't quite a stalker. The room was bright and whimsical and sweet. Nothing looked familiar here. He stood there staring down on a bed that looked like a bower, covered in something green and gossamer, and thought how her whole house should have looked like this. It made him realize, as nothing else had, just how ambivalent she must have been, torn between the magical world she inhabited and the earthy, human one she coveted. He felt sad for her here, as if her sense of displacement saturated the room.

Backing out, he gave her a grin, even though he didn't feel like it. "Well, at least that doesn't look like my bedroom."

Nuala managed a small smile. "I don't know how to quilt."

He walked right up to her, suddenly certain. "Come back with me," he urged, his hand cupping her face.

Tears welled in Nuala's eyes. "I can't. You know that."

"Then let me stay. Let me protect you. Something's going on around here, and I think it's bad."

Nuala pleaded with those liquid spring eyes of

hers, humbling him. "It may be. But it's nothing you can fix, Zeke."

"I can't leave you in danger," he protested. "Kieran is a scared little kid, and I have a feeling that's not common."

"You can't stay. If you do, you'll never get back."

He leaned closer, close enough that he couldn't help but smell the whisper of cloves on her, so he could see the tiny flecks of sunlight in her eyes. So he could exclude everything but the two of them, bound by something he didn't even have the courage to name.

"Would it really be so bad if I stayed?" he asked, and saw her all but shatter at his fingertips.

"You don't understand," she whispered, her voice bleak.

"Then make me."

Her breath hitched, as if caught on a sob. But she didn't look away. She didn't back away, when even a brave woman might have. Zeke thought he could lacerate himself on her pain. Without a word, she took his hand and led him out of her house. Behind it stood a small copse of trees. She led him to the center, where they stood in front of something that looked very much like a bird bath.

"Look into it," Nuala commanded, still holding on to him.

Zeke waited for an explanation, but she remained silent. Shrugging, he bowed his head and focused on the glassy surface.

"Look," she whispered, her voice thin with distress. "Understand."

He smiled, just to reassure her. Then, connected by no more than their fingertips, he shut out the sight of her anxious eyes and concentrated on the water. The woods waited around him in an odd, profound silence that unsettled him. The very air seemed to chill.

And then, like a film coming into focus, he saw it.

"No…"

His brother Jake, bent almost double, his hands on his knees, his back against a sterile wall. His mouth open, his eyes closed, he was keening. God, honest to God keening, as if he were suffering such pain it couldn't be contained. The sound was terrible; raw and primal and terrifying. Zeke could feel it impale him on a hard blade. He was swamped by the sense of sudden, crippling loss.

Jake's wife Amanda stood with him, her arms around his shoulders, her head resting against his back, her own eyes awash. She was murmuring, as if it would help. Zeke thought maybe he could see Gen and Lee in the distance, enfolded in their husbands' arms. He thought he heard tears. But it was Jake who tormented him.

He looked so lost. This brother, who had stood like a granite wall against all adversities, who had single-handedly impelled them all past their parents' deaths and the bitter poverty of a failing ranch, looked beaten. Crushed. His hands were clawed fists. His granite face was crumbled, his eyes blind.

And Zeke saw it. He heard it. He felt it, so deep it threatened to shatter him, too.

"What is it?" he demanded, not hearing the high distress in his voice. "What's wrong?"

From far away, he heard Nuala's voice, and the minute he heard it, he knew it was true. "You," she said, her voice just as pain-filled. "Didn't you know, Zeke? You're lost to them."

Chapter 10

Nuala had thought she couldn't feel any worse. She should have known better. It had been bad enough when Zeke's eyes had still been focused on the water, his visions private and restrained. But suddenly his eyes were focused on her, and they were accusing. Betrayed. Hard as ice.

"What have you done?" he demanded, pushing her away.

Nuala held her ground, no matter that her knees were trembling. "I did nothing. It is what your absence is costing your family."

"You act like I'm dead!"

She shrugged. "If you stay, you might as well be."

Nuala was reminded then what a good man Zeke Kendall was, because she saw the terrible struggle in his eyes. The yearning to stay here and share the glades of faerie with her. The terror of what it would cost his family, of what it would cost *him* never to see them again. He wanted to stay. She knew, though, he needed more to go.

He stalked by her to walk back into her house. The

glade was so small that Nuala had to step aside or be mowed down. She let him pass and then followed. She held her breath. She waited, struck so silent by Zeke's turmoil that her harp hummed with distress alongside her.

And then, as if he couldn't help himself, Zeke turned to her. Nuala wanted to keen like a *bean sidhe* at the agony in his dear eyes. She wanted to gather him into her arms and give him peace. She wanted…oh, she wanted.

But she stayed so still that no one could later accuse her of coercing him. No one could blame her when he came to her.

He came to her. In long, ground-eating steps, he returned to find her arms open to him, her face lifted to him, her heart exposed to him. He pulled her into his arms and all but crushed the air from her.

"I'm sorry," she whispered, leaning her head back so he could see that she grieved, too. "I would have it any other way, if I could. I would spare you all this." Then, because she had to for him, she smiled. "You *would* have to insist on fallin' into the queen's own living room."

"I have to go back," he said, sounding so torn.

She nodded, drinking in the sight of him to keep her warm in the long years ahead. "You have to win the next two tests."

Bending enough to rest his forehead against hers, he sighed. "I still haven't been praised for passing the first one."

Nuala's heart stumbled. "You haven't?" Her palms went damp. The temperature in her little house rose. She couldn't breathe, and Zeke hadn't even kissed her.

He still didn't. Instead, he gently traced her lower lip with a finger, watching it as if expecting divination from it.

"No. And considering what Orla offered, I should at least get a 'good boy' out of it."

His hand began to wander, tracing her throat, the ridge of her collarbone, the slope of her shoulder.

Nuala fought for breath. "Was it so much, what she offered?"

He looked down at her, his eyes incandescent, and he smiled, still sore, still torn. But, for that moment, at least, hers. "Not much at all," he said. And finally kissed her.

Nuala knew she should stop. This would only make his leaving all the harder for her. Already her body hummed for him like her harp as she waited for his fingers to unleash a melody from her. Her skin glowed as his hand passed, as if he had lit her to shine in the dark. Her breasts ached, full and heavy in his hands, anxious for his mouth. Her mouth opened at his approach, and her knees melted.

She had never loved in her own home. In the hills, where it was a rite. In the glens, where the sacrament of it gave birth to the new year. Never in a place so private and meaningful to only her, where there was no more reason than hunger and wanting and love.

But what did it matter? Even if their loving created a child between them? She was the issue of such a match, after all. Only Orla had a fairy father. The only difference would be that Nuala would forever love the father of her child. And so, she knew, love the child that much more.

Yes, maybe that was what would be best, after all.

"Will you give me a kind farewell?" she murmured against his strong lips, her hands laid against the wall of his chest. "Will you make me magic?"

He wrapped her in his arms and lifted her from the floor. "We'll make magic together."

Zeke Kendall knew women. He loved them, one and all. He cherished the memory of their touch, their smell, their sated little sounds when they rested, damp and smiling from lovemaking. Zeke knew, as he carried Nuala, daughter of Mab, in his arms, that every other woman he'd ever had was about to fade into insignificance.

She smelled like grass. Like fresh air and morning and the silent dark places of the earth. She felt like satin: the hollow of her throat, the sleek line of her legs, the ridge of every rib he measured with his callused fingertips.

He laid her down on her gossamer bed cover that was the color of fresh spring grass, and he kissed her. He tasted cloves on her tongue and sought out the honeyed recesses of her mouth. He nibbled and supped and plundered, losing himself in the secret mysteries of her. He could have spent the rest of his life feasting on her mouth. She was so responsive, so eager and soft and hungry, her own tongue dancing against his, sucking and sipping and sweet, her lips lush, her breathy sighs his for the tasting.

He knew he shouldn't do this. He should walk out and take to the hills on Cadhla, if the horse would have him, and wear away this hunger with work. He should track down Kieran and demand answers. He should save them both from the worse pain to come.

He couldn't. He had to touch her just a little more. He had to explore the wondrous landscape of her and claim each inch. God, oh, God, he had to fill her until there wasn't a cell of her that didn't store him in its memory.

He stripped her, a ridiculously easy thing to do. Pragmatic beings, these fairies. They must know that a dress is only good for being divested. They certainly didn't seem to mind displaying their delicious charms to the day. He let her undress him, her small, slim hands torture as she struggled once again with unfamiliar cotton and wool, as she giggled over the magical properties of a zipper.

"It's a devilish thing, Zeke," she whispered, her eyes alight, her hands ravenous. "Made to drive a woman mad."

He decided that music was the growl of a zipper slowly being loosed. He thought there couldn't be anything more addictive than the torture of her fumbling attempts. She was tenacious, though, frantic to get beyond the barrier of clothing until she was finally able to meet him, skin to skin, hip to hip, mouth to mouth. He wondered how he was ever again going to enjoy the feel of another woman's skin, when it wasn't Nuala's skin, Nuala's mouth. He ached with grief even as he burned with hunger.

"I've been dreaming of touching you again," she admitted shyly, her small hands inciting sparks all up and down his torso. "I never knew you could actually feel a man's muscles before. Like a living statue, you are, carved just to please a girl."

Zeke did his best to hold still before the onslaught, wanting nothing more than to imprint the feel of those magic hands on his memory.

"I live to serve," he assured her, kissing his way down her throat.

He wrapped himself around her, fighting to be closer, to consume her like air. He filled his hands with her breasts, memorized their perfect contours and lifted them up for feasting. He felt the flutter of a moan lift from her as he licked the pale peach of one nipple, as he tormented the other with his thumb. As he gave in to his most basic urge and closed his mouth around her to suck.

He felt the flight of her hands over him, branding him as she tested muscle and tendon and bone, as she winnowed her fingers through his hair and measured the breadth of his chest and the length of his belly. As she wrapped those long, magic fingers around his cock and took his breath from him.

She damn near stole his control. Laughing as if she were in a land of discovery, moaning as if she were being tortured and couldn't beg him to stop. He gasped for air when she cupped her hand around his balls. Orla had done that in his head out on the path that morning. One touch of Nuala's hand and he could cleanse himself of that other touch. That other memory.

His hands and mouth and breath only remembered Nuala. His body met hers as if returning home. He swallowed her up, breast and hip and mons, and then, because they so fascinated him, her feet. Her tiny, elegant fairy feet that should have been callused and dark from carrying her without shoes. Which weren't. Which were sleek and satiny and sensual enough that he had to take the time to suck on each toe as if it were a personal treat created just for him.

He courted her, coerced her, cherished her, drinking in her surprised whimpers of pleasure, the arching, writhing response of her lovely body, the wet welcome at her core. And just so he would never forget, not even when he was an old man telling stories nobody believed, he pulled her to the edge of the bed, and he knelt before her. He laid gentle hands on the inside of her velvet thighs and spread her before him. He bent his head, that head she held in her hands, and he sipped from the sleek petals of her. He tormented her with his tongue and little nips of his teeth. He drank his fill even as he heard her gasps gather and felt her body tauten. He smiled against her, inhaled the earth scent of her as she shattered, her cries high and reedy and surprised. He laughed with her as she pulled him up to her.

And then, when he felt it was time for him to complete his mastery of her, body and soul, instead she flipped around and did the same to him, her mouth on him, hot and wet and wild, her hair a waterfall of silk against his belly, until he was gasping her name in desperation and clawing at her for control. She laughed again, the melody of pure joy, and gave herself up to his lead. She lifted her head so that he thought he was saved, and then dipped it again, tormenting him with the fan of her hair, back and forth, back and forth along the length of him, until he knew he would explode before he ever got inside her.

He at least had that much command left. Suddenly Nuala was sprawled on her back, her hair a bright blanket beneath her, her eyes wide and smiling as he nudged her knees open. As he tested himself with her, nudging just the tip of him into her, bathing himself with her until his body was taut as steel above her.

"Goddess!" she gasped, clawing at his back, pulling him hard against her. "Be done with it! Love me."

"My lady's wish," he panted, kissing her hard, "is my command."

And he sank into her, her tight, hot depths damn near splintering his control. But he held on. Wrapping his hands around hers, he imprisoned them above her head and bent to kiss her, a hot, open-mouthed, drugging kiss that only sharpened the slide of entering her. Deeper, deeper, and then away. Again. Again. Faster, harder, seeking the core of her, the honeyed depths of her, the last, most perfect memory of her. He lunged and lunged, until the fairy bed slammed against the wall and she arched beneath him, her breath caught, her fingers curled into his, her eyes closed tight. Until he felt her convulse around him, until he forced those high, sweet little cries from her again, until he pumped himself into her, all of himself, every last measure of himself, until he knew that his were the cells that would hold the memory. And then he collapsed against her, his chest heaving, his brain empty, his body replete.

For a long, long time, he couldn't move. Couldn't so much as lift himself off her so she didn't smother. His nose was in her hair and his legs tangled around hers. His heart didn't slow for at least an hour, he would swear.

"I've heard of *la petite mort*," she murmured by his ear. "I always thought it was a fairy tale."

Zeke couldn't help it. He laughed. Rolling over, he pulled her with him to nestle her against his side. "It is," he assured her. "You just have to have the right fairy."

I love you.

He heard it in his head and didn't know which one of them had said it. He closed his eyes, terrified it had been he. He couldn't stay. He couldn't bear to leave. He had a feeling, though, that what he really couldn't do was survive a statement like that. She was right. He had to leave before he said it out loud.

"I should go," he said, not moving.

"No," she begged, her hand open against his chest. "Not for a little while."

Zeke sucked in a thready breath. "A little while," he agreed. And for the first time in his life, Zeke Kendall fell asleep with a woman in his arms.

The night was deep, the moon an inch from setting. None in the world of faerie could see the stars, but the moon was an old friend. She beamed down now on the couple who stood at the edge of the earth, wrapped in their dun cloaks and watching the water.

"I'm still not sure we should do this," Darragh whispered, his voice edging up toward a whine.

Beside him, Orla stood straight as a spear, her ebony hair rippling in the wind. "Yes, you are," she said, not bothering to cloak her voice in kindness. "You want the mortal hurt as badly as I do. This is the only way."

"But the Dark Sword..." He'd barely said it before looking around. "You swear it won't be discovered who did this thing?"

"Not if you do your work properly. I wouldn't even be letting you help if your grandsire wasn't a *Dubhlainn Sidhe*, himself who gave you control of storms."

He scowled. "Do you think I'm unfamiliar with my own genealogy, then? I tell you still, Orla, it's not enough for keepin' them in control. The Dark Sword are..."

But Orla's cat eyes were glowing. "Powerful. Potent."

Maybe, she thought, susceptible to a *leannan sidhe's* sorcery. A tempting thought, that. After all, nothing excited Orla as much as conquest, and there could be no greater conquest than one of the *Dubhlainn Sidhe*. He would undoubtedly make a worthy challenge, and with all that virility running rampant in his clan without the modifying effect of the female Dearann Stone, maybe a potent enough lover to finally satisfy her.

Yes, she thought, all but licking her lips. She would spend the time she waited by the sea considering just what a *Dubhlainn Sidhe* lover might offer. If she had been a creature in the habit of self-examination, she would have admitted that the wound was far better than revisiting the sharp edge of empathy she'd cut herself on that day. She would have to admit that it still bled, an infuriating trickle that refused to stop.

But a *leannan sidhe* was not made to bear the burden of guilt. Far better to fill herself with anticipation than waste her time admitting to feelings of loss. Much better to focus on the bargain she was about to make. A bargain that would, with luck, enable her to break the mortal right before her mother's eyes.

Balance had to be restored, and it seemed she was the only one to do it. As odd as it sounded, Orla knew herself to be the only one to realize that the good of Faerie was being suborned to the whims of a few. Her mother wanted the mortal for play, and her sister wanted him for…whatever it was Nuala wanted. Orla seemed to be the only one to know that the mortal was leading them down the path to disaster. He was distracting them all from the real issue, which was the succession.

Nuala was not fit to be queen. She didn't want it. She wouldn't be able to deal with it. She would always have one foot in another place, and in this perilous time, the world of Faerie couldn't stand that. It would never survive a queen who had lost her way.

Was Orla the only one who saw that? Was she the only one of them who realized that she alone would be able to step out from the long shadow her mother cast? Did no one else see that the world of Faerie needed her almost as much as she…well, that was something Orla was not yet ready to consider.

"How do you know they'll cooperate?" Darragh demanded in a hushed whisper as he wrapped his cloak more tightly about him, so as to camouflage the sight of him from fairy eyes.

Orla didn't bother to look over at him. "Because I understand the need to commit mischief."

She was distracted, barely hearing his complaints. Was it the sound of hoofbeats she heard? Was that how they arrived? On the backs of those benighted beasts? She heard the sound out where the moon spilled diamonds across the water.

"They're coming."

Darragh whipped around, paling. He could hear it, too, Orla knew. The fire-eyed horse of the *Dubhlainn Sidhe*. Black-coated and fierce, the kind of phantom that destroyed dreams.

Orla peered out to the water. Was that he? That shadow across the moon? That phantom billowing like a cape in the wind? It was certain she felt a sudden dread, an exhilaration unlike any she'd ever experienced. A breathlessness that had nothing to do with the sudden wind in her face.

It was a single hot-eyed horse that galloped across the shoulder of the sea, its black mane billowing like the cape of its rider. Its black-haired rider. Its black-eyed rider who had the face of an angel, the body of a panther, the arrogance of a king. Orla was struck silent at his beauty.

It was said that any human looking on the face of a

Dubhlainn Sidhe would go mad. Orla understood why. It was his fearsome splendor that overwhelmed, not any ugliness or sorcery. Orla was shaken to her core with the unaccountable hunger that suddenly washed over her.

She was never plagued with such feelings, such uncontrolled yearnings. She was the *leannan sidhe*. She wanted no one. Nothing. She chose. Even now, no matter what had happened with that ill-begotten mortal. She was in control.

But she stood stone still before this fairy that approached over the churning water and wondered if she was already lost.

"You called for me," he said in a rich, dark voice as he pulled the sleek horse to a pawing, snorting stop at the edge of the waves. The fairy's black, black hair tumbled in the wind; the night shadowed his eyes. "Speak your mind."

"Who are you?" Orla couldn't help but ask.

"I am Liam," he said in a curiously soft voice that still sent chills down her spine. "The protector. The avenger."

Finally, slowly, Orla smiled. "Then we are well met, Liam. For I have something to avenge."

Zeke woke slowly. It had been a long night, full of the most exceptional lovemaking he could remember. They had been insatiable, storing up every moment they could before he had to leave. Bodies and memories and the agony of dreams. Zeke learned that

Nuala's father had been half human himself, a beautiful harpist who had wandered down the wrong lane on a dark night and found himself in the fairy kingdom. Zeke had told her of things he had a feeling she already knew, his love for his work, his almost obsessive need to travel, his guilt at not spending more time with his family. They had slept entwined like vines and woken to rediscover the wonder of each other's bodies.

He ached with exhaustion and satiation. He smiled with the images he kept in his heart. The pert peach nipples that just begged to be tasted. The deep, verdant green of her eyes. The precious metals that glinted from her hair, and the surprisingly whimsical fire of that triangle between her thighs.

He especially cherished that particular landscape. Brazen flag and primal mystery. Sleek satin and fundamental homecoming. Even thinking about it, he went hard all over again. He wanted to be inside her in the worst way, but he was sure he'd just left her to sleep only an hour or so ago. She had to be at least as tired as he was.

She was asleep, her back to him, her hair setting the pillow alight, her body a symphony of curves and sweet shadows. He needed to touch her again, to measure the arc of her hips, the incline of her waist, the delicious weight of her breasts. Breasts that weren't as lush as her sister's or as proud as her mother's. Perfect breasts, nonetheless. The only breasts that made his mouth go dry and his heart stutter. The only breasts that fit so perfectly in his hand and his mouth. Peaches and cream. His new favorite treat.

Gently, because he wanted to ease her awake, Zeke reached out to slide a hand along her hip and ease the cover away so he could feast on just the sight of her in these early morning minutes. He could hear the birds wake outside, could see the first blush of sunrise peek through the windows. He felt the minutes escape him as he hesitated, minutes he would never recover, minutes he needed to memorize of her before she was gone for good.

He curled his hand around the ridge of her hip and tormented himself with the satin of her skin. He closed his eyes, focusing on nothing but the pads of his fingers, the hollow of his palm as it skimmed the dimple at the base of her spine. Her scent drifted up to him, soft morning and darkest night. Enticement and enchantment. He felt her lift in a sigh and knew he'd accomplished his mission. She was waking.

"The sun is almost up," he whispered.

So am I, he thought inconsequentially.

She must have heard him, because she chuckled. "Yes," she whispered back. "I can tell."

And then she rolled onto her back, and he was struck dumb. Could a woman look more perfect? Her skin literally glowed. Her cheeks were rosy with sleep, her hair tousled and gleaming with a thousand shades of sunset. Her smile was soft and private, her lips still swollen from all the feasting he'd done on them the night before. Her eyes glowed, mysterious in the half light.

"Shall we sleep in this morning?" she asked, reaching out to stroke his stubbled cheek.

"Sleep?" he retorted, leaning into her.

Which was when he had his first niggle. No more than that, just a quick feeling that something didn't fit. Zeke took a look around, almost expecting to see that they were being spied on. The shadows were empty, though. No one watched, even though Zeke suddenly felt as if someone was.

He didn't like it. It was one thing to have a queen climb into your head when you were out in public, quite another to have it happen when he was in bed with her daughter. But he swore he could feel her hanging around somewhere.

"What's wrong?" Nuala asked, her brow furrowing.

Zeke shook his head. There was nothing there. He was just getting paranoid, which shouldn't be surprising, considering what had happened to him so far.

"Nothing. Nothing. Now, where were we?"

He leaned over her, resting his arm on the pillow by her head. He soaked in the smile in her eyes and tasted anticipation. He bent, seeing her lips open to him, feeling her arms wrap around him, hearing her sigh for him. He teased himself with the waiting, his mouth only a breath away from hers, his arms closing around her.

He bent to take her mouth, his heart pounding so hard he wondered if he would just explode. And then, from one second to the next, as if a light went on, he froze.

What? he wondered, suddenly sweating. *What was wrong?*

"Zeke?" she asked, anxious.

"Your mother," Zeke said, taking another look around. "I swear I can feel her nearby."

Nuala chuckled again. "Of course she is," she said, stroking his cheek. "But she'd never peek. She's not a voyeur."

Zeke returned his attention to her. To the spring green of her eyes, to the milky perfection of her skin. The perfect oval of her face. And then he realized what had been wrong. Not the feeling that something was wrong with Nuala's mother. The feeling that something was wrong with *Nuala*.

It was her scent. Cloves and honey and gorse. That was the scent of Nuala. What he smelled now as their breath mingled. But there was something else always present, something indefinably Nuala. Something elusive and elemental. Something suddenly missing.

Zeke was off the bed so fast, he tumbled right over. Stark naked, suddenly limp as seven-day-old lettuce, shocked as a virgin.

"Who are you?" he demanded, ass-down on the floor.

Nuala looked confused. "Zeke?"

He glared at her, his heart double-timing in his chest. "I'll ask you again. Who are you?"

She blinked, as if trying to figure out how to humor him. "I'm Nuala. You spent all of last night with me, remember?"

"I spent all of last night with Nuala," he agreed. "Which means I did not spend it with *you*. Now, who the hell are you, and where is Nuala? Or is she part of this little prank?"

She wasn't. He knew it before the words left his mouth. But still, he felt abruptly panicked. He grabbed one of the silky wrists she'd lifted to him only moments earlier and began to twist.

"Last chance," he growled. "You're beginning to piss me off."

And just as if he'd been David Copperfield, the arm in his grasp seemed to change and reform before his eyes. The rest of her followed, from the achingly beautiful Nuala of his dreams to the predatory brittleness of someone entirely different.

Naked.

In Nuala's bed.

Mab. Nuala's mother.

Chapter 11

Zeke let go of Mab so fast he almost ended up on his head. For the first time in his memory, he thought he was going to be violently ill. He sat there, naked and frozen, swallowing down bile as the very naked queen of the fairies lounged in his lover's bed.

If he hadn't realized... If he'd actually made love to her...

He closed his eyes. Not to avoid seeing her. After all, by this time it was useless to avert his eyes. He'd seen much more of her in his head than he did now anyway. More to avoid what had almost just happened.

Did Nuala know what her mother had planned? What would she have thought if he'd failed? Hell, he thought, swallowing again. If he'd failed, it wouldn't have mattered. He would have been shackled to the queen. At least until he'd managed to throw himself into the ocean. Suddenly he couldn't think of anything worse than spending eternity at the beck and call of a predatory monarch. Especially one who would so blithely betray her own daughter.

With her daughter's lover. Who'd been so horny he almost hadn't taken the time to notice the difference.

Well, that sure as hell made him feel better.

"And isn't it a sad thing to know you aren't all that holy yourself, little man?" the queen purred from Nuala's bed.

Zeke opened his eyes on her. "I wouldn't be calling this particular kettle black right now," he advised.

Sucking in a breath to settle his stomach, Zeke pulled himself to his feet. Then, not knowing what else to do, he snatched his clothes from the floor. He thought it wouldn't be a bad idea to be girded for the next few minutes. He yanked his jeans on and zipped them, ruefully aware of how much less intriguing the scratchy glissando sounded than it had when he'd been unzipped a few hours earlier.

"All I have to say," he snarled as he slid into his shirt, "is that I'm glad I didn't have a mother like you. I would have drowned her in the river. What the hell were you thinking?"

The queen, it seemed, chose not to answer. All Zeke heard was silence punctuated by distant birdcall and the jangle of cowbells. The sun strengthened, sipping away at the shadows in the room. Zeke made it a point to watch that, rather than the woman in Nuala's bed.

"Where is she?" he demanded.

Finally, Mab sighed. "You may face me now. I am decent."

Zeke laughed. "Boy, if that's not a relative term, I don't know what is."

"Mortal," Mab said in a tight voice, "you begin to weary me."

"Imagine how *I* feel," he snapped, finally turning to find her reclining on Nuala's pillows in her white robes. "Now tell me before I really lose my temper. What have you done with Nuala?"

He would have asked how the queen had pulled the switch, but he didn't think he was up to the answer.

"You asked what I was thinking," the queen reminded him, her beringed hand stroking Nuala's soft sheets.

Zeke wanted to slap her hand away. She was fouling something precious.

"I asked what you've done with your daughter."

She lifted an elegant eyebrow. "You think I disposed of her? The heir to the throne?"

"I think you used her like the pawn she is. Your maternal instincts are sadly lacking, madam."

Well, if he'd wanted a reaction, he got it. Her eyes glinted like sun off steel as she straightened to her full regal height. "Never," she said, "*never* question my relationship with my daughters."

"Why?" he asked, feeling reckless. "Because you're their queen?"

"Because," she said, her voice terrible, "I am their mother. And now, little man, if you would rather not suddenly find yourself cropping grass with big rabbit teeth, I'd suggest you find another avenue of discussion."

"Fine," he retorted, stepping forward. "If you're such an exemplary mother, then what the hell was *this* all about?"

"This," she retorted, climbing to her feet with all the

imperiousness of an absolute monarch, "is about your tests, you insignificant insect."

Suddenly Zeke felt like smiling. "Ah," he said, doing just that. "So you were my second beast."

Triumph tasted pretty sweet, especially when it was savored in the presence of the enemy. She was furious, which meant that he hadn't been as close to succumbing as he'd feared.

The queen was not amused. "I wouldn't be after throwing around such nomenclature if I were you, little man."

Zeke gave her his best innocent look. "I only repeat your own words, my lady."

The queen looked as if she wanted to huff in disgust. "I think Nuala picks her mortals too fresh."

Zeke found himself frowning. "Mortals?" he echoed. "Does she bring home strange men often, then?"

The queen smiled, looking suddenly calculating. "Would it matter to you?"

Zeke thought about it a moment. "Actually, no. But then, I realized the minute I said it that she wouldn't even think of it. Nuala isn't quite as...gluttonous as some of her relatives."

The smile died a terrible death. "You go too far."

"Oh, I don't think so. Now, you were going to tell me where she is. I need to apologize for not waking her this morning like I wanted to."

They had a glare-off, he and the queen, who suddenly seemed to tower over him, her displeasure a darkness on the sun. But Zeke held on, because he thought maybe it was time this fairy knew that there was somebody out there impervious to her tantrums. Besides, he figured winning two of the three tests had gained him some mojo.

Evidently he was right. "Why do you insist on breaking yourself on her, mortal?" the queen asked, her voice curiously subdued. "You know you cannot win."

"Is it about winning?" he asked, giving her his innocent look. "Odd. That idea never crossed my mind."

"You cannot have her."

"I can remember her."

The effect of those four words was damn near cataclysmic. Zeke felt as if he'd just been pushed off his feet all over again. He'd only said it to annoy the queen. He hadn't meant to terrify himself.

But he had. He'd said it without meaning it, then wondered, suddenly if that was true. If he actually *had* meant what he'd said. If he really *could* mean it. Ever. Without realizing it, he walked right out of the house to stand there in Nuala's little copse of trees, his gaze on the distant hills, his thoughts on his past. To the moment his mother had died, sallow and sweating and skeletal in the remnants of her marriage bed. There had been no words in his head then. No vow to never go through that again. After all, he'd only been eight. But he'd known it anyway. Terrified, holding on to Jake's big, hard hand as if it were the only real thing left. Gaping like a fish out of water, sure there wasn't any air left in the world, because the last of it had just seeped from his mother's tortured lungs. All the air that had been left in the universe after his dad had died, anyway.

Alone.

No matter that Jake and Gen and Lee had stood there with him in that echoing, empty room. No matter that the town had gathered to help them bury his mother, bestowing casseroles like bouquets, tutting and hugging and promising better things, which in the end only Jake had provided. Zeke had still been alone. Without even realizing it, he'd promised himself that he would never allow himself to be left alone again. Better to never have, so that you could never know what it was you would inevitably lose.

How stupid was that? he wondered. As if just by making the vow he could assure it of coming true. As if he could control the world with nothing but the strength of his fear. As if by staying away from the people he loved the most he could keep them in a safe place where he could pretend they would never be hurt. Where he could pretend *he* couldn't be hurt.

It sure hadn't worked so far. His family had suffered, with or without him. People came; people left. There wasn't a damn thing you could do about it. And, inevitably, you were hurt. It was that simple. And that awful.

And now, because of Zeke, Jake was being forced to suffer the same hell. Zeke couldn't bear it. He couldn't allow it.

"Little man?" he heard behind him.

But he didn't move, not just yet. There was something big trying to work its way past his defenses. Something that caught in his chest like a balloon, expanding so wide that it threatened to choke off his air. To take the last of it from the world all over again. It tasted like panic. It smelled like revelation. It hurt with the crusted-over edges of old grief. He didn't know if he wanted to examine it. He didn't know if he had the courage.

"Attend me, little man," the queen commanded.

Zeke decided that it was about time to do just that. Easier to do than fight whatever it was he'd just decided to discover. He should probably be ashamed of how fast he'd given up. He was too old a hat at rationalization, though. This time he called his evasion pragmatism. After all, if he didn't attend the queen, he could be munching on kale and eyeing cute bunnies for a tumble. Personal trauma would always be there to examine.

"Nuala is at the great hall," Mab said when he rejoined her in the house, her expression no less unfriendly. "You have the right to see her. Until the next test, anyway."

"And that will happen…?"

The queen's smile was not pretty. "Whenever you least expect it, I imagine."

She was about to glide out of the room. But Zeke wasn't letting her go quite yet. "Why is your seer so upset?"

The queen never turned from the door. "He is a child. His powers are still maturing. Sometimes he… imagines things."

"I don't think so." Zeke stepped closer. "I think there is some danger in the air, and you're not stopping it."

For a second there was absolute silence in the little house. "You make many accusations, little man. Did I not tell you to be careful?"

"If I win my challenges, you said I could choose to stay. It's my right. Could I take Nuala back with me instead?"

This time the queen spun around. "You would not dare! She is to be queen."

"Not if she's mortally injured, she's not. If you won't protect her, I will."

"You have no right!"

He shrugged. "I don't really care."

She shimmered with rage. Finally, though, she lifted a hand. "Succeed in the third challenge and I will make all clear to you."

"It's that easy?"

The queen smiled again, savoring her next words. "I never said it would be easy."

And then, satisfied with the effect of her words, she opened the door and walked out, leaving Zeke alone with the scent of flowers and lovemaking, and the taste of a tainted victory.

He should have made straight for the hall, if for no other reason than to make sure Nuala was safe. Instead, he walked, head down, hands in pockets, Cadhla following in his wake. Zeke appreciated the fact that the horse had nothing to say. Sometimes a horse should just be a horse. Especially when a man was wrestling with big problems.

What was he going to do? What did he *want* to do?

He couldn't get that image of Jake out of his head, his brother bent and broken. It sliced into him like a sword, a deep fatal thrust of guilt. He'd never been the best kid on the planet growing up, but he'd never once thought to hurt Jake like this. How could he, after all? Jake was his hero. Jake was the mountain that protected him, the oak that shaded him. He was the only reason Zeke had made it to adulthood with some semblance of honor. And here Zeke was threatening to desert Jake when he knew more than anyone in any world what that would do to his brother.

Nuala was right. He had to go back. He had to pay his debt to the brother who had loved him enough to clobber him the day he'd tried to play "high school jock jerk" with Judy Mercer. He had to wrap his arms around those seemingly impregnable shoulders and tell Jake he wasn't alone.

If he did, though, it would mean leaving Nuala. Leaving her in danger. It would mean losing her, when he couldn't afford to lose one other soul in his life. Because he knew that her honor would forbid her the chance to flee. She was Nuala, heir of Mab, and her duty was to her people.

So either way, someone he loved would be hurt. And just like with his parents, there wouldn't be enough of him to prevent it.

The more he thought about it, the angrier he became.

Not just because it wasn't fair, but because he couldn't believe he'd let himself in for this kind of grief. He couldn't believe he had allowed Nuala past his hard-built armor. He couldn't really have been so stupid as to fall in love with her, could he?

Without realizing it, he had walked in the general direction of the great hall after all, where it seemed that Nuala was teaching the children something about flying. She was laughing and pointing skyward, where her sister Sorcha was doing loop-de-loops like a country fair barnstormer. The children clapped and oohed, and Nuala bent to ruffle hair and tweak ears. Zeke stopped a good twenty feet away, absolutely not wanting to step closer. Not in the least needing to hear the bells in her laughter or see the emerald of her eyes. It was bad enough that when she bent over, her hair tumbled over her shoulders like a fall of fire, or that he could swear he could feel her hips sway in his hands. It was worse that his own body remembered all too clearly what it felt like to be sunk into hers.

He wanted to kiss her. He wanted to grab her and never let go. He wanted to bury himself so deep inside her that the borders between them blurred. He wanted it so badly that it took his breath. It took his courage.

He had to go back. She had to stay. He wanted to haul her into his arms and run as far as he could from everything, someplace safe for just the two of them. Someplace where neither of them had a single responsibility.

And yet he stood there, just watching her, his hands

shoved in his pockets to keep from reaching for her. As if that could ever be enough.

Obviously he hadn't stopped far enough away. As if he'd spoken out loud, Nuala looked up. Smiled. And Zeke was forced to admit that he really could be that stupid. That balloon filled his chest again to the point of pain. His palms went damp, and his mouth went dry. He wanted to howl. He wanted to throw himself on Cadhla's back and ride so far that no fairy could find him. He wanted to destroy something.

But Nuala was smiling, and Zeke couldn't move, because, damn it to hell, he was in love with her.

"I expected better of you," he accused as she stepped closer.

That stopped her dead in her tracks. "I'm sorry?"

The confusion in her eyes tugged at him. Still, he couldn't seem to stop. "I expect collusion from your sister and your mother. Not from you."

She stood so close he could see those flecks in her eyes, sunshine on a green sea. "What are you talking about, Zeke?"

"Test number two, Nuala. Did you think it was amusing for your mother to impersonate you in our bed?"

He'd already known she was innocent, but the absolute proof was on her now. Nobody could fake that kind of sick pallor. "You were asleep when I left," she said, stricken. "I...I thought to let you rest."

"Well, resting wasn't what I did."

What was wrong with him? He wanted suddenly to

hurt her, to make her pay for what her mother had done, when he knew damn well she'd had no part in it. Behind him, Cadhla shoved a hard nose into his back.

Zeke whipped around. "Thank you. I don't need your services anymore."

Even the horse looked affronted. Without so much as a tossed head, he turned with great dignity and stalked off.

"Zeke?" Nuala laid her hand on his arm.

Zeke reared back as if she'd burned him. "Don't," he snapped, feeling suddenly frantic. "I don't think I'm good company right now. I should probably walk this off."

"Walk what off?"

"The feeling that I want to haul off and belt somebody."

She stood there in her bare feet like a gypsy, her hair tumbled, her cheeks sunkissed. But it was her eyes that compelled him. They were huge, luminous. Looking down at them, Zeke couldn't breathe.

"Did you…?"

"Screw your mother? No. I did not. Not for want of effort on her part, though."

He saw the brief flash of relief in her eyes and fought fresh rage. "Don't trust me much, do you?"

It was Nuala who flinched, just as if he'd hit her. "Yes," she said. "I do. But I'd be a sorry failure to trust the likes of my mother, now wouldn't I?"

That fast, the balloon exploded and Zeke could breathe. He actually shook his head, completely disoriented. What the hell had happened just now? He felt as if he'd just broken a fever. His skin was flushed and damp, and he was sure his hands were shaking.

"Zeke?" Nuala whispered, standing so close that she shielded him from the eyes of her kin. "What's wrong?"

For a minute all he could do was stare at her. She smelled like gorse, like fresh grass and summer. He couldn't get enough of her smell. He wanted to bury his face in her breasts and sate himself with that scent. Sate himself with *her*, as if he hadn't done that very thing the night before.

The sad truth was that he would never have enough of her. Not in the time left here, not in the time left in his entire life.

"Can we go walking?" he asked.

With no more than a tremulous smile, Nuala put her hand in his.

"I'll be back in a while, Sorcha!" she called.

"But I'm about to do a death spiral!" came the voice from above.

"Well, for all our sakes, don't be slammin' into the ground."

Zeke wanted to laugh. Awfully, he also wanted to cry. He hadn't felt the same since he'd realized that the wrist he'd had hold of belonged to Mab. Could you go crazy on no more than one surprise? Okay, one big surprise. Zeke felt that there was a good chance he could.

"Now, tell me," Nuala urged as they strode away from the little village.

He rubbed at his head. "Tell you what?" he asked,

wincing against a fresh headache. His heart was still racing, and he felt nauseous. "That I'm a bastard for yelling at you? I'm a bastard."

How could she smile? She did, though, all bright whimsy and soft understanding, and Zeke thought he might die from it. "Ah, no, I think your good parents would have a fair argument against that, wouldn't they?"

"Not that kind of bastard, Nuala. The 'what the hell are you thinking'? kind of bastard. The kind that is such a jerk he gets chastised by a horse."

"Well, there you are, then. Cadhla has always been a bit of a prig, altogether."

He laughed. It felt sore and raw, but he laughed. "I feel like I'm being torn apart."

"You've had quite a bit to deal with in a wonderfully short time, Zeke."

"True. But I always thought I was one of those grace under pressure guys."

Nuala stopped in her tracks, pulling him to a halt beside her. "And you don't think withstanding the lure of a *leannan sidhe* is grace enough?"

He frowned. "I guess I'm not as impressed by her legendary skill as you all are. She doesn't hold a candle to you."

Nuala went perfectly still, flushing a delightful shade of peach. She opened her mouth, then closed it, then shook her head.

"Neither," Zeke added, leaning close, "does your mother."

Nuala laughed, a huff of surprise. "Don't say that too

loudly, Zeke. She'll be after teaching you *that* lesson all over again, for sure."

Delighted at her real astonishment, Zeke shook his head. "She's given it her best college try, Nuala. I'm not impressed."

Well, that wasn't perfectly true. He was impressed. He would have to be dead not to be. It was just that he wasn't interested. Orla was predatory. Mab was relentlessly carnal. And no matter his past history with humans, he found that on fairies, that just didn't stack up to one bright-eyed, intelligent, empathetic redhead with a talent for the harp.

Nuala, undoubtedly knowing just what he was thinking, looked up at him with a disbelieving smile. "Thank you. It's a small, petty thing, I think. But I've never compared well to those two." She shrugged and chuckled. "Sorcha doesn't care. Even though she's as much fairy as I, she seems to have missed out on the need for such pleasures. She's happier with her stones and her children. But I admit that sometimes, deep at night, when those kind of thoughts take hold, I wish... well..."

Zeke leaned his forehead against hers. "Well, wish no more. You are a gem to rival the ruby in your mother's crown."

She closed her eyes and just rested against him. A breeze tugged at his shirt. Trees rustled and swayed, a dance of approval. Tucked in the branches, a thousand birds set up a chattering chorus. Zeke reached out to lift a lock of hair off her forehead.

"Come," she whispered. "We should be walkin' on. I'd be happier without such an audience."

So Zeke took her hand and they walked. He didn't know how long they wandered, for they were silent, content with nothing more than the touch of each other's hand. He heard the dryads whispering at them, of course. He caught sight of birds darting and wheeling about, as if just happening by. He even thought he saw Sorcha swoop past once, camouflaging herself in the trees, but figured that was fanciful thinking.

He felt the sun on his face and soaked in the million shades of green. He could live here, he thought. He could be so happy just walking with Nuala in the afternoons.

They were on it before he realized. They'd just topped a rise when he saw it spread out before him, a quiltwork of stone across a narrow peninsula. Beyond it the sea glittered. Above it a smooth-topped mountain stood, wearing a cairn on its crown like a domed hat. Maeve's Cairn. They were standing at the edge of the Carrowmore burial field.

But it wasn't Carrowmore. Where Zeke was familiar with the site of half a dozen half-excavated mounds, here rose at least fifteen perfectly formed cairns, their doorways clean and their stones bone gray. And around those, stood dolmens, the classic pie-shaped burial chambers that to this day offered up more questions than answers.

Again he swore he could see a pattern. A wheel whose spokes were graves that still made him think he could make sense of thing if he could only look long enough.

"What *are* they?" he demanded, seeing again how

everything faced the center of the site. How the mountains ringed it, each with its own cairn.

Nuala looked up at him with a gentle smile. "The gates?"

Zeke whipped around so fast he fought dizziness. "Gates?"

She nodded. "Of course. For our court. For the other worlds."

He stood very still, Nuala's words sinking in. He let them mix around with the scene in front of him. He considered what else he saw down there. Each cairn was attended by a mail-clad soldier, the tallest fairies he'd ever seen, who stood like guards at Buckingham Palace, stone-faced and perfectly still.

"Why do they have to be guarded?" he asked.

Nuala greeted the closest guard, who saluted back. "Because they're too much of a temptation. The elves have the honor of protecting them. Otherwise, the fairies could be far too tempted to wreak havoc in all the other places we visit. Especially on you mortals. The only time the gates open is on feast days, especially Samhain. Or when the queen rides."

"Samhain...Halloween?" He kept staring, the pieces of the puzzle tumbling and tumbling.

"Aye. Halloween. The preparations are being made even now, you know. It is almost upon us, and the fairies love nothing more than making mischief on that particular night."

"Gates," Zeke mused, still focused on the plain that spread out before them. "Thirteen."

"Here. Yes."

He stood there, trying to remember what she'd said about worlds. How this one wasn't his. How he'd tumbled across into it.

He could see how closely this world mimicked his, yet obviously wasn't his. But was, maybe, one very close to his.

Zeke turned to her in consternation. "You're telling me that you cross dimensions in those things?"

"Of course. The cairn you fell from is in the mortal world, of course." She pointed. Zeke saw it tucked up within its fuchsia hedge, even though he shouldn't have been able to.

"Good God," he breathed. "You're talking about alternate universes. The string theory people were right."

What was it? he thought, frustrated at his lack of physics training. There were at least ten alternate universes, all bound by the strange power of connected strings of matter. He'd pretty much discounted it. After all, it wasn't his field. Old bones and pots were. Who could ever figure that the one would turn out to prove the other?

"What other universes are there?" he asked, his voice almost hushed.

Nuala considered him, much as a college professor once had. "Are you ready to know?" she asked. "Many aren't."

"Ready?" he echoed, the thrill of discovery churning in his veins. "Are you kidding? It's what I've been searching for all my life."

She took a glance at the cairns again, her brow furrowed. "Well, now," she said. "Of course, there is the world of Faerie...separated, into the realm of the Tua and the world of—"

"Yeah," he said, knowing she didn't want to invoke the bad fairies. "Go on."

She nodded. "And yourself, of course. Closest to ours, yet separate. And, oh, so many more, all in their way unique altogether. In one, the colors are different, and isn't the grass red and the sky green? I'm thinkin' you'd enjoy the sunsets, all right."

"And you've been all these places?"

"Ah, no. Not 'til I'm queen. She is the only one with full access. She and the king...well, he did when they had the power to come here, anyway. They haven't crossed since before my time."

"I bet that sure eases the tension between you."

"Well..."

"Why do the gates all point to the center cairn? Where does that one go?"

Nuala's expression softened; her eyes grew wistful. "To the Land of the West, of course. It is the door the queen will step through for the last time on this earth."

"And the...uh, king? How does he get across?"

Nuala looked uncomfortable. "Ah, well, that's a problem, so. He can't. Not since..."

"Before your time. Doesn't he deserve to go to the Land of the West if he wants?"

Nuala wouldn't face him. "It's not my place to say.

Not 'til I'm queen." He heard her small sigh. "Would it be so hard to let himself rest, though?"

Zeke found himself shaking his head, overwhelmed by the simplicity of it, the elegance. "I sure hope this isn't a dream after all," he admitted, his brain spinning faster than Sorcha on a good thermal. "I'd hate to think I made it all up."

Nuala shot him a saucy grin. "And the gates are the only thing you'd miss, is it?"

A long, open-mouthed kiss answered that question to both their satisfaction.

"Who put the gates here?" he asked, when they could both finally focus on something besides the heat two mouths could generate.

"They've always been there," she said, leaning against his chest within the protection of his arm. "We were simply the ones who learned their import."

"But you don't just go whipping back and forth among all the worlds."

"It would be foolish. And for all our reputation among you mortals, foolish we are not."

He knew damn well he should run down the hill and challenge one of the guards to examine the site. To see if he felt a weird energy or saw the ripple of space inside the doorway.

"What a great way to escape," he mused. In his mind, he saw himself pulling Nuala through one of those doors. Any of those doors. He would even deal with red grass to have the chance to be with her.

"A lovely idea," Nuala said, hearing him, of course.

He nodded. "Yeah."

They remained where they were for a long while. And then, wordless, turned away.

They spent the afternoon with Sorcha and the children, and then gathered with the others in the great hall. Again Zeke was forced to listen to Nuala's music until it seemed to tear open his chest, and the other fairies sat silent and awed. And afterward they left together without interference and returned to the homey comfort of Nuala's little house. Again they spent the hours into the deep night making love as if they would never touch each other again. They stored up sensations and memories for the long days they would survive each other, and then fell asleep in each other's arms.

Zeke wasn't sure when it started. Later he couldn't describe the first of it except that it seemed to creep in over him like whispers, as if somebody were standing just out of sight and slipping the seeds of malice into his dreams. It gathered, like birds circling, black crows blotting out the sky, stirring up the most awful terror in him. Rage. Frustration. He thought there were people there, shadowy faces that indicted him, that tormented him, faces he couldn't identify but should have been able to. He thought there was darkness, a darkness so deep he despaired of seeing light again, all in dreams that wouldn't stop, wouldn't let him rest, wouldn't ease his fear. He felt caught in a whirlwind that swept him up in a terrifying vortex.

And then he saw it. He heard it. As if a screen cleared, his saw his brother Jake, caught like a deer, facing down a threat even Zeke couldn't have anticipated. A siren, a sorceress, a psychic vampire who was bent on his destruction.

Nuala.

She had her long fingers all over Jake, stroking, just like her sister, like the *leannan sidhe*. She whispered in his ear, and it was like a steady drip of acid.

"You," she whispered in a terrible, soft voice that burned in Zeke's brain. "You've finally lost him. You let him go, you know, you let him fall, you gave him to me to suck the soul from." She leaned closer, right in Jake's ear, where he couldn't help but hear. "Such a simple man. Such a needy man, as needy as you, my fair mortal. What do you think he'd do if you bedded me? How do you think he'd feel?" Nuala, her hands all over Jake, her body wrapping around him, her words eating at him, her eyes devouring him.

His eyes closed, his head back, his cheeks streaked with tears, Jake seemed to howl in torment as she kept whispering, kept stroking, kept scourging. Zeke fought to get to them. He tried to scream, but his voice was gone. He tried to beat at her, but he couldn't reach her. He tried to reach Jake, but his brother simply opened his eyes, eyes empty and lost, and turned them on Zeke so that Zeke knew he was responsible. And still she whispered, a succubus who sought Jake's soul.

Nuala.

His Nuala, whom he'd thought so good, so guileless, pouring her terrible poison into his brother's heart.

Zeke should have known that it couldn't be, but

suddenly he wasn't sure. She sounded like Nuala, but she had that predatory gleam in her eyes he'd seen only in Orla's. She had the dark intent of her mother. She attached herself to Jake like a parasite and drained him dry.

And Zeke, struggling so hard to stop it, to save the brother he worshiped, battled an anguish that choked his lungs, felt the hard fire of fury ignite, so that he wanted to rush her, to take her apart with his bare hands for betraying him, for destroying his brother, even knowing it couldn't be happening. Sure she wouldn't do this. Certain she was better than the rest of her race. Wasn't she?

"What would happen," she whispered, the sound echoing in Zeke's head, "if I just…sucked you until you wasted away to dust?"

"Nooooooo!"

Zeke felt frantic fingers along his wet cheeks. "Zeke? Zeke wake up. It's all right, Zeke…."

Zeke exploded off the bed like a catapult. One minute Nuala was stroking his cheek, the next he had her pinned beneath him, his chest heaving with exertion, his brain white-hot with rage.

"What were you doing, Nuala?" he demanded, her face pale and indistinct in the darkness. He knew this was wrong, but the rage consumed him. He wanted to hurt her. He wanted to see her howling in despair. "Did you *like* breaking my brother?"

"Breaking…?" She struggled to reach him, but Zeke shoved harder, yanking both her hands over her head.

Sweat dripped off his chest and forehead. His body was hard, his cock harder. Rage hard. Revenge hard.

"Zeke, you were having a dream." She looked so suddenly frightened. "Please, Zeke, let me up."

He didn't hear her. Not really. Nothing but the memory of that voice taking his brother apart.

"Let you up? I don't think so. I think you need a little payment in kind, Nuala. I think you need to know what it feels like to be a victim."

He ripped the sheets back and stripped her bare. Her skin looked pearlescent in the dim light, her eyes huge pools of smoke. Her breath came in short, whimpering gasps. She looked like an animal in a trap. She looked terrified, which just stoked Zeke's satisfaction.

No, he thought, his whole body trembling. His knees shoving hers apart. *No, this is wrong.*

She had to understand. She had to suffer for the torment in Jake's eyes. In Zeke's head.

He should pummel her. He should ram himself into her until she screamed, until she bled, until she paid in kind for what she'd done.

He was shuddering, sweating and taut. He was so hard the pain of it took his breath. He was so fueled with rage he couldn't think.

He had to act. He *had* to.

He *couldn't!*

With a howl of despair, Zeke tore himself completely off the bed. He could see her, splayed out on her sheets like a broken doll, frozen and small. Eyes closed. Waiting for devastation. He turned away. He ran.

He got no farther than the little copse of trees before he was tackled by what felt like four linebackers.

"For that, mortal," growled one, pressing a very sharp blade to Zeke's neck, "you will die."

Anguish scouring away the rage, Zeke just closed his eyes. "Then do it."

Chapter 12

Nuala found him out among the trees, flattened beneath four of the strongest elves who guarded the court. Xender the Elder was lifting his sword over his head.

"Halt," she said, although her voice only sounded weary.

She felt battered, beaten. She had pulled on her dress, but she still felt naked. Naked and ashamed and furious. Yet she suddenly couldn't hold it against Zeke, who lay passively waiting for death.

Zeke wouldn't have hurt her. Not really. Not finally. She had to believe that or she would go insane. But she had to understand what had just happened.

Still, none of those thoughts prevented her from landing a good kick to his beautiful rump as he lay flattened like a frog. "Get up, mortal," she snapped, doing her best to hide her trembling hands.

The reek of violence permeated the air. The rank stench of terror and rage. And Zeke had no reason for it.

The elves stepped back, but Zeke didn't move. He lay curled on his stomach, naked on the grass, and suddenly Nuala heard it. Keening. Not *bean sidhe* keening, a sweet solemn melody, but survivor keening, the high, thready notes of grief. Of guilt.

From Zeke. From beautiful, powerful, enchanting Zeke. She wanted to go over and lift him. She wanted to wrap her arms around him and rock them both until the sense of violation eased. But she couldn't. There were bruises on her wrists. She could still taste the sour remnants of futility in the back of her throat.

Lifting an arm, she waved the elves away. Xender straightened and held, obviously questioning her judgment. It was Xender's primary duty to protect her life. He wasn't sure she would be safe without him.

A few moments ago, she wouldn't have been sure herself. But reason was beginning to seep back through the confusion. And reason said that what had just happened had not been Zeke's fault. She had to find out whose fault it was. And then deal with it.

"Wait in the house, good Xender," she commanded. "The rest, return to duty. I thank you most sincerely."

She waited for the salutes and silent departures before moving. When she did, it was to kneel alongside Zeke.

"Zeke?" She kept her voice soft, nonthreatening. She couldn't keep it from trembling almost as much as her hands. "What happened?"

He didn't move, his eyes closed, his hands fisted, his body trembling worse than hers. "I think I'm going mad."

The breeze was growing cool. Nuala saw the gooseflesh rise on him and knew that the sweat had to be chilling him. She held her place, though, still instinctively uncertain. She'd seen his eyes, after all, and there *had* been madness there.

"Tell me," she insisted softly.

"I wanted…" He sucked in a terrible breath and opened his eyes. Lurched upright. Nuala instinctively scooted back and saw his shamed reaction in his eyes. He gained his feet, but he posed no threat. There was defeat in his posture, despair in his eyes. "I almost raped you, Nuala."

She looked more closely, past the beauty of his handsome body, past the damage to him from his fall, new bruises and a scrape along his cheek. Confusion radiated from him. She could all but smell the residual horror. She climbed to her own feet.

"I know," she said. "I was there. The question is, why?"

Shivering now, he dragged his hands through his hair. "There were such images in my head. Such feelings of…oh, I don't know. Sickness, fear, rage. God, there was such rage. Because you were seducing Jake. Just like Orla. Tormenting him. Breaking him. Trying to break me with it." He shook his head. "I don't know. I'm so confused. All I know is that I can't shake the feeling that you've done something horrible and I have to hurt you."

Nuala wasn't sure how she could feel worse, but she did. Not for herself this time. For him. For what someone had just done to him. Goddess, this brave, bright man was all but crushed by what had just happened. He was more traumatized than she, and she'd almost been his victim. Rage lit in her, stiffening her spine and bringing icy calm to her limbs.

"But you didn't," she said to him. "In the end, you couldn't commit such terrible violence."

He closed his eyes rather than face her with his shame, she thought. "It was a close thing, though."

That was when she went to him. Reaching up, Nuala wrapped her arms around those cold, sunken shoulders. "Oh, I don't think so," she assured him, even though he refused to ease in her hold. "You're cold now. We need to dress and find out why this happened, Zeke."

He didn't move, just shook his head, a wounded animal. "I don't know," he muttered. "I just don't...I never dream. I'd never...*ever*..."

She reached up to touch him, laid her hand against his stubbled cheek until he looked down at her and she saw the anguish in his eyes. She thought of all the years she'd watched him, all the pain she'd seen him survive, and she raged even worse for somehow bringing this to him. "I know. Come inside. We need to speak. Xender will be with us, but not to protect me from you, but you from something else. Something darker than anger, I think."

Zeke followed her, seemingly unaware of his nudity. His attention was drawn inward, as if he kept reviewing what had just happened, just as she was.

The sense of uncertainty simply wouldn't leave. The

instinctive need to flinch from him. Nuala knew perfectly well that he could never hurt her, but she still feared it. From no more than that one incident. From the memory of madness in his eyes.

Someone had to pay for that. Someone would. Even if it was her mother. Especially if it was her mother. No test was important enough to destroy a man's soul.

She didn't see Xender when she entered the house, which meant he waited beyond the entrance, close enough for security, distant enough for privacy. Nuala led Zeke to her bed and urged him to sit. Then she sat next to him.

"Do you remember anything else?" she asked, taking hold of his hand. His cold, cold hand.

He focused on the early sunlight out her window. "You," he said, his voice tormented. "Jake. I tried like hell to stop you. Then I tried like hell to hurt you."

She reached up again, to turn his face to her. Still he looked ravaged, his beautiful features torn with what looked exactly like grief.

"Zeke," she said, rubbing her thumb across his cheek, "make love to me."

It was Zeke who flinched. "We need to find out what that was about."

"First we need to reassure ourselves that it wasn't about us. Please, Zeke. Make love to me."

Dear Goddess, there were tears in his eyes. She would slaughter with her own hands whoever had put them there.

"Are you sure?" he asked, tentatively lifting a hand to stroke her hair.

"Love me, Zeke. Give us both the courage to fight this."

He did. Cupping her face in his callused hands, he bent his lips to hers. He closed his eyes. Nuala did not. She knew she trembled. She knew the instinctive doubt hadn't eased. She needed to see Zeke in the clear morning light to dispel the memory of that other Zeke, the one who had visited violence on her.

He was not violent now. He was unspeakably gentle as he took his exquisite time in worshiping her with his hands, with his mouth, with his gentle, great heart. With his eyes. His dear, verdant, wise eyes that now carried fresh shadows.

He opened his eyes when Nuala asked and kept them open as he slipped her dress away and laid her on her bed and feasted on her body. As he incited a completely different madness with his careful, tender attention. Nuala arched beneath his hands as he found her breasts, as he trailed kisses along her throat, her ears, her eyes. As he reminded her why she'd fallen in love with him so many years ago and eased the memories of the morning.

"Come, Zeke," she begged, opening her thighs, taking him in her anxious, ready hands. "Come home to me."

And with a harsh groan of repletion, he filled her. He consumed her. He surrounded her with his strength and his heat and his care. Nuala gave herself up to the joy of him, smiling. Keening. Yes, high and sweet in the back of her throat as they moved together, as the fire built between them, as it swept them before it into the cataclysm of climax. Head thrown back, eyes held open, her body sweating and satiated, Nuala sang to him the symphony he had set loose in her. She welcomed his shuddering sighs and held his slick body in her arms. And somewhere in the gasping aftermath, when his tears mixed with hers, she knew somehow that a child had been made.

And she was glad. Especially now, when she captured his tears with her fingertips and offered her own in answer. When they righted what something or someone had sent so very wrong.

Hours later, it seemed, Zeke roused himself. Fingering her hair, he wrapped protective arms around her. "Thank you," he said, sounding awed. "I couldn't have borne those memories any longer."

"You shouldn't have to."

The time had come. The question had to be raised. Nuala resented it, resented that would take Zeke from the safety of her arms. But if her mother had set the abomination of those dreams loose on Zeke, Nuala had to know. She had to know why.

"We need to—"

"I know."

Nothing else was said. They rose and dressed in silence, afraid to sully the fragile peace they'd reclaimed here. And in silence they left the house and went to find the queen, Xender following like a shadow.

They did not find the queen alone. She rested in her lover's arms, naked and lush and smug in the crook of an old oak. Nuala wasn't pleased, especially by the way her mother was smiling. Nuala stopped a good ten feet from her, standing as rigid as judgment.

"You have gone too far," she greeted her mother, her expression hard.

The queen didn't so much as blink. But Nuala knew she was displeased. Without seeming to move, she set herself apart from her consort. "Explain, my young Nuala, why you disturb me at my rest."

"No," Zeke interrupted, stepping forward. "This is my fight. I think you can talk to me."

He didn't even seem to notice that the woman he talked to was naked. Or that she was the most glorious creature in nature. Nuala couldn't help a flash of selfish satisfaction. He'd chosen her, Nuala, over the legendary beauties of her family. And because of it, her mother had almost destroyed him.

Mab snapped to attention. "You make a hard accusation, little Nuala. I think you must want to explain."

"No, really," Zeke said. "Let me. Because I have to make something perfectly clear to you. I don't care who you are, or what you think you can do to me. If you *ever* so much as cause your daughter a moment of distress or willingly put her in danger again, I'll tear you apart. And please believe me that I can do it. And I will."

Nuala heard the implacable threat in Zeke's words and fought new tears. New anxieties for his safety. Behind him, Xender shuffled a bit but held still. Ardwen stiffened. The queen grew dark.

"And, now, why would I distress my daughter, little man?"

But evidently Zeke was not in the mood to be intimidated. "You think that rape is a valid third test? You think to put her in such danger, just because you're angry at me? What the hell kind of mother are you?"

Suddenly Mab was not just on her feet but garbed, her white robe all but blinding, her hair unadorned and flowing. Beyond her, Ardwen scrambled to catch up. The oak tree trembled.

"I think you must explain, little man," the queen intoned, her emerald eyes flashing lightning.

Nuala took hold of Zeke's hand, claiming allegiance. She was so proud of her man, so heartsick at his pain.

"I don't have to explain a damn thing," he informed her mother. "You were the one to send that madness, the one who put your daughter at such risk just to prove a point. How could you even think to do it? Do you think I'd be a happier prisoner if I'd succeeded in raping the woman I love?"

Nuala's heart stopped. Her breath froze at Zeke's temerity. At the truth she never should have wanted to hear. Just the weight of those beautiful words opened a fissure in her heart.

"How *dare* you?" the queen trumpeted, startling clouds of birds into noisy flight. "You have the effrontery to suggest I would put my own *daughter* at risk? For *you?*"

Her wrath was terrible. Clouds covered the sun and the trees moaned in distress. Nuala knew that every fairy in the land had taken to trembling before that anger, not even knowing why.

She herself took a close look at her mother, at the surprising glint of distress betrayed in those regal eyes. *Goddess*, she thought, even more stunned. *She meant it. She really wouldn't hurt me. Even for the court.* Not since the day Mab had handed her the royal orb of succession had Nuala thought her mother sentimental. Her guidance had been hard, her lessons harder. But it seemed she really cared, after a fashion.

Mab turned to her, and Nuala saw a hint of injury. "You thought I did this?" she demanded, her voice low and urgent. "That I set this mortal against you?"

"What else?" Nuala had to ask. "Such thought would never cross his mind."

"You so swear."

"I know him, Mother." It was as simple as that. Finally.

That fast, the sun returned. The queen sat. The court crept back.

"Goddess," Mab breathed, stunned. "He really did do this thing?"

"No," Nuala said. "He could not. It is important you know."

Mab's frown was terrifying. "Are you sure…?"

Nuala scowled at her mother. "You think I would face you for a fantasy? Would you like to view my bruising, my lady? Or his? My guardians were efficient."

"Well, thank the goddess for that. You have my gratitude, Xender."

"I will attest, lady," the elf spoke, his voice calm. "The mortal was maddened. Yet he ran rather than hurt the lady Nuala. We captured him thus."

Mab considered Zeke closely. "Then you have my thanks as well, mortal. Can you explain?"

Zeke never had to open his mouth. Nuala saw it this time as he remembered it, every vivid, paralyzing moment, the sights and sounds and sensations that had filled his head to bursting. She held on more tightly to him, reminding him that this time he didn't face them alone. Then she turned to see the memories strike her mother like a blow.

The queen actually paled. "Goddess," she breathed.

"So that wasn't the third test?" Zeke asked.

The queen glared. "And wouldn't you be back picking at my hill with your little ax if it had been? I tested *you*, little man. Never Nuala. I have no need to test my daughter."

"Then who?" Zeke demanded. "Why?"

Nuala felt the dread creep back. The shadows slid closer, until the very air seemed heavy with portent. Even Mab looked suddenly uncertain.

"You woke to see these things in your head?"

"I didn't wake. I was dreaming."

A sick hush fell over the land. Mab froze, her eyes stricken, and suddenly Nuala saw what she should have seen right away. Certainly before she accused her own mother.

"They have no access here," Mab protested, her distress plain. "We are fortified."

"They need only one," Ardwen said, his voice hushed.

"No one," the queen insisted, "would commit such betrayal. It is inconceivable. Who would have the heart for it?"

"Inconceivable or not," Nuala said, the cold creeping up her spine, "it happened. A crime against this mortal who sought nothing but peace with us. At least set him free, Mother. Send him to safety."

She should never have said it. Zeke turned on her. "Safety?" he demanded. "From what?" He faced down Mab. "Is this the thing you were going to explain?"

"This is nothing more than an aberration," the queen pronounced. "An attack we swear was not of our making."

"Then whose?" he demanded.

The silence was absolute. No one wished to name the thing that had despoiled Zeke's dreams. Certainly not Nuala, who had been taught since her first memory to flinch from the very name.

"This we will discover," the queen promised, her threat terrible.

Zeke looked down at Nuala, and she knew what he would ask. She knew, too, that no matter the cost, it was her place to tell him.

"Nuala, explain it to me," he demanded, even though his voice was gentle. "I think I have the right."

"You do," she admitted as she girded herself. "It is the *Dubhlainn Sidhe*," she said, the very words sending a harsh wind across the glen. "They have the gift of dreams. Of controlling them, invading them. Despoiling them."

Zeke stared at her. "Do they incite violence?"

"Well, now, isn't it their special gift?" the queen snarled.

"They have no balance," Nuala said. "No feminine caution. Not since the loss of their stone. Their powers have gone dark."

"Have the seer come to me," the queen intoned, her light radiating silver. "And call for my daughter Sorcha. I would have my crown."

The indication of judgment. Around and behind her, Nuala felt the court gather in silence, their queen's call heard. Mab faced them all, blind to them. She had lifted her hands, turned them up as if to cup the sun in her palms. She turned her eyes inward, listening. And Nuala, still holding tight to Zeke's hand, waited in silence with her lover to discover how this terrible thing could have happened.

The *Dubhlainn Sidhe*. The Fairies of the Dark Sword, who should never have had access to this place, had somehow sown Zeke's dreams with malignancy. They had incited him to a violence that wasn't his own. And someone, one of Nuala's own court, had let them through to do it.

And now the queen, standing like a brightening beacon in the twilight glade, was searching for whoever that was. Her eyes half closed, her body swaying a bit, she searched the realm for betraying thoughts. For evidence of an unspeakable crime.

The wind stilled, the air held suspended. Not an insect moved as the queen swept her gaze over her province. As she sought sedition. Nuala stood before her, waiting should her mother call her to help, allowing herself the comfort of Zeke's hand while he yet kept with them. Waiting for Sorcha to return with their stones, with the talismans of their power. Waiting for the chance to protect Zeke if necessary.

Suddenly Mab's head came up. Her eyes lit with a terrible fire. "Orla!" she cried, and it reverberated through the trees, over the glen, until the land shuddered with it. "Orla!"

Nuala knew that her own mouth had dropped open. Oh, no. Surely not.

"Yes," Orla answered, appearing on silent feet. "I fought for what was mine."

The queen faced her daughter with the wrath of a monarch. "You imperiled my realm?"

"I did my best to ensure a secure throne. This mortal has no business here, and I tried to prove it. Who better to do it, I ask you? And I might have succeeded, if he'd not been so fainthearted."

"You'd see me violated, Orla?" Nuala demanded, stricken. She and her sister had never seen eye to eye, certainly, but she would never have thought Orla would visit this on her. Never.

Orla waved her concerns aside. "Oh, not really. Xender would have stopped it, all right. I simply meant that he should prove unworthy. Then wouldn't you and our mother finally have focused again on the realm?" She faced her mother. "And wouldn't you have seen that Nuala isn't fit for your throne?"

"As you are?" Mab asked, eyes narrowed.

Orla strode up to her queen, unbowed. "She doesn't want it. You know that. Sure, it's why you brought him here, to make certain. Well, I was helping, wasn't I? Just like when you demanded the first test of me."

"Faith, I never remember asking you to invite the enemy among us, now, Orla," the queen answered, her voice deceptively soft. "Did I?"

It was the first time Orla looked as if she might squirm. "It was nothing more than a dream possession. A quick visit and gone, I swear. We watched them leave, just to be sure."

"We?" Nuala asked.

"He has also been judged and will find banishment," the queen declared. "You're so sure they've gone, daughter?"

"Of course. I have that much power. There'll be no more problems," Orla promised, giving Zeke a look. "Especially if you rid us of this pestilent mortal."

But Orla was wrong. Nuala heard the commotion even as Orla was defending herself. Harried footsteps, raised voices, the tones desperate and afraid. Nuala turned in time to see her sister Sorcha running toward them, a troop of armed elves at her heels. In her hands rested the queen's crown, the glorious starlight diadem that lit the hall at night and bore the great Coilin Stone of power at its apex. The bloodred ruby that glowed like blood.

"Oh, dear goddess," Nuala breathed, blanching.

The stone…

"It's gone!" Sorcha sobbed. "The Coilin Stone has been stolen!"

Chapter 13

The queen literally flared scarlet with rage. "You sent them on their way, did you, Orla?"

But Orla was mute, her eyes riveted to the empty crown Sorcha bore before her. Nuala felt sick. Unbalanced. The stone that governed them, that gave them balance and unity, the stone that defined them. Gone. She didn't know what to do. She hung on to Zeke's hand, as if he could offer the balance she'd lost.

"What do we do?" Ardwen asked, his voice a hush.

"Yes, Orla," the queen echoed in a frightening voice. "What do we do?"

Nuala could feel the news spread like a plague over the land. Trees bent, and shadows collected. Even the small animals, usually safe in their burrows, fled the terror of this thing.

"I...I saw him," Orla protested, her voice thin and wavering. "Leave. He left. I swear it."

"You swear, do you?" the queen demanded. "On what? The Coilin Stone?" Orla flinched, but the queen did not stop. "Oh, but you cannot, my lovely daughter. Because you gave it away to our enemies, now, didn't you?"

"You don't know that," Orla protested.

"Of course I know that, you foolish, selfish girl." The queen shook her head, her hands out in frustration. "You might actually have made a queen. But you had not the patience to work for it, did you? You thought to trick your way to it. Well, Orla, whatever happens in my court this day, know one thing. Your tricks will serve you no more."

"What do you mean?" Orla demanded.

But the queen only glared, her wrath so fulminant that even Orla paled. "Call the guard," she told her minions. "Send our horses to search. He'll be gone, if he's any kind of thief, but we must look. And isn't it a grand thing we've already readied for battle? Otherwise Orla's little surprise could have caught us unprepared."

"You called me, my Queen." It was Kieran, looking impossibly young and guileless for the burden he carried.

The queen waved an agitated hand. "You have our blessings to gloat, young Kieran. Hasn't our own daughter brought us to disaster?"

"You know the way, lady," he said, his voice calm, his eyes so impossibly old in his half-grown body. "You've known it all along, I think."

Mab frowned at him. "You're so sure, are you?"

And Kieran grinned. "Good grief, no. But it's the best I can say right now. You must go on."

"Can you send the mortal home?" Nuala asked, as if the question weren't crowding her throat like acid.

"We have not the time, girl," her mother snapped.

"We must make the time," she insisted, her spine

creeping with cold. "Please, Mother. We have no right to further endanger him. Set him free. Send him to safety."

She should never have said it. Zeke turned on her. "Safety?" he demanded. "From what?" He faced down Mab. "Are you saying this is going to get worse?"

"After the third test, you'll know, mortal," the queen said. "And you haven't passed it yet."

"Then give the damn thing to me and let me help."

"A fine sentiment," she assured him. "But it's not something you can simply swing a big stick at, little man. This is faerie business."

"Watch me," he snapped.

Nuala tried to take hold of him, but he shook her off. "No," he insisted. "I'm not leaving you to face this alone. Whatever it is."

The queen settled herself as if donning her warrior robes. Nuala knew they were running out of time.

"Xender," the queen called out. "Report to my captain Tearsigh. Bear him this dread news."

"Aye, lady. It will be done."

"We must warn the land," Ardwen said, suddenly looking like the court senior he was. "We must prepare."

"Please, Kieran," Nuala pleaded. "Tell them the mortal should leave."

"Has he had the third test yet?" he asked.

"No!" she retorted, her control snapping. "It doesn't matter!"

Kieran looked regretful. "But it does, Lady Nuala.

Once the tasks have been set, they have to be completed or something bad happens."

She raised a disbelieving brow. "Something *bad?*"

He shrugged. "A rip in the fabric of time. Something like that."

Sometimes Nuala forgot that the seer really was only a nine-year-old boy.

"Quiet," the queen snapped. "Both of you. It is time to move. We'll deal with the mortal later." She squinted at Zeke, assessing. "Sure, won't you look grand in a set of elven armor, little man. Now, has someone had the sense to call for mine?"

"At the hall, lady," Ardwen assured her.

Mab rose to her feet, her face glowing and proud. Nuala had seen her mother in many moods. She had never seen her in command of the army. She beheld now what majesty a queen had to possess. What purpose and unyielding strength. And Nuala knew she had none of it. She would never be able to do this, to send her own into battle to die. To risk the ones she loved. And yet Mab stood tall and composed, her command complete, her glory the very beacon that would guide her people. And, with the goddess's grace, would lead them to victory.

"Let us go, then," she announced, and then turned a look on Nuala that made Nuala wonder just what her mother saw in her. It was an almost wistful smile that unsettled Nuala anew.

"I go to lead the horse troops," Nuala offered with a formal bow. "At the queen's pleasure."

Mab nodded.

"I guess I'll go with her," Zeke said.

They'd been about to move when Orla reminded them all that she was still there. "What about me, then?" she demanded.

Mab turned cold eyes on her daughter and actually sighed.

"You, is it? You'll stay here, of course. It would be unwise of me, sure, to let you loose among the enemy you brought to me."

"You don't know they'll come!"

"I was told they wouldn't steal more than the poor mortal's soul. Well, now, that was wrong, too, wasn't it?"

"You have to let me do something. Faith, lady, you can't afford not to! I am the *leannan sidhe!*"

"Ah, now, so you are. But I'm thinking it hasn't done you any good to be such a one. It's brought you a surfeit of arrogance, my girl, and no softness. So I'm thinking it's time you learned how to get on without tricks. Today you'll lead the great archers, who remain in the rear. And if we all make it through this day and you don't find yourself handing my archers over to the lad who's sporting my stone, it might be best for you to see what the world is like without the power of the *leannan sidhe.*"

Orla, if possible, grew paler. "You cannot!"

The queen's smile was terrible. "Ah, but I can. In fact, my little Orla, I did. After you serve a bit of time, I'll tell you what else must be done. Because if the stone has already left this realm, you're the one who'll be fetching it back."

Orla swayed on her feet. "In the land of the dark sword?"

"In the land of hell, if I say so. Now, go, before I lose what love I have for you."

Orla, foolish, covetous Orla, had the courage to stand tall before her mother. "I only did it to save the throne."

"That is why I haven't banished you, foolish girl. Now, go."

Orla turned, and Nuala saw the court that had gathered in their flowing, jewel-toned robes part for her. Not in honor but in condemnation, their shoulders turned against her. Orla disdained their judgment and stalked through them as if in royal procession.

Waiting still for the queen to move, Nuala realized that Sorcha yet stood beyond them, the starlight diadem in her hands, her beautiful face stricken. Ah, wouldn't Nuala take that burden from her? It was Sorcha who protected the stones, and yet she'd been unable to protect the most important of all.

"Mother…" Nuala said before thinking.

On the brink of departing, Mab looked back. Saw what Nuala had seen. Bent a bittersweet smile on her middle daughter. "Ah, now, my little Sorcha, there's small point in sporting an empty crown, now, is there? I think I'll be getting more use from a helmet this day."

Sorcha lifted grieving eyes to her mother, to her people. "I should have known."

"Indeed you should. But yours was not a malicious failure, child. It was the children distracted you again, wasn't it? Well, now, child, you also will bear respon-

sibility for the return of our fearsome Coilin. But do not
grieve. You were never meant to keep him safe this day,
I'm thinking. Don your armor and join your mother,
now."

Sorcha bowed her head to the queen, her huge blue
eyes glistening with heavy tears. Nuala thought her
own heart would break for her sister. No one carried her
burden more devotedly than Sorcha, child of Mab. But
her mother had said it true. The children held a more
precious place in Sorcha's heart. Now, though, Sorcha,
like the rest of them, would have to leave the children
behind in the *bean tighe's* secure embrace. It was time
to arm and march.

Nuala wanted to call her mother's attention again,
to beg once more for Zeke's safety away from the
concerns of Faerie. To send him back to the comfort
of his family, to the safe familiarity of his science and
his mountains. Anywhere but into the catastrophe that
loomed over her land.

Already she could see the light dim just a bit. The
power wane. Would the *Dubhlainn Sidhe* come, or
would they simply hoard their power, gathering it so that
it incubated in dark places and darker hearts? Male
power aligned with male ambitions, never leavened by
the softer science of women. Dear Goddess, what would
happen to them? To the world? Would there be storm
without sunlight? Power without patience? Would they
give in to their rage, and then inflict it on their world
and the other worlds so carefully guarded by the *Tua*
guardians?

The queen was right. The challenge must be made. But Nuala was afraid it was too late. And she was terrified that Zeke would suffer for it, that their unborn child would never see the beautiful glen where she was conceived. That the worlds of mortal and faerie would be forever sullied and sad, and her precious court and dear Kendalls sorrier for it.

Zeke would have felt like a fool if he hadn't seen the frantic preparations going on around him. He stood alongside Cadhla testing the weight of a three-foot war sword and wearing the damnedest suit he'd ever seen. Chain mail, for God's sake, complete even to the helmet that wasn't nearly as comfortable as his old dig hat. But light as air, this elven stuff. He guessed Frodo wasn't so deluded after all. Even the horse was so clad, his pale, pale gray even more indistinct within it, as if it were a cloaking device.

Around them, all the horses had gathered, to be met each and every one by an armored fairy. Flying fairies hovered in agitated clouds, and herds of metal-working gnomes clattered and jangled over armor and armaments. Armies marched and rode and flew, dispersing over the valley of the gates. Carrowmore burial field. Appropriate, Zeke guessed. After all, what better place to have a war than over a burial field, even if it wasn't really just a burial field but a sea of inter-dimensional gates?

At the head of each army, foot, horse and archer, rode the daughters of Mab. Each in glittering mail, each adorned with her stones of power. Zeke couldn't take his eyes off Nuala. His soft, sweet, comforting Nuala looked like the embodiment of Joan of Arc, perched on her magnificent fairy stallion, her standard raised high, the troops behind her focused on her to lead. How could he not love her more? He knew she hated this. He knew she wanted nothing more than to tuck herself into the folds of the glen and celebrate the seasons of the earth. She didn't want to fight, couldn't want to lead her troops to their death. And yet, fire-haired and silver-mantled, she rode before them, resolute and calm. The eye of the army's hurricane.

As were Sorcha before the foot and Orla before the archers. Princesses of the realm in every way. And at their head, the incandescent radiance of the queen. The single focus of all eyes. The inspiration and cynosure of every living being in the realm.

He never would have believed it if he hadn't seen it. If he hadn't stood by his horse itching to get in the saddle and ride. Zeke had never been in an army. He'd been a scientist, not a warrior. And yet he felt inexplicably tied to this field of proud beings, anxious to honor them, exhilarated to be part of them. Terrified to let them down. He shifted next to Cadhla and waited as the troops were called to march.

"Patience, Muuyaw," Cadhla cautioned. "There will soon be carnage enough for all."

"Have you done this before?" Zeke asked, his attention still on his arrow-straight Nuala, her hair a flaming beacon in the mist.

"There have been no wars in my lifetime. It has been many lives since the fairy clans fought."

"And you think they'll fight today?"

"I think we must all prepare for it." The horse shook out his mane, his mail setting up a sweet glissando that should have had no place on the field of battle.

"Who knows?" Zeke mused. "Perhaps the elves have caught the culprit."

That got an equine snort. "Doubtful. It is said that it was Liam the Protector himself who came."

Zeke scowled. "This is the guy who...?"

"Infected your dreams? Aye, Muuyaw. It is so."

"Then I'd be grateful if you'd point him out to me when the time comes."

The horse shook his head. "I doubt it will be that simple."

"Why?"

He got only another head shake. He didn't really notice, though. Nuala had turned in her saddle to scan the cavalry behind her. She said not a word, yet a rustling set up in the ranks. Horse to horse and rider to rider.

"She seeks you, Muuyaw," Cadhla said. "Mount, and we shall advance."

Sounding much like a demented glockenspiel, Zeke sheathed the sword, vaulted into the high-cantled war saddle and turned Cadhla toward the front. Naula caught sight of him the minute he did, and Zeke couldn't help but smile at the relief in her eyes. Did she really want him up there? An anthropologist? He didn't quite know how to tell her that the only thing he'd led in his life had been a dig. He doubted armies were quite the same.

"She needs your strong arm," his horse told him as if answering. "Do not fail her."

Zeke was surprised to see the ranks of cavalry part to let him through, each bowing in a kind of salute that would have been inconceivable only a few days ago.

Days? Had it only been days? He was beginning to feel as if he'd belonged here all along. That Jake and Gen and Lee were the dream, not this insubstantial phantasm of a place.

And yet Nuala wasn't insubstantial. She was no phantom, fading into the twilight. She was fire and earth, as elemental as air. She turned as he approached, and he saw the need she barely allowed to escape into those spring green eyes of her.

"So," he said so quietly the others couldn't hear. "I hear we're about to throw a party."

She flashed a brief smile. "You must attend some strange functions."

Zeke saw her lift her free hand, clad in bronze leather, and then let it drop again to her thigh. Reaching out to him, but not allowed to show such weakness before her people.

"Can I help?" he asked.

Her eyes were eloquent. "I'm sorry, Zeke. I shouldn't be wanting this. I should command you to retire from the field, where you'll be safe."

"But you won't?"

She looked so regretful. "Will you ride with me?"

It was better than a declaration of love. Zeke gave her his very best, brightest smile. "I thought you'd never ask."

He saw her battle an answering grin. "But after this, you're going home. You hear me?"

"Only if I pass the third test."

"If this isn't test enough for herself, then she doesn't deserve the right to set them. Now, come."

With no more than a look over her shoulder, Nuala kept her troops in place as she advanced on her mother. On the other side, her sisters joined her, and behind them the senior court, all arrayed in battle mail and bright colors and snapping pennants. No one would ever accuse the fairies of meeting battle with faint hearts, Zeke thought, his own beginning to pick up speed.

"Where's Kieran?" he asked Nuala as they trotted side by side.

Again she was betrayed by a grin. "Back with the children. He is not pleased, I can tell you. But who would risk losing the seer?"

"I bet he didn't agree."

"Maybe he needs a mortal man to show him the wisdom of our course without bruising his pride."

"I'm sure there's some kind of basketball analogy I could come up with."

Nuala smiled over at him and lifted a hand of command. With a curiously musical dissonance, the ranks of cavalry came to a halt. Zeke looked across the valley, almost expecting to see an answering army. It was quiet, though. The cairns gleamed in the gathering light, and shadows crept across the ground from the dolmens. The grass shuddered with an unseen wind, and clouds chased across a perfect azure sky. What was the Lakota saying? *Hota hey.* It was a good day to die.

Then, in a second, it all began to go wrong. At first it was just whispers, faint voices that made him turn to see nothing. A feeling of dread snaking its way along his spine, as if something he couldn't see were creeping up on them. Something he could sense in every nerve ending in his body.

He looked around, but nobody else seemed to be reacting. Nuala was scanning the horizon; he thought she might be assessing the field. She didn't seem to notice that a fetid wind was rising, that there were voices in it, voices he suddenly recognized. Moans of anguish, cries of despair.

"Nuala," he warned, peering into the valley. "It's them."

She turned to him, followed his focus, swept the vista with keen eyes. "I see nothing."

"I hear it," he insisted. "The voices from my dreams. The rage. The need to avenge. They're in that cloud."

The cloud he could suddenly see skim the far edge of the landscape. Zeke felt its approach like a red tide crawling along his skin. He smelled it, brimstone in the air, and he wanted to yell out, *There, can't you see it? Am I the only one who recognizes it?*

And yet no one else moved. No one heard. No one saw the deep shade that already dimmed the sun. In an instant he recognized that his dream had given him an edge. He recognized what none of them had experienced in their lifetimes, the voice of the *Dubhlainn Sidhe*.

He couldn't hold. He couldn't wait. Suddenly he knew without question what was going to happen, and he knew that no one else would react in time.

"Nuala!" he yelled, spurring Cadhla to action. "The queen!"

All he would remember later were his cries and the brief astonishment in Nuala's eyes before she, too, kicked her horse into flight, the blank hesitation of all around him as he drew his sword and sent his horse straight for the queen. Kneed Cadhla along a line to intercept that shadow. That threat.

Nobody saw it. Nobody but him. But now, there was Nuala, crying out like a warrior as she raised her glowing red sword. As he swung his own sword like a berserker. He heard Cadhla trumpet his challenge, felt the pounding of the horse's hooves upon the earth. Saw the queen begin to turn. Saw the shadow gather, heard the war horns finally call out, echoing again and again across the plane. Inciting the sudden, deafening roar of the fairy army.

They wouldn't be in time. Nuala was before him, between him and the queen. The perfect target for the enemy, because Zeke knew them, recognized their voices. He heard them in his head where those terrible dreams still lingered, and his fury was roused.

He couldn't allow them to hurt Nuala. They would not be allowed to kill the queen. If they killed the queen, then

all would be lost, but they would steal her. He didn't know
how or why he knew this, but he did. And he couldn't let
Nuala's world vanish before such a wave of malevolence.

"Xender!" he cried out. "To your princess!"

And even in that chain mail, wielding a sword he'd
never lifted in his life, Zeke was able to outpace Nuala,
to swing around her, using only his knees to guide the
courageous Cadhla, and he thought in passing that it
was a wonderful thing he'd been trained on cutting
horses, because nothing was as close to a war horse in
the world, taking direction from knee and instinct and
a hunger for action. And then they were there, cutting
Nuala off from the enemy, where she would be safe,
bearing down on the queen, who had lifted her eyes to
the still unseen force. The force that balked of destroying Nuala, now sought only her.

"*Hota hey!*" Zeke howled into the face of the enemy.

And then, not even thinking about what he was
doing, he scrambled right up on Cadhla's back,
balanced on his feet and, in the last seconds before the
enemy swept over the queen, launched himself from the
saddle and knocked her right to the ground.

The enemy hit him with the force of a cannon, a tidal
wave pummeling him into the earth, prying at him to
get to the queen, who he had wrapped completely in his
arms, just as Xender had protected Nuala and others
had shielded Sorcha and Orla. The attack was only on
them, the women of fairy power, but it wouldn't
succeed. As Zeke protected, others fought. He heard the
terrible clash of swords, the cries of rage and frustra-

tion and pain, the thundering of horses and the whistle of arrows. Ah, for one good howitzer, he thought, just before whatever was attacking him landed a stunning blow to his head. Ah, for a tank.

Trumpets blared, but they blurred in his head. The ground trembled with the force of attack, with the screams and yells and curses of the combatants, but Zeke was suddenly having trouble discerning them. He thought, through the din, he could hear Nuala's voice, and it was screaming his name, but he couldn't look. He couldn't lose focus for a second or Nuala's world would be lost. He hoped she understood. He thought the queen told him she would, but it was indistinct amid the cacophony of war.

And then, to seal the deal, he was hit again, the same place on the side of his head that had taken the brunt of his fall when he tumbled down that hill, when he fell, just as he was falling now, down into the darkness where a beautiful girl with a magical smile lived.

"Ze-e-e-e-e-e-ke!"

There it was again. Her voice. He would find her when he woke, he thought, still clutching tightly to the queen. He would hold her and cherish her and walk the twilight with her.

When he woke.

But when he woke, Nuala wasn't there.

"Oh, my God! Zeke!"

His sister Gen was.

Chapter 14

He blinked. Then he blinked again, trying like hell to clear the chaos from his brain. Where was the noise? The panic, the ferocity, the smell of horses and upturned earth and anger?

"Where's Nuala?"

But Gen had left his side and didn't answer. He was lying on his back, Zeke realized, weighted down and worthless, his vision filled with electronics and his ears filled with the dissonance not of chain mail and battle cries but chirping alarms. Every ounce of him ached as if he'd been run over by a truck, and his head felt like a pumpkin that had been tossed from a roof. And there was no homely *bean tighe* to heal him this time. There were white-coated medicos with Irish faces and astonished smiles. No fairy clothes and hobbit houses but IVs and curtains and clean white walls. From his experience with his pediatrician sister, his best guess was that he was in an ICU.

His first instinct was to jump up and get back to the battle. His second was to cringe from the pain of trying. He ached in every cell of his body, and he could still feel that pummeling he'd been taking. It must have been bad, because his limbs felt leaden and useless. The rest of him was trembling with weakness, as solid as a deflated water balloon. It made him sympathize with the Scarecrow from the *Wizard of Oz*. Zeke suddenly had the feeling he knew what it was like to have your stuffing ripped out by flying monkeys.

He tried turning his head, only to have it explode out one side. "Ohhhff," he groaned, closing his eyes against the suddenly too-bright lights. "That last guy must have been wearing roach stompers."

"Last guy?"

Zeke's eyes flew open at the sound of *that* voice. His heart all but stopped. Jake. Leaning over the bed, looking like a man who'd just survived a month's trek across the desert, his face bristly, his eyes red-rimmed and drawn, his hair tangled and a good two days past the need for washing. He seemed to be having trouble keeping his hands still, but he was smiling. The same smile Zeke had seen on Gen. As if he were witnessing a miracle.

"Where's your hat?" was the only thing Zeke could think of to say.

It took a lot, after all, to get Jake out of his flat-crowned cowboy hat. It was his signature. It was also his camouflage. Jake could hide a lot of anger and terror and joy beneath the brim of that hat. Zeke felt naked himself to see all those emotions right out there on his big brother's square-jawed face. He wanted to hide from the pain he'd etched on those hard planes.

"My hat," Jake said, reaching one hard, work-rough-ened hand out, as if he couldn't help it, and laying it on Zeke's sore shoulder, "is at the B&B. We're staying with Mrs. O'Brien."

"I hope she hasn't poor-me-ed you guys out of breakfast."

Zeke huffed a surprised laugh. "No. Your friend Colm forewarned us." That quickly, he lost his smile. "We...uh, we didn't expect you back, Zeke."

And Zeke, still trying to assimilate his precipitous change of surroundings, realized that he was at once profoundly glad to see his family and crushingly dis-traught by finding himself back. "Nuala wouldn't let me stay," he admitted, hating the sound of tears in his voice.

"Nuala?" Jake shook his head. "I'm afraid you're confused."

"Not a huge surprise," Gen piped in from where she'd come up behind Jake, her hazel eyes brisk with pragmatic good sense. "We had a pretty active hospital pool going on when you'd wake up."

"*If* you'd wake up," his little sister Lee added from behind Gen, her features stricken. Now *her* features were elfin. Blonde, bright-eyed and pixie fair. Not those guys in armor who looked like linebackers from the 49ers. "You really feel all right?" she asked, patting Zeke's hand where it lay uselessly on the bed.

"I'm fine," he assured them. "Except where the *Dubhlainn Sidhe* place-kicker drop-kicked my head, I'll be up and around in no time. Thank God for chain mail, huh?"

He saw somebody at his periphery—one of the staff, maybe—turn suddenly at his words. Probably not any happier to hear about the *Dubhlainn Sidhe* than Nuala had been, he thought, which brought him right back to where he'd been before. How could he get back to Nuala and her world? Why had they sent him away? God, he hoped they'd succeeded. That the queen was safe and they were on their way to restoring the balance. That Xender had kept his oath to protect Nuala. He closed his eyes just a moment at the exquisite pain of not knowing. Not hearing whether she was alright. He hated it that he hadn't been able to stay and help.

How, he wondered, had they sent him back? Why? And why hadn't Nuala at least taken the time to tell him goodbye?

He could only think of one reason, and he decided that he simply wasn't going to consider that.

"Zeke?" Gen leaned closer, lifting one eyelid, then the other. Gen never could resist checking reflexes.

"You're a pediatrician, Gen," Zeke drawled. "Don't pretend you know what you're doing."

"A pupil's a pupil," she assured him. "And yours have been doing some pretty spectacular things. I wanted to make sure they were finished."

"I'd lay five to one she's checked on him more than the staff," Jake offered dryly.

"Don't be silly," Lee retorted with a quick, bright grin. "Nobody takes a sure bet in this family. The staff even gave Gen her own coffee mug in the doctors' lounge."

"Hey, you've hit the big time now, Gen," Zeke taunted his older sister. "You might want to quit your fancy job at home and take your show on the road."

Just as Zeke knew she would, Gen scowled. "Thanks, but no. The fame isn't worth all that jet lag."

Zeke smiled, comforted by the family banter. It was better than worrying about Nuala. Better than seeing Jake standing there at the periphery, as if it was just too painful to come closer.

"When did I show up?" Zeke asked.

The three siblings exchanged looks. "You, uh, fell four days ago," Gen said, evidently claiming the post of family spokesperson. "Since then you've been right here...well, when you haven't been in surgery."

Okay, that he hadn't expected. "Surgery?"

"Everything's okay now," she assured him with a too-bright smile and a pat on his arm, the kind he remembered all too well from his own stint walking ICU waiting rooms the time his sister Lee had been almost fatally injured. "Especially now that you're awake."

Not the question he'd asked. "But I had surgery."

She shrugged. The rest looked even more uncomfortable. "Well, you hit your head pretty hard tumbling down that hill. "They had to go in and relieve the pressure. You're... well, you're kind of bald."

He'd been there for four days? Who were they kidding? He hadn't even been in the same time and space continuum.

"When did I have this surgery?"

"The first day. You scared the snot out of us, Zeke. Now we just need to know that you didn't suffer any damage."

"You mean, like, do I like Jell-o? No. I still don't. But you're wrong, ya know. I haven't been here all along."

Another series of looks were exchanged. Evidently a decision was made to placate him. "Well, fine," Gen said in her best professional voice. "You can tell us all about it after you get a little more rest. For now, I need to get Jake back for a shower. He's beginning to offend the staff."

Lee's grin was a bit giddy. "Ten bucks says he falls asleep first."

Zeke couldn't help it. "Gimme a little of that action."

Nothing said Kendall like an active betting pool.

His siblings patted him again, as if reassuring themselves that he was there. They had no idea. If it were up to him, he wouldn't be. At least until he knew what had happened back on that field of battle. Until he said a proper goodbye to the next queen of the fairies, the kind that would keep him for the rest of his life and go down in the annals of legend. But when he gauged the expressions on his siblings' faces, he knew that was something he couldn't share. Not yet. Not until he understood better what had just happened.

Not until his head stopped hurting.

Gen bent and kissed his forehead, and then Lee. Zeke thought to reach up and pat them back, but his arm was just too heavy. So he smiled and watched as they turned for the door, Jake behind them. Zeke thought he would try to sleep, but suddenly the sight of his family disappearing through the door panicked him.

"Jake?"

Jake stopped. He must have seen the anxiety in Zeke's eyes, because he waved everybody off. "Go on down. I'll catch up."

Gen scowled. "Jake, your own children refused to hug you this morning."

Zeke knew what she meant was that Jake needed to sleep before he collapsed. He should have waved his brother on to his rest, but he couldn't. Not just yet. There was something he really needed to know first.

"It'll only take a minute," he told his sister.

"Well, what's so important?" Gen demanded.

Zeke did his best to grin. "Guy stuff."

The girls snorted, sounding much like Cadhla in high dudgeon, and walked on out the door. Jake returned to lean a callused hand on the bed rail.

"What's up?" he asked.

But Zeke didn't know how to ask. What should he say? *Have you been dreaming of a beautiful woman who was trying to suck out your soul? Are you as afraid to close your eyes as I am?*

"I'm sorry" was what he could say. "Jake, I'm so sorry."

But Jake didn't understand what Zeke meant. "For what?" he asked, looking so exhausted that Zeke couldn't believe he was still upright. "Finally taking your turn in an ICU? It was only a matter of time, after all. I'm just surprised it took you so long."

Zeke tried to suck in a breath for courage. He had to know. "Have you been having any...uh, dreams? Nightmares?"

"Nightmares?" Jake asked.

Zeke held his breath, completely unsure of what he wanted his brother to say. But when Jake grinned, he knew Jake was still blissfully and thankfully oblivious.

"Yeah, I have nightmares. The three of you. And my three kids. I got lots of nightmares."

Which meant that whatever else had happened, the *Dubhlainn Sidhe* had not crossed worlds to torment his brother. Which also meant that it was going to be even harder to convince his brother of what had happened— what *was* happening—in that other world inhabited by the kinds of beings Jake Kendall simply wouldn't recognize.

Jake Kendall was a rancher. He still lived on the land where he'd been born, drove a battered pick-up truck and ate every Saturday at the town diner, ordering the same meal for the last twenty years. Jake Kendall's first and only flight of fancy had been marrying his beautiful wife Amanda. If Zeke had had trouble believing in fairies, the idea would give Jake a stroke.

Amanda. Zeke would tell Amanda. Let her tell Jake. Amanda believed in fairies, after all. She wrote about them. She'd written that book that claimed his great-great-grandma had been a witchy woman.

But for now there was nothing Zeke could do to make Jake understand. His own brain felt like sludge, and his brother smelled like a locker room. So he

dredged up a semblance of a smile so he could send him
off to rest.

"Yeah, fine. Thanks." It was an effort, but he waved a
hand in Jake's direction. "Go get a shower before the staff
just turns a fire hose on you. I'll see you in the morning."

"It *is* the morning."

"Then this afternoon. And, Jake?"

Jake held. Zeke exchanged one of those male
moments, when there was so much to say you simply
couldn't say it. "Thanks for being here."

Jake's smile was wry. "Amanda would have cut out
my liver with a kitchen knife if I hadn't come."

He smiled, and Zeke smiled back, their comfort recovered. It was enough for Zeke to let his brother out the
door.

Waiting until Jake was gone, one of the nurses, a
beautiful young woman with near-black hair, sassy blue
eyes and a name tag that read Maureen came over to
check Zeke's status.

"Well, now, isn't it grand you've decided to attend
the party?" she greeted him. "From what I've been
hearing, sure, you're the life of it."

At any other moment in his life, Zeke would have
risen to her flirting like a like a large-mouth bass to a
spinning lure. She was everything he liked: smart and
pretty and interested. She was even gentle enough that
she didn't set up a clamor of pain in his head. Rolling
him one way and then the other, she changed the bed
beneath him as if he were an infant. She checked
monitors and cuffs and IV lines, and something that

seemed to be taped to his head. And all the while, she hummed a familiar tune in a sweet voice.

A tune Zeke had just heard the night before.

"Where'd you hear that?" he demanded.

She smiled down at him. "Hear it? Everywhere. It's an old Irish air my da plays on the fiddle."

"But I just heard it...."

That got a musical chuckle out of her. "Of course you did," she assured him. "Haven't I been hummin' it around here ever since you came? It's a favorite of mine. 'May Morning Dew'. Pretty, isn't it?"

She had no idea. Especially if heard on a fairy harp. Zeke closed his eyes against fresh grief.

"You all right, then, Mr. Kendall?" she asked.

"Fine." Disoriented. Frustrated. Furious. "Just tired."

"And why shouldn't you be? Even sleeping through the festivities, you could still use more."

"Festivities?"

She grinned and pointed to where what looked like a turnip sat on the station desk with a face carved in it. "Sure, wasn't last night Halloween? I don't suppose you were conversin' with the dead, now, were you? It would have been the day to do it."

"No," he said, unable to look away from the grimacing vegetable. "But I rode with the queen of the fairies. Does that count?"

Maureen laughed, obviously delighted at Zeke's sense of humor. "Ah well, that would have been enough to exhaust you, right enough. Go ahead and rest up now. We won't be bothering you for a while."

And then she patted him on the shoulder, too. Did everybody have to do that? he wondered irritably. As if he were a six-year-old who'd just lost his way in a mall?

Maybe he was, after all. God knew he felt lost. He felt abandoned and betrayed, and he had no earthly idea how to go about doing something about it. He was reduced to lying like a lump of protoplasm while other people took care of his most basic needs. A far cry from a sword-wielding berserker. A farther cry from the man who'd made Nuala, daughter of Mab, scream out in ecstasy.

He couldn't believe it. He was fighting tears. He hadn't even cried when his mother died. He'd walked through those harsh days dry-eyed and cold, more intent on being Lee's big brother than Mary Rose's son. He'd made it through those days and all the days after without once breaking down. But now, trapped in the hushed chaos of a hospital, more alone than at any time he could ever remember in his life, he fought the ache that crowded the back of his throat. He squeezed his eyes shut, furious that he could be so weak. Frightened that it could actually come to this.

She was gone.

He'd wasted so much of his time with her, when he'd known he would have to leave. He'd taken everything she'd offered him without giving back the one gift he actually could offer a fairy princess. He hadn't told her that he loved her, that he would take that love with him wherever he went, to warm those empty cold nights out under a desert moon, to soothe those moments when he thought no one else in the world understood him. He would take her with him in his heart when he joined his family in their celebrations and claimed none of his own.

If only he could, he would go back and hand her his gift like a silver-wrapped package. And then he would stay to soak in the sight of her reaction. He would sate himself on her, just once more, to hold him for the rest of his life.

Because she was gone. And he had to go on. Alone.

Maureen was as good as her word. She left Zeke alone for quite a long time. Long enough for her to return to find him asleep, his cheeks streaked with dried tears.

Zeke didn't dream. He didn't revisit the glens and hills of the world of Faerie, or visualize Nuala as she sat astride her war horse preparing for battle. He didn't suffer instruction from Sorcha or Mab herself on what he needed to know. He lay completely insensate for hours, his battered body healing as his family tiptoed in and out of his room to make sure he didn't slip away again. And then, from one breath to another, he woke knowing what he should have realized before.

"It's the third test," he said, startling Lee where she sat next to his bed, reading.

"What?"

He thought he felt better. More substantial, as if somebody had stuffed some of his straw back into him while he slept. He felt more aware, more discerning.

Obviously a few more synapses were firing in his battered gray matter.

Or he'd just had enough time to figure out the obvious.

"I thought Mab had just sent me back," he said, rubbing at the lingering ache in his forehead. "But she didn't. She meant this to be my third test."

Lee wasn't keeping up. "Third test?"

Zeke wanted to laugh, but he figured it would hurt too much. So he smiled. He knew now. He was going to get another chance to see Nuala. Neither she nor Mab was finished with him yet.

"Don't you see?" he demanded, blithely unaware that Lee had no idea what he was talking about. "I imagined the third test would be something about sex. God knows I thought the other two were. But they were really about how much I knew Nuala. How much I cared for her. I needed to want only her, be true to her. The third test is for me to believe in her. And if I'm right—which I know I am—then when I've proven I love her enough to never hesitate in trusting her, then I'll at least get to say goodbye."

"To whom?"

Zeke gingerly turned his head. "To Nuala, of course."

But Lee was blinking, as if he were speaking a foreign language. "Zeke?"

"Uh huh?"

"Who's Nuala?"

Which was when Zeke remembered that Lee had no

idea what he'd been through. And he had no idea how
to tell her. For a very long time, he simply stared at her,
overloading his poor battered brain all over again.

"It's a long story, Lee."

She grinned. "I bet it is. Is she a stewardess or an ar-
cheologist? Did you meet her here or at home?"

"I met her…I met her at her mother's house.
She's…" He was surprised by the ache of more tears.
How did he tell Lee what Nuala was? She was his soul,
his laughter, his magic. She was Grace Kelly in *The
Swan*, Audrey Hepburn in *Roman Holiday*. Whimsical
and regal and seductive as an Irish air on a fairy harp.

"Good God, she *must* be something," Lee blurted
out. "You're all poetic."

For a second Zeke thought maybe she'd picked up
that annoying habit of mind reading that fairies excelled
at, but then he realized he must have spoken aloud.
And Lee deserved an answer. Before the last few days,
he would have blustered and protested and pretended
to be joking. He couldn't do that now. It would be an
insult, to him and to Nuala.

"She *is* something," he told his little sister. "She's the
woman I love."

As simply said as that. As basic.

And he'd been too afraid to tell her. God, he hoped
he had the steadfastness to pass this third test so he
could at least rectify that mistake. So they could have
that to bind them between worlds when they lost the
sight and sound of each other.

"I don't suppose she has red hair, does she?" Lee asked, absolutely delighted.

"Yeah. She does."

Lee clapped. "Wait 'til I tell Gen," she chortled. "You owe her fifty bucks, ya know. She said you'd be bringing home a red-headed Irish lass within six months."

Zeke battled the ache of loss and smiled for his sister. "I won't be bringing her home," he said, costing Lee her smile.

"What do you mean?"

He shrugged, and it hurt. "She, uh, she can't marry me."

Lee frowned. "Is she already married?"

How to explain it? How to open his mouth without weeping again? "Let's just say she has a responsibility I can't be part of."

Lee looked as if she was about to protest again. It made Zeke smile. Little Lee, who had suffered as much as any of them, had strode through her life with a defiant joy that had helped buoy them all. She had dosed her handsome husband with it, literally saving his life in the process. She had brought it to her work as an actress and playright. No matter what tragedies Lee performed on stage in Chicago, she simply refused to believe that she couldn't make everything turn out all right. And Zeke just couldn't explain why this time she would fail.

So he reached through the railings and took her hand. "It's all right," he told her, feeling a tear slide

down into his hair. "I had her for a while. I can remember her."

And Lee, unused to seeing her big brother cry,
reached over the bed and just held him.

"I'm sorry," she told him. "Oh, Zeke, I'm so sorry."

He shook his head. "I'm not."

And he found that whatever happened, he wasn't. He
would grieve, and he would go on. He might marry
someday, find a woman who could be his friend and his
lover. But he knew he would never have another
soulmate. A man only got one chance for that kind of
luck.

"Besides," he said, trying hard to make light of the
anguish that thought brought, "if I just believe, like
with Tinkerbell, she'll be able to come say goodbye."

"That's it?" Lee demanded, backing up. "You're just
going to leave her?"

"Well," he mused, more to himself, "I do know
somebody who knows her. I can keep track through him."

"Another anthropologist?"

"A nine-year-old basketball fan."

"Zeke," Lee protested. "You're not making sense."

Which finally made him laugh. "Oh, Lee, you have
no idea."

"No idea about what?" Jake asked, stepping into the
room.

Lee lifted tear-blurred eyes to their big brother.
"Zeke's in love, but he can't marry her."

Jake prided himself on never showing a reaction. He
gave away his surprise by stumbling. "I'm sorry?"

"Her name's Nuala," Lee told him. "He met her at her mother's, and he loves her. But they can't stay together."

"Why not?"

Oh, what the hell? He would have to tell them sooner or later. "Because she's a fairy and I'm not."

Zeke realized that slack-jawed was a very descriptive term. Lee was stunned. Jake looked like he'd been slapped in the face with a wet fish.

"Pardon?"

"More to the point, she's a fairy princess who will rule when Mab, Queen of Fairies, goes away to the Land of the West. She has to stay, and I had to come home. To the warm bosom of my family."

Jake didn't even look over to Lee for her reaction. "Uh huh," he said, slipping his hands into his jeans pockets. His personal ritual of governing. Whenever Jake was about to gather the information he needed to make his decisions, he slid his hands into his jeans pockets. "And you met her when?"

Zeke flashed a bright grin that belied the dread that curled in his belly. "When I fell down the cairn and was kidnapped by the Queen of Fairies." He looked over to Lee. "That's her mother. Nuala's mother, that is."

Lee's eyes were the size of dinner plates. "Oh."

Zeke had the overwhelming urge to laugh. God, the look on Jake's face.

"The Queen of the Fairies," his brother said, his voice flat.

Zeke managed a limited nod. "Mab. She's also called

Maeve. Quite a gal. Horny as a hoot owl, as Amanda would say. Matter of fact, all the fairies are. Horny, that is. Quite a randy lot. But they throw great parties."

Jake looked like he wanted to test Zeke's forehead for fever. "Zeke…"

Lee had gone from sympathetic to furious. Wearing a scowl the size of Utah, she slammed her hands on her hips, her traditional position of judgment. "Zeke Kendall, how dare you? I was really feeling sorry for you. And then you pull this stunt."

Zeke lost his smile. "It's no stunt, squirt. I'm serious."

Jake actually sat down, as if his legs had just given way. He didn't say another word. Just watched Zeke. Zeke wanted to laugh again. He wasn't even sure why. He wasn't doing himself any good telling his big brother about Mab and Nuala, he knew. In fact, if he knew his brother at all—and oh, he did—there would probably be a psychiatric evaluation in his near future.

But he had to tell somebody. He had to paint Nuala's picture here in the mortal world so she stayed alive to him. So her colors held strong and vibrant. He needed the people he loved the most to know about her. To believe in her as much as he did.

They didn't.

"Is Amanda with you?" he asked Jake. "She'd understand."

Amanda, who collected folktales and turned them into award-winning fiction. Amanda believed in fairies.

At least until her brother-in-law claimed to have been kidnapped by one.

"Now, Zeke," she soothed, patting him. He was getting damned tired of the patting. "This has been a traumatic experience. And naturally, you might, well, have assimilated some of the more fanciful stories of your environment when you were unconscious. To help explain what had happened. It's how folklore starts, of course. An attempt to define the natural world in a way that gives us at least some illusion of control over it."

Zeke had moved past impatient a while ago. He was heading into frustration. In a minute he would step right into panic. She had to believe him. *Somebody* did.

Zeke glared at his collected family. "Amanda, have you ever seen me read a folktale? Ever heard me wax rhapsodic about elves and gnomes, or so much as dress up as Captain Kirk for Halloween? Hell, I didn't even read *Lord of the Rings*. I'm not making this up."

"Of course not," she assured him. "I believe that you believe it."

She made a move as if to pat him again. The glare on his face evidently pulled her up short.

It wasn't going to work. He wasn't going to get through even to the people he should have been able to count on.

"Never mind," he sighed, turning away.

"You'll feel so much better when we get you home," Lee assured him, looking pinched and unhappy.

"I'm not going home."

Silence.

"Of course you are," Jake said. "As soon as we get the clearance from the doctors. They think in a week or so. Maria's getting your old room ready so you can rehab at the ranch."

"Fine. Make my reservations," Zeke agreed, knowing he didn't look the least agreeable. "As soon as I say goodbye to Nuala."

Jake was beginning to look ferocious. "Don't be an ass."

For once in his life, Zeke refused to back down to his big brother. "I leave after I see her. Not a minute before."

Lee looked like she was going to cry. "Zeke..."

He glared. "I'm waiting. This is my third test, and I'm not failing it. I don't care what you say."

He waited.

The psychologist did come to see him. He listened with calm gravitas as Zeke related the whole story of how he'd fallen down the queen's cairn and into the lap of a fairy princess. Of how the factions were warring, how Nuala had been about to assume the throne, how she'd sent him back for his own good. Zeke saw the man write "possible fugue state or delusional disorder" in his notes and didn't care. As long as he faithfully wrote down the account of Zeke's story.

Zeke graduated from flat on his back in the ICU to sitting in a big, uncomfortable arm chair on the floor. Outside his window, he could see the hills beyond the rooftops of Sligo. In the distance, Maeve looked down on him from her perch atop Knock-narea. If he squinted his eyes, he could almost believe

he saw the fairy horde march. He recounted his ad-
ventures to himself and mapped the memory of
Nuala's body in his head.

And he waited.

Rain moved in outside and blotted out the mountain.
Colm came to visit with his unlit pipe clenched in his
teeth and a slice of soda bread smuggled in from Mrs.
O'Brien. Zeke told him his story to find that Colm wasn't
any more comfortable with it than his own family.

Zeke took physical therapy to strengthen his left arm
and leg, which were still weakened, and sat with the
nurses in the lounge drinking strong tea.

And he waited.

Jake began preparations to take everybody home.
The doctors told him that Zeke could be transferred to
private rehab in the U.S., and the hospital helped Jake
make arrangements. Zeke reiterated the fact that no
matter what, he wouldn't go until he saw Nuala.

He knew he had to leave her. He had to live without
her for the rest of his life. But he wasn't going to do it
until she said goodbye to him. He had to trust that she
would. Because if he didn't, there would be nothing else
to believe in. Not what had happened, not her, not what
they'd felt for each other.

And he flat out refused to doubt that.

"Zeke, I'm running out of patience," Jake said one
morning as the two of them sat in a glass atrium. The
weather was gray and grim again, the rain pouring
down the vaulted glass ceilings. "Unless you can

knock me down, you have no say in the matter. You're coming home."

Feeling weary again, Zeke faced his brother head on. "No."

Jake sighed, raked a hand through his hair. He still hadn't worn his hat. "We can sedate you to get you on that plane."

"You do that and I'll never forgive you, Jake. I mean it."

"Zeke, please. You have to know that you dreamed it all up. The brain is an amazing thing. Yours can create entire worlds. It just happened to do that when you were…asleep."

"I did not dream it. All I'm doing here is trying to be worthy of the woman I love. Is that so much to ask? Wouldn't you do as much for Amanda?"

Jake looked like a doctor delivering fatal news. "It's been eight days, Zeke. Nobody's coming."

Zeke turned away to watch the rain sliding down the windows. "She's coming."

And then I'll say goodbye.

Come soon, Nuala, before I lose my courage.

Before I'm too sore and heartsick to savor the time we have together.

They came for him three days later, bearing his clothes and a wheelchair and reams of instructions to dismiss him from the hospital. Zeke begged to be allowed to stay. He couldn't imagine how Nuala would be able to find him if he left. But rules were rules. The hospital called him cured enough to go home. His bed was stripped and his flowers piled onto a rolling cart.

"I can't go," he pleaded, frantic. Knowing he looked wild-eyed, sure the staff—if not his sister—was hiding a big syringe of sedative behind their backs. "Please."

He hated that his family looked so torn. He would never want to put them through this. They thought Nuala lived within the swollen cells of a brain injury. But Zeke knew.

He *knew*.

He listened for her even as the nurse helped him struggle into the same jeans he swore Nuala had so laughingly divested him of only a week before. He looked up as the door opened, only to see Gen come to get him with regretful eyes and gentle humor. He took as long as he possibly could to get into his shoes and his shirt and his jacket, to slip his battered old field hat onto his newly bald pate. He'd been half bald after the surgery anyway, and it had seemed easier to start all over again than grow half a head of hair. Lee said it made him look like Vin Diesel. Zeke didn't care. He just wanted Nuala to be able to recognize him when she came.

She *would* come.

So he eased into his wheelchair and prayed for a miracle. He held his breath all the way down the long hall as nurses and doctors stopped by to wish him well, to smile at his story of a misadventure on a fairy rath, to meet the man who waited for a fairy princess.

He saw the outside door approach like the gates of hell and knew he couldn't go through it. His heart began to hammer. His back broke out in a sick sweat. He couldn't give up. Not yet.

Not yet.

He was almost to the door when he heard it. The light, almost invisible patter of feet, running. He swore he smelled it. Cloves.

He knew it. She'd come for him.

"Stop!" he yelled, planting his size twelves on the terrazzo floor and bringing the procession to a drunken halt.

"What the hell now?" Jake demanded.

But Zeke was already on his feet and turning. He was looking for her, because he knew, he just *knew*, she was there.

"Nuala!"

But before he even had a chance to see her, his damn left leg gave way. He saw the almost comical dismay on half a dozen faces as they took just a second too long to react. His knee buckled. His right foot slid on the new polish. His arms windmilled, and down he went. Right on his ass. Just like before.

He lay flat on his back, the wind completely knocked out of him. He didn't see anything above him but Jake and the nurse, and Amanda, hands out, face crumpled with distress, and Lee's husband, Rock, scowling, ready to bend to pick him up.

He didn't see *her*.

"Nuala!"

But the only answer he got was the indifferent chatter of a hospital corridor.

Slowly, as if he'd aged thirty years in the last week, Jake knelt down by Zeke's head. "Zeke," he said bending closer, and Zeke knew how hard it was for his brother to do this. "There's no one there. I'm sorry."

Zeke didn't close his eyes. He didn't jump up and begin to batter at something. He simply lay there, defeated. She wasn't coming. Something had kept her in her world, something dread. And he might never know what.

He would never see her again.

Fighting the scalding pain of loss, he lifted a hand to Jake. "Okay. Let's go."

It was over.

Chapter 15

"Wait!" a gentle voice pleaded.

Zeke collapsed back onto the floor. He didn't even have to look. He just smiled up at the ceiling tiles and waited. Everything was all right. He could rest now. It was going to take all his strength just to do what he had to, after all. To tell her that he loved her and then send her away.

But she was safe. It was all that mattered.

Well, and that she'd come. Just as he'd known she would. He thought he'd been finished with tears. But they threatened again, like a hot tide rising in his chest. He was shaking, and it had nothing to do with weakness.

Zeke saw the astonishment blossom on Jake's face. He heard the hush fall over the hall. And then silver fairy bells danced in a breeze, and she was there beside him, right down there on the floor, pulling his head into her lap, smiling. Whole. Here.

"Ah, Zeke," she greeted him, the light dancing in her eyes. "Do you forever have to be falling down at the feet of a fairy?"

"Only one fairy," he assured her, his heart lifting, soaring, shattering. "I'm glad you came."

"Aye," she said with that heart-stopping smile. "So am I."

She bent over him, her thick ocean of hair screening them from the rest of the world. "And what have you done with your beautiful hair, I'd like to know? I loved your hair."

"I shaved it off in mourning."

Her eyes glinted with amusement. "Mourning? For what?"

He reached up and tested his fingers against the satin of her cheek. "The woman I love."

Her eyes swelled with tears that refused to fall. "Ah, what a silver tongue you have, Zeke Kendall. I should be leery of it, I think."

"No, you shouldn't," he said. "Not ever." Then, because he couldn't help it, he smiled. "I knew you'd come."

"You did, did you? Even in the middle of such a fierce battle, I'd like to know?"

"Is *that* her?" Zeke heard Lee whisper.

"Mary Mother of God," a nurse intoned in awed tones. "If he hasn't found himself a fairy for sure."

"Is everything all right?" Zeke asked Nuala, searching her for signs of injury. Breathless with relief that she appeared untouched.

And smiling. She was smiling, and his world lit into spring again. "It's all right now."

"The world of Faerie is safe?"

"Well, there is an uneasy peace. But the attack was repulsed—by the heroic charge of a madman in elven armor, I'll have you know." They shared another smile, and she skimmed her fingers over his stubby head. "Cadhla sends his best, by the way. He would like to be remembered to his cousins on your ranch."

"Of course he would. What next for them all?"

She shrugged. "Mab is consulting with the council. The seer watches and waits."

Zeke nodded, wanting more: more time, more words, more future. "I love you," he said before, he lost the chance. "I had to tell you. I should have before. Whatever else happens to us, I need you to know."

The tears spilled over this time. "I'm glad, so."

Zeke nodded and swept the tears from her cheeks with his fingertips. "Did I pass the third test?"

"Oh, aye. Even Mab couldn't argue against it."

"And do you love me?"

She stroked his forehead with her healing fingers, and he felt their ease. "What a question that is, when I've taken the great trouble to come this far to find you. I'll have you know that these hospital places are fierce confusing. I've been wandering through this one for hours."

Zeke lifted a brow. "Hours? You don't measure time."

For the first time Nuala looked uncertain. "I do now."

Zeke went very still, unsure of what he saw in Nuala's expression. "Why?"

She looked away for a moment, and Zeke loved her even more. She looked as if she carried new burdens. New griefs. New half-admitted hopes.

"Well, now," she said, trying to be bright, "haven't I lost my job, then?"

Zeke sat straight up, eyeing her from no more than six inches away. "What?"

That was when he finally took in what she was wearing. Not her lovely peacock dress nor her multitude of silver rings.

Jeans.

Dear God, she was wearing blue jeans and a T-shirt and tennis shoes. Zeke found himself gaping like a trout. What was worse, she looked anxious, vulnerable. As if his reaction to her attire made all the difference in her life.

Zeke couldn't decide what to do. What to say. He was too afraid to ask what he wanted to. Too suddenly beset by the sharp edge of hope. So he just lay back down and closed his eyes.

"Zeke?" There was such need in her voice.

"You're here, right?"

"I am, so."

He nodded a bit. "I'm going to get used to that. Then we'll move on to the next bit."

He felt her laughter vibrate through her and smiled. Then, gathering his courage, he opened his eyes to find her still there. Still wearing blue jeans and sneakers.

Suddenly Jake was bent over the both of them, all but blocking out the light. "Nice to meet you, ma'am. And I'm glad you came to see Zeke here. But it seems to me that you might want to have your say in a quieter place."

"Jake?" Zeke greeted his brother without bothering to turn from the sight of his Nuala dressed like a mortal. "This is Nuala. Nuala, my brother Jake. You remember him."

Nuala flashed Jake a blinding smile. "The very man who bred Grayghost, is it? An honor to meet you."

"You, too," Zeke managed. "However, it's time to get Zeke off the floor."

For the first time since he'd gone ass over teakettle, Zeke took a second to look around. Strangers were stopped cold in the hall. Patients stood in doorways, some holding up their IVs to get a look. His own sisters were looking on like spectators at a whorehouse raid. And he was still lying on the floor with his head in Nuala's lap, just soaking in the sight of her.

"Well," he grudgingly admitted, "if you insist."

Jake actually smiled. "I do."

It was a production, but Zeke managed to get back in the wheelchair, which upset Nuala all over again, since he'd suffered the fresh injuries saving her mother, and the staff allowed them a few minutes in a conference room. To confer.

"Nuala," Jake said, with a wave of his hand, the other holding firmly on to hers. "My family. Family... Nuala."

He got the most startling silence from his siblings. Even Amanda, who looked more intrigued than anything, couldn't seem to form words. It was Lee, of course, who broke the impasse.

"It's so good to see you," she greeted Nuala, folding her in an enthusiastic hug. "You have no idea."

Nuala smiled, and Zeke battled an urge to laugh.

"Thank you," Nuala said. "It's a pleasure, sure, to finally meet Zeke's family."

He wondered if he should tell the family the truth. That Nuala knew them better than their spouses.

"And now, family," he said pointedly. "I'd like a few minutes with Nuala. Then, I promise, we'll go."

Jake still looked shell-shocked, but he nodded and, just as Zeke knew he would, ushered everyone out the door. Zeke didn't even hear the door close. His eyes were only for Nuala.

"Now, my lady," he said. "Explain yourself."

Nuala pulled up a chair and sat, her hands folded tightly in her lap. "Mab decided," she said, suddenly quiet, her focus on her hands rather than on Zeke, "that the next queen of the fairies shouldn't be so in love with a mortal that she'd prefer to become one."

Zeke thought his heart had stopped. "Become one? What do you mean?"

She offered a small, uncomfortable shrug. "My allegiances are torn. I long too much for this world to rule my own effectively. So I was given the choice." Even though she lifted her eyes to him, Zeke saw the terrible hesitation that still lit them. "It is the only way I can live in this world, Zeke. To be mortal."

For a long moment he couldn't even think to answer. Hell, he could hardly breathe, what with the enormity of what she seemed to be saying. He'd been about to say goodbye. He'd bolstered himself for it. Prepared. Grieved.

How did he greet this?

"And are you?" he asked, terrified that he was hoping too much. "Living in this world?"

Still looking like a fawn in a hunter's sights, she nodded.

Her leap of faith took Zeke's breath. She'd done it for him. To be with him. She'd done it not even knowing if he would have the courage to commit himself to her.

"Oh, Nuala," he breathed, shaking his head. "Will you regret it, do you think?"

Because she was Nuala, she took her time to answer. "I'll miss my world, although we're invited over on the odd Samhain. I'll miss my family, although Kieran promised to exchange messages. I'll miss the glen, although there's much to this world that delights me even more. Did you know there's a machine that lifts you straight off the ground?"

Zeke chuckled. "It's called an elevator."

She shook her head. "You don't even need fairy dust."

"Nuala," he nudged gently. "Why?"

Why give it all up? Everything she'd been bred and trained for. Everything that defined her magical life.

This time there was no hesitation. Merely a smile, lit with the pure joy that fired her heart. "Because it gave me the chance to be with you."

It took Zeke time and effort, but he managed to get himself out of his wheelchair and onto his feet. "Come here," he said, when Nuala protested.

She stepped close, close enough that he could fold her into his arms. So he could bring her home.

"I'll never be good enough for you," he said, resting his cheek against the sunlit satin of her hair. "But I'd like to try. I'd like to devote all that time I've been wasting on other women just to you." Her hair still smelled of gorse. Her skin was as soft as satin, and her lovely small ears were still pointed. He swallowed down his wonder. "How would you like to see the Four Corners in person? And the Andes Mountains, and maybe the islands of Tahiti? Would you be willing to travel with me, to take on my interfering, bossy family, and withstand their interference enough to join them for holidays?"

"I have no earthly talents, Zeke," she said, her own arms tight around him. "Nothing but an ear for the harp and a way with a healing herb."

"Which would probably come in handy on a dig. Especially the harp part. You got to bring it with you, didn't you?"

"Sure no one would think to separate a fairy from her harp. Even when she's no longer a fairy."

Zeke heard the wistfulness in her voice. But he thought he also heard anticipation. He pulled back to consider her. "You'd really give up the Land of the West to grow old with me? To rock with me on our front porch and pass fairy stories to our grandchildren?"

Her eyes glowed like gemstones. "I would be honored, Zeke Kendall."

"Then there's just one thing for it. Will you marry me, Nuala, daughter of Mab? Will you be my last lover and the future of my family?"

When Nuala smiled, Zeke had his answer. "Sure, I thought you'd never ask."

"And what about the queen?"

Nuala smiled. "The queen will have to wait a while longer before she leaves."

Zeke was still in the process of welcoming his fiancée with a heartfelt kiss when the door burst open to admit his family. Their reaction to the news was supportive and enthusiastic.

It was Gen who expressed it for them all. "You owe me fifty bucks!"

As for the queen, at that moment she was standing over Nuala's scrying water. The seer stood with her, and her daughter Sorcha, who looked on her sister's joy with a bittersweet smile.

"Well now, little Sorcha," the queen said, turning away. "It's your turn, then."

Sorcha looked wary. "For what, my lady?"

The queen raised an imperious eyebrow. "Why, to be queen."

Sorcha, who had never stood up to her mother in her life, straightened to her full height. "Thank you, my lady," she said with proper obeisance. "But no."

The queen didn't even seem to notice. She was looking back on Nuala, who was caught up in her mortal's arms. What a waste, Mab thought. She could have enjoyed that one for a good few years. And she wasn't much happier about losing her daughter to him. Mab had truly thought that Nuala could have made a good queen. But no fairy queen should be prey to the kind of love that would put a mortal before her own realm.

Ah well, it was for the best. Hadn't she brought the mortal through to find out this very answer? Orla was right in that, after all. In the end, Nuala would have failed as queen. And Orla was still too selfish. It was left to Sorcha.

"I wouldn't challenge me on this, Sorcha," she said. "After all, you are still responsible for helping to right the imbalance in the realm. It will be easier to do if you're queen."

"No, Mother," was all Sorcha said in answer. "Thank you, but no."

Mab just smiled. "We'll see, little one. We'll see."

And before Sorcha could argue, she just disappeared. There was much to be done, after all. Mab thought that the best way to recover the Coilin Stone was to recover the lost Dearann Stone. And wasn't it a good thing she had an idea of where it was? Then they could force an exchange with Cathal, king of the *Dubhlainn Sidhe*, and reestablish balance.

Or steal Coilin back and have both stones. That would bring a power that would tempt a queen, even away from the Land of the West. For now, though, the queen was satisfied. The borders were safe again, Darragh exiled and Orla stripped of her powers. And soon Mab would know whether she herself yearned more for ultimate power or ultimate rest. Either way, she knew it was her time to relax in her power.

Left behind, her daughter turned to the seer. "What will happen?" she asked. "When I continue to say no?"

Kieran, as was his way, simply studied the gathering shadows. "All will change."

Sorcha sighed, the weight of the future settling hard on her shoulders. "Aye. I thought as much."

As the twilight settled over the land, the two walked away from Nuala's empty house. It was time for the banquet. The life of Faerie went on. There were legends to be made, magic to be wrought. As the mortal world settled to sleep, the fairies danced in the glens and lit the glades of autumn with their flickering lights. And as they danced, they wondered what would happen next. The *Dubhlainn Sidhe* had the Coilin Stone. The queen had none. Not one among them discounted the gravity of the situation. Not one thought it finished or even safe. But as the moon rose smiling over the verdant glen, it was something they knew would wait for another time. Tonight was for dancing.

nocturne™

USA TODAY bestselling author

MAUREEN
CHILD

ETERNALLY

He was a guardian. An immortal fighter of evil,
out to destroy a demon, and she was his next
target. He knew joining with her would make
him strong enough to defeat any demon.
But the cost might be losing the woman
who was his true salvation.

On sale November, wherever books are sold.

SNETERN

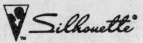

Romantic
SUSPENSE

Excitement, danger and passion guaranteed

INTIMATE MOMENTS™

WARRIOR

WENDY ROSNAU

MERCENARY

**Beginning in October
Silhouette Intimate Moments®
will be evolving into
Silhouette® Romantic Suspense.**

Look for it wherever you buy books!

Visit Silhouette Books at www.eHarlequin.com   SIMRS1006R

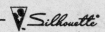

SPECIAL EDITION™

Silhouette Special Edition brings you a heartwarming new story from the *New York Times* bestselling author of *McKettrick's Choice*

LINDA LAEL MILLER

Sierra's Homecoming

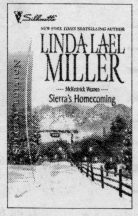

Sierra's Homecoming follows the parallel lives of two McKettrick women, living their lives in the same house but generations apart, each with a special son and an unlikely new romance.

December 2006

Visit Silhouette Books at www.eHarlequin.com   SSESHIBC

nocturne™

Save $1.⁰⁰ off

your purchase of any
Silhouette® Nocturne™ novel.

Receive $1.00 off
any Silhouette® Nocturne™ novel.

**Available wherever books are sold, including most
bookstores, supermarkets, drugstores and discount stores.**

Coupon expires December 1, 2006. Redeemable at participating
retail outlets in the U.S. only. Limit one coupon per customer.

RETAILER: Harlequin Enterprises Ltd. will pay the face value of this coupon plus
8¢ if submitted by the customer for this specified product only. Any other use
constitutes fraud. Coupon is nonassignable. Void if taxed, prohibited or restricted by
law. Void if copied. Consumer must pay for any government taxes. Mail to Harlequin
Enterprises Ltd., P.O. Box 880478, El Paso, TX 88588-0478, U.S.A. Cash value 1/100
cents. Limit one coupon per customer. Valid in the U.S. only.

5 65373 00076 2 . (8100) 0 11265

SNCOUPUS

nocturne™

Save $1.⁰⁰ off

your purchase of any
Silhouette® Nocturne™ novel.

Receive $1.00 off

any Silhouette® Nocturne™ novel.

Available wherever books are sold, including most bookstores, supermarkets, drugstores and discount stores.

Coupon expires December 1, 2006. Redeemable at participating retail outlets in Canada only. Limit one coupon per customer.

RETAILER: Harlequin Enterprises Limited will pay the face value of this coupon plus 10.25 cents if submitted by the customer for this specified product only. Any other use constitutes fraud. Coupon is nonassignable. Void if taxed, prohibited or restricted by law. Consumer must pay any government taxes. Mail to Harlequin Enterprises Ltd., P.O. Box 3000, Saint John, New Brunswick E2L 4L3, Canada. Limit one coupon per customer. Valid in Canada only.

52607136

SNCOUPCDN